MINE TO HOLD

CYNTHIA EDEN

Published by Cynthia Eden.

Cover art and design by: Pickyme/Patricia Schmitt

Proof-reading by: JRT Editing

PROLOGUE

The gun pressed into the center of Claire Kramer's forehead. She didn't move, not an inch, too afraid to even breathe as she knelt in the middle of the old, rickety wooden dock.

It was her grandfather's dock. Her grandfather's fishing cabin. Her haven.

She should have been safe there. Instead, it seemed she was about to die there.

"Why did you leave me, Claire?" Ethan Harrison asked her as he held that gun to her head. "*Why?*"

Her gaze darted to the right. His bright, red sports car gleamed in the nearby parking lot, sticking out like a sore thumb.

Please, please, someone notice that car. You have to see it. But there just weren't any people out then. No one was there to help her. *If someone would just pull into the lot. If someone would just come—*

"I love you, Claire," Ethan whispered, his voice actually sounding sad as he stared down at her with his soulful green gaze. "You know that."

Claire was sixteen, but she still knew that love didn't involve a gun. It also didn't involve hitting, punching, *hurting*. Her parents had wanted her away from Ethan. *She'd* wanted away from him.

But in Alabama, escaping from a Harrison wasn't exactly easy. The cops hadn't believed her story about Ethan's attacks. His daddy was a state senator. Ethan was old money. Power.

And she...she was the girl kneeling on the dock, with a gun to her head.

My family believed me. She'd been trying to get her parents on the phone just moments before Ethan had surprised her. He shouldn't have been able to find her. Only her parents, her sister, and her grandfather knew she was at the little cabin on the water.

"Why did you leave?" Not a whisper this time, but a bellow.

Claire flinched. Her hands were twisted behind her, her fingers fisted, and her nails sank deep into her own palms. "I-it was over, Ethan. You said you-you didn't want me anymore."

The sunlight glinted off his blond hair. "I will always want you, Claire." Ethan never eased his grip on the gun. "You're my one and only."

My one and only.

"You shouldn't have run. Never run again, understand? Because I can find you anywhere, Claire."

A tear leaked down her cheek. "Don't hurt me." She was begging. She knew it. "Please, don't. *Please.*"

He smiled. Once, that wide grin had made her heart melt in her chest. Now it just made her body ice with fear.

"I like it when you beg me, Claire."

She knew he did.

She also knew that he liked to hurt her.

This isn't the way love is supposed to be.

She'd seen her parents together. Her dad loved her mother so much. He would *never* hurt her mom. But Ethan wasn't like Claire's father.

Claire still had the bruises from Ethan's last attack on her skin.

Ethan exhaled slowly. "Begging won't work this time. You shouldn't have left. You knew that you belonged to me."

No, I don't. Claire shook her head.

His handsome face twisted with fury. *"You're mine!"*

And he pulled the trigger.

Claire screamed. The frantic cry burst from her throat as her eyes instinctively squeezed shut. She knew that she was dead. She'd never see her parents again. Never see her sister, Sara. She'd never do anything but—

He was laughing at her.

I'm still alive.

Her eyes opened. More tears coursed down her cheeks.

"Oh, Claire, I forgot to mention…I already used the bullets that were in this gun."

The chill on her skin got worse. So much worse.

He glanced toward the phone that had fallen from her fingers when he'd surprised her before. The phone sat on the edge of the dock. "You were trying to call your parents, right? Sorry, sweetheart, but they'll never be answering you again."

I already used the bullets that were in this gun.

He pulled the gun away from her head. Numb, she could only kneel there and gaze helplessly up at him.

Ethan tucked the gun into the back of his jeans. Then his head tilted to the right as he studied her. His hair fell loosely over his forehead. The good-looking college boy. The heart breaker. "You have a choice," he told her flatly as that good-looking veneer twisted with rage. "You can be mine, or you can be dead. Because I swear…*you will never leave me for another.*"

She hadn't been leaving him for another boy. She'd been afraid of him, and she'd fled. For her own survival. "I-I didn't—"

Claire couldn't say any more. His hands were at her throat. Squeezing so tightly. "Mine or dead, Claire. Mine. Or. Dead."

Her fingers flew up. Her nails clawed at his skin.

He jerked her, twisting her body, and hauling her down the dock with his fierce grip on her throat.

He was going to take her away. This was the end for her. No matter how hard she fought, Claire couldn't break free. Her throat hurt so much—

A gunshot rang out. The bullet sank into Ethan's thigh, just a few inches away from Claire's face. Blood sprayed onto her.

Ethan screamed and he let her go.

Claire jumped to her feet. She ran for the end of the dock even as Ethan bellowed her name. She didn't stop. *Faster, faster.*

Then she saw them. Men in uniform who were coming from the woods near the small parking lot. Their badges gleamed. They had their weapons out.

"Keep my boy alive!" That shout, it was familiar. Her gaze whipped to the left, and she saw Senator Colby Harrison standing behind a uniformed officer—that officer had a rifle in his hands.

"Claire, it's okay now." The sheriff came toward her. Jim Brady's face was lined with concern. "We've got you."

Jim hadn't believed her when she'd tried to press charges against Ethan. But...but the deputies were all there. They all *had to* believe her now.

I already used the bullets…

Claire grabbed Sheriff Brady's shirt-front, clenching it beneath her fists. "My...my parents…"

Other deputies rushed past her. They raced toward the dock. Toward a still-screaming Ethan.

Sorrow flashed on Sheriff Brady's face. "Claire, I'm so sorry…"

No, no. Her body started shaking. "I-I need to call my mom."

Sheriff Brady shook his head.

"I *have* to call my mom!" Now she was screaming.

Sheriff Brady wrapped his arms around her. "They're gone, Claire. He...he got to them first."

And at that moment, Claire broke.

CHAPTER ONE

I can do this.

Claire Kramer stared up at the tall, imposing lines of York Towers. The building seemed to touch the sky, and windows—far too many to count—gleamed as they reflected the bright sunlight back on her. The Towers were located in the heart of New York, and the streets were packed with people.

So many people. Their bodies brushed against her as they passed her on the sidewalk.

Claire took a deep breath. That breath was supposed to fortify her. She'd come this far. She had to go inside the building. It wasn't like she had much of a choice at this point.

Her savings were gone. Her apartment—um, she didn't have one. She had nothing but a hotel stay that would last for two more nights.

She was desperate, and desperate times sure called for desperate measures.

After one more glance up at York Towers, Claire straightened her shoulders. She smoothed down her jacket for what had to be the tenth time. Fall had hit the city, and the brisk air chilled her skin. Or maybe that chill just came from the fear she felt. *What if he doesn't help me?*

Going to York Towers…it was her last option.

So do this. With her chin up, Claire approached the entrance to the hotel.

The rich and famous usually stayed in places like this one. Claire wasn't rich, and she sure wasn't famous.

Just infamous back home.

But New York was a long, long way from Fairview, Alabama. No one knew her in this city. No one but Noah York. The man who *was* York Towers. Young, dynamic, mysterious…Noah York was a powerhouse in this city and around the world. He had dozens of luxury hotels and getaways.

He was also the sexiest man Claire had ever met. That sexiness made him dangerous. The last time Claire had fallen for a good-looking, rich boy, she'd lost everything.

This time, I have nothing to lose.

A doorman hurried to open the door for her. He tipped his hat, a friendly smile on his face. Claire found herself nervously smiling back. She'd worked in plenty of other hotels during the last few years. It wasn't as if she was totally out of her element.

She'd seen gleaming marble floors before. She'd seen other lobbies filled with complimentary welcome champagne and roses.

It was just that…this was Noah's hotel. And Noah made Claire very nervous.

She headed toward the concierge desk. The woman there immediately stood to greet her. "May I help you?" she asked. Her ID listed her name as Janelle.

Claire cleared her throat. "I'm here to see Noah York. My name's Claire—"

The woman's brown eyes lit with curiosity. "Of course! Mr. York told me that you'd be here for a meeting this morning."

Because she'd broken down and called him last night. She and Noah had met a few months ago. They'd both been caught in a terrible nightmare in Chicago. She'd been stabbed. He'd been shot.

They'd both survived.

Sometimes, Claire felt like that survival had linked them. Or maybe it was just the odd, instinctive awareness that she'd felt for Noah since the first moment that they'd met. When he was close, Claire was hyper-aware of the man.

An elevator dinged behind her. She heard the doors slide open.

And goosebumps rose on Claire's arms.

Instinctive awareness. Almost like prey, sensing danger.

Claire glanced over her shoulder. Sure enough, Noah strode from the elevator. His golden eyes were locked on her. Such unusual eyes — they reminded her of a lion's. Noah was certainly a top notch predator, both in the boardroom and, judging by the gossip columns, in his personal life.

As she turned to fully face him, Noah smiled, a flash of his perfect, white teeth, and his steps quickened as he approached her. "Claire, you're late," he chided as he closed in.

She shook her head. "I…it's only nine."

"Five minutes after nine." He raised one dark brow. "And here I thought you'd be more punctual."

Oh, crap. What a way to begin a job interview. Claire felt her cheeks sting with embarrassment. How did she go about explaining that she'd actually been outside of the hotel for thirty minutes? She'd just been trying to work up the courage to step inside the place.

Noah scares me.

Her gaze drifted over his face. He was too handsome. Handsome men were dangerous. That was rule one in her book.

Rule two went something like…*Never trust handsome men.*

And Claire didn't trust Noah. The man was too much of a mystery for trust to enter the equation. But then, Claire didn't actually trust anyone. Not completely.

Noah's cheekbones were high, sharp slashes. His nose was straight and strong. His jaw was perfectly square. His lips appeared hard but sensual. His hair was midnight black and his eyes —

They were like a lion's. A deep, beautiful gold.

Those eyes seemed to be looking right into Claire's soul then.

Nervously, she pulled at the sleeves of her jacket, making sure they covered her wrists. Then she stopped, catching herself.

Noah reached for her hand. "Come along, Claire." He nodded to the concierge. "Morning, Janelle."

"Sir…" Janelle said, giving a quick nod.

Then Noah pulled Claire toward the elevator. A private elevator, she noted, because he had to use a keycard to get the control panel to function. Once they were inside, he pressed the button for the top floor.

She knew that floor would house the main luxury suites.

The elevator doors closed, and they were sealed inside. The space seemed far too small to her, or maybe Noah was just too big. His broad shoulders stretched the tailored suit that he wore, and the guy had to be at least six foot two, maybe six foot three. A raw power clung to him.

Claire inched back a bit.

"Don't."

Her gaze flew to meet his.

Noah shook his head. "You have nothing to fear from me, Claire." He smiled at her. "Besides, from what I remember, you're pretty strong in your own right."

She blushed. Again. She couldn't help it that she had the annoying skin type that flushed way too much. No, she couldn't help it, but she could hate it. "I was…" Claire cleared her throat. "I didn't know who you were then." When a strange man appeared out of seemingly nowhere and came at her, Claire's immediate instinct had been to attack. She hadn't wasted moment on questions. Instead, she'd gone in fighting.

These days, Claire knew it was better to be safe —

Than dead.

"And to think," he murmured as he advanced in that little space, "you look so…deceptively delicate."

Claire was tall, about five foot ten, but she still had to tilt her head back a bit to keep meeting his stare. "Appearances are always deceiving." She'd learned that lesson at sixteen.

His mouth hitched into a half-smile. A smile that made her heart race too quickly. He was definitely a handsome bastard, she'd give him that. And the fact that he could make her heart jump so easily —

That tells me to be careful with him. So careful. The last time she'd fallen for a man with a heart-jumping smile, she'd nearly paid for that mistake with her life.

"You remembered my offer," Noah murmured.

How could she forget?

The last time that she'd seen Noah York, Claire had been at her sister's funeral. Grief had nearly choked her as she stared down at Sara's coffin. Noah had been there. Right at Claire's side. *I want to help you.* His words whispered through her mind. He'd slipped his card into her hand. *I owe you. I owe your sister. If you ever need me, I'm a phone call away.*

When the funeral had ended, Claire hadn't stayed around to talk with Noah or any of the others at that gut-wrenching graveside. She'd run away from them all. Claire had gotten good at running.

But there was nowhere to run now. She needed him. A week ago, she'd lost the job that she'd *counted* on, and Claire had forced herself to come to Noah. Even though he scared her.

"My, what big eyes you have," he murmured. His smile slowly faded as he searched her gaze. "I've never seen anyone with eyes quite like yours. That deep blue is really quite incredible."

Her lashes lowered, hiding the blue in question. She found herself staring at his throat. At his tie. At anything but —

His fingers slipped under her chin. Claire jerked at the contact and tried to back away from him.

Her elbow rammed into the wall of the elevator.

"I don't...I don't like to be touched." The words were sharp. They were also true.

Normally.

But she hadn't jerked away from Noah because the press of his fingers brought the usual cold fear.

She'd backed away because his touch had scorched her.

"It's a pity," he told her as his hand dropped back to his side. "Because I think that I could enjoy touching you."

The elevator had stopped. She just realized that. How long had it been still? "Ah, why aren't the doors opening?"

He glanced at the control panel. "Because I haven't opened them."

So he wanted the two of them to be trapped together in that elevator?

"Are you afraid of small spaces?" Noah asked her suddenly.

Claire shook her head.

"Good to know." He inclined his head. "I'm making a list, you see."

She was totally lost. "A list?"

He pressed a code into the control panel. The doors opened seconds later. "I'm finding out what scares you. What you like. What you don't like."

She hurried from the elevator, but then hesitated on the lush carpet in the hallway. "Why does any of that matter to you?"

He shrugged. "Because it does."

Talk about an incredibly vague answer.

"We're almost to my suite." He headed down the hallway.

Claire didn't follow. "I'd expected that we'd meet in your office." Not in his suite. If she hadn't been so nervous on that elevator, she would have brought up this point sooner.

Noah glanced over his shoulder at her. "I can get the best privacy in my personal suite."

They were having the meeting in his *personal* suite? The breath that she sucked in felt icy, but Claire soldiered on. Noah opened the suite door for her. She slipped past him, casting a quick glance up at the chandelier that hung in the entrance way. The huge chandelier gleamed, casting light all over the massive foyer of the suite. *A suite that is way bigger than the home my family used to have down in Alabama.*

Noah shut the door behind her.

"Do you always have business meetings in your suite?" She asked him, not buying the privacy line for a minute.

"I didn't know we were going to talk just business." He slid by her. Not touching, but close. He headed into the next room. She did, too, then momentarily lost her breath at the stunning view she discovered. The New York skyline was spread out before her, on perfect display thanks to the floor to ceiling windows that lined the wall. Just to the right of that wall, Claire saw a glass door that led out onto a balcony area. When she'd been staring up at the hotel, she hadn't even noticed the balcony. She glanced back at Noah. He was watching her.

Noah motioned toward the windows and said, "I saw you."

Her shoulders tensed.

"You stayed across the street for so long. I was wondering when you'd get the courage to come to me."

She crossed to the windows. Stared down. They were up so high. "How could you see me clearly?"

"When it comes to you, Claire, I can see plenty."

Now she looked back over her shoulder at him.

"Want a drink?" he asked her.

"No, I want a job." Okay, those words had just blurted out. She'd meant to broach the subject of her employment in a much more elegant way. She was sure that had been her plan. But when she got nervous, elegance tended to vanish from her repertoire.

Noah crossed his arms over his chest. "That's a problem."

Oh, damn. She'd had such high hopes. *Keep your pride, Claire. It's all you have.* Her chin notched up. "It doesn't have to be anything fancy. Just something temporary. You've got dozens of hotels, I'm sure that you can—"

"I don't fuck with my employees."

Wait, *what?* Her jaw dropped.

"And I very much want to have sex with you."

She shook her head. Claire wasn't sure if she was denying his words or just—"You didn't just say that to me."

His lips quirked. Amusement flashed in the depths of his golden eyes. "I assure you, I did. I believe in honesty."

She didn't know what to say. "I'm not…" Okay, this was getting way past her control. "I'm not here for sex. I'm here for a *job.*"

"Do you feel it?" Noah asked as his gaze seemed to heat with emotion. "Or is it just me?"

"Is what just you?" Claire whispered.

"I look at you, and my whole body burns. I want you naked. I want you screaming. I want to see pleasure make your eyes flash even brighter."

Her breath came faster. Rougher.

"So I wondered if that was just me. Is the arousal all on my side? The attraction?" His gaze dipped to her mouth. "Or do you feel it, too?"

I feel it. But Claire had rules. So many rules. She licked her lips. Saw the gold in his eyes go molten. "I'm not…I'm not interested in having sex with you."

His dark brows rose. "Are you very sure about that?"

No. Yes. Claire hadn't taken a lover in years.

Nine years, to be exact.

Not since she'd learned how dangerous a lover could be. She pulled at the left sleeve of her jacket. "Sex won't be an issue." Claire cleared her throat. "I *need* the job. You said that you owed me." She didn't actually think that he did owe her. He certainly hadn't caused her injury in Chicago, but in that desperate moment, she'd try to play on any sense of debt that he might feel. "I-I need the job."

He took a slow step toward her.

"Please," she said, truly desperate and—

A flash of anger crossed his face. In the next instant, Noah was right in front of her. "Don't ever do that."

Do what? Lost, she could only shake her head.

"You don't have to beg me for anything. Remember that." His hands lifted, then his fingers fisted as if he were trying to resist the urge to touch her. "If you want a job with me, it's yours."

Her breath expelled in a relieved burst. "Thank you."

"I don't want your gratitude." His eyes still burned. "I want you, and that wanting isn't just going to stop."

She could actually feel the heat from his body. It warmed her when she'd been cold for so long.

"But I meant what I said," Noah continued, his voice deep and rumbling. "I don't fuck with my employees."

"Y-you won't be f-fucking with me."

His lips thinned. "We'll see. I don't want you to beg, I think I was pretty clear about that…you should never have to beg for anything. But I will wait and let you ask me to be your lover."

That shocked her. "It's not happening."

"We'll see." He turned away from her. Paced toward a desk that waited in the corner. "You graduated at the top of your class at Washington State University. Received a Bachelor's degree in Business Management, then got your MBA."

He'd checked her out?

"But you've barely stayed at any job longer than six months since you got your MBA." His fingers tapped lightly on the edge of the desk. "Why is that?"

"Because my past keeps catching up with me." And she did not, *could not*, talk about her past then. She'd lost her last job because her boss found out about her.

Noah's expression hardened. "Are you in danger, Claire?" A new note had entered his voice. Rougher. Harder.

A shiver slid over her. "No." Not any longer. At least, she shouldn't be. She cleared her throat. "I have…a powerful enemy. He likes to punish me, so he tends to make sure I don't exactly have the best employment prospects." *Please, please, Noah, just accept what I say and don't ask any other questions.*

Her gaze dropped to the manila file on his desk. Understanding hit her hard and had Claire backing up a step. If he'd learned about her college, then… "You already know."

His shoulders tensed as he straightened to fully face her.

"You know everything that happened to me, don't you?" And she *hated* that. Claire rarely talked about her past. It hurt too much. For Noah to know. For this sexy, strong man to know all her dark secrets—

The knowledge of her exposure to him just made her feel weak. Too exposed.

He held her gaze. "I know you're a survivor, and that's all that matters to me."

She blinked quickly because, for some reason, his words had her eyes tearing. Claire would *not* cry in front of him. She didn't cry in front of anyone.

"I don't really give a shit how powerful the enemy from your past is," he continued, voice deep, "because I'm pretty sure I've got just as much…if not more…power."

Claire thought he did, too. That was why she'd come to him. If anyone could stand up to the man after her, it would be Noah. "I just want a chance."

Noah inclined his head. "Like I said, I'll give you a job."

Her shoulders slumped. The relief that hit her then was so dizzying she felt a little light-headed for a minute. The last nine years had been so hard. And with her sister's death just a few months before…the demons that chased Claire seemed to have just grown stronger.

"I know I have to start at the bottom," Claire said, her words coming fast now, "and that's fine. You just tell me who to report to, and I'll—"

"You'll report to me, Claire. Only me."

Her lips parted. "But—"

"I need an assistant, and you just got the job."

That was...*wow*. "I can do it," she promised him. "I'll prove that I can—"

"I already know you can do it." He tilted his head as he studied her. "But you should be aware that we'll have to work very closely together. My hours are crazy, and I'll expect you to be at my beck and call pretty much twenty-four, seven."

She nodded. She had no social life, so that was a done deal.

"Where are you staying?" Noah asked.

"The Hamlet, over on—"

"It's a dump, Claire." The anger was back on his face and in his voice. "A man was shot there last week."

And two men had been arrested there last night. But when you were trying to save every bit of money you had, well, you didn't have the luxury of being choosy about your hotel.

His jaw locked. "I'll make sure you have a room available here at the Towers."

"But..."

A muscle flexed in his jaw. "You aren't staying there any longer."

"What will the other staff members think?" Claire asked as she shifted her feet nervously. "If I just move in here, even if it's just for a few days, they'll talk."

"There's nothing to talk about. Other staff members stay here." He waved that concern away. "Like I told you, I don't sleep with my employees. No one will think anything of your sleeping accommodations at the Towers."

Right. Claire nodded and sighed in relief. "Th-thank you, Noah. I won't forget this." Claire squared her shoulders. She walked toward him. Offered her hand.

He stared down at her hand for a moment, then his fingers curled around hers. His hand was so big that it seemed to swallow her own. His flesh was golden, warm, and at that touch—a touch she'd instigated—a surge of sensual awareness flooded through her.

Just from his hand? Such a simple touch…

"And we will get to this part," he murmured as his fingers tightened around hers. "Then you'll have to choose…if you want to keep working for me or if you want to fuck me."

***

He had Claire Kramer, and he wasn't letting her go.

Noah York was used to getting what he wanted in life, and for the last few months, he'd wanted her.

Noah led Claire to the room he'd arranged for her. She probably didn't know that he'd had that room—a suite also on the same floor with his—cleared out when he'd gotten her call. He and Claire now occupied the only two suites on that floor.

He needed her close. He'd have her close.

And, eventually, he would get exactly what he wanted from her.

He'd watched her that morning as she stood outside, the wind sending her blonde hair flying around her shoulders. He'd been afraid that Claire wasn't going to walk into his hotel.

Come to me, Claire. Come to me.

Then she had.

He opened the door to her suite. Heard her soft gasp. Good. That sound better mean she liked the place.

"There is no way I can afford this!" Claire turned in a circle as her eyes swept around the suite. "Give me another room. This hotel is huge, just put me—"

"I need my assistant nearby," he said smoothly. "I do business at all hours, just like I told you. This floor is reserved for me and my associates." A partial lie. "If you're going to work for me," Noah added, "you really do need to start learning how to follow my orders."

She bit her lower lip. That lip was sexy and full, and he'd like to be the one biting it.

"Staying close is an order," he told her as his stare swept over her once more.

In the past, he'd gone more for the dark-haired beauties. But Claire — Claire with her blonde hair and blue eyes — she was different for him. Her heart-shaped face kept catching his gaze. Those high cheeks, that small nose. When the light hit her hair just right, she almost looked like an angel.

One who'd fallen so very far.

Claire had lush curves that he couldn't wait to explore. Rounded hips and tempting breasts that he knew would be perfect for his hands.

But *not yet*.

Because Claire still feared him. He had to work past that fear.

He would.

"I'll get your things brought over from the Hamlet," he told her, aware that his voice had hardened. He couldn't help it. When he thought of Claire and sex, his response was immediate.

"I only have one bag there." Her shoulders lifted in a faint shrug. "I've learned to travel light over the years."

Because she'd been forced to do so.

Things were going to change for Claire. Noah believed in protecting what was his.

Claire, you don't know it yet, but you will be mine.

"I don't need you to get the bag, though," Claire said as she notched up her chin. "I'm perfectly capable of doing that on my own." She cast one more nervous glance around the suite. "I'll…um…I'll go do that now, and I'll come back and get settled. That way, I can get started working this afternoon." Her eyelashes — so long — flickered. "If that's okay with you?"

"I'll come with you to the Hamlet." He wasn't ready to let her out of his sight yet. The last time he'd done that, when he'd thought she might want a little time to grieve privately in Chicago, Claire had vanished.

It had taken him weeks to track her down. Claire had a talent for disappearing. He wasn't about to let her use that talent again.

Instead of arguing with him, Claire surprised him then. She smiled.

Noah stiffened.

Claire's smile was slow, beginning with a faint curve of her lips. The smile spread, showing a dimple in each cheek. He'd never noticed those dimples before.

Because Claire had never smiled for me before.

And her eyes lit with her smile. Shined even brighter.

"It's going to be okay now," she said.

He couldn't speak. Noah just nodded. Hell, yes, he'd make sure that everything was okay for Claire.

She'd already suffered enough.

***

Claire wasn't embarrassed by the sight of the Hamlet Hotel. She'd stayed in far worse places in the course of her life.

Even once, for five terrible months, in a place where her other roommates would scream for hours and hours.

Claire shoved that memory into the back of her mind. All of the memories from Shady Pines deserved to stay back in the darkness.

She rose from the car—Noah's car, a sleek limo that had been waiting outside of York Towers. She cleared her throat and told him, "You know, this car really doesn't seem to belong here."

Noah had exited a few moments before her. He glanced her way. "*You* don't belong here. You should've come to me as soon as you arrived in New York."

That statement had her frowning. How did he know when she'd arrived in New York?

He took her elbow. Claire stiffened. "You know I don't—"

"Like to be touched," he finished grimly. "Yes, I know, but, Claire, you have to get used to me." He nodded to his driver. Claire wondered if the hulking guy was also a body guard.

She knew a few secrets about Noah's past. Enough to tell her that the man hadn't always worn fancy suits. He knew how to fight.

How to kill.

"We're getting in and out as fast as we can." He led her into the building. Growled when he found out that she was on the first floor. "Open access to anyone," he snapped.

The room had been cheap, so she'd taken it.

They hurried past the desk clerk. Turned the corner and—

Her door was ajar. Room one-oh-four. Claire stopped.

Noah immediately stilled beside her. "What is it?"

Claire shook her head, fighting the surge of fear she'd felt. If she wasn't careful, Claire found that fear could creep up on her far too often. "I think the maid is in there."

He advanced. Claire tried to hurry with him, but Noah pushed her behind him.

He entered the room first. His body tensed. "It's not a damn maid."

She peered over his shoulder. Her clothes were tossed around the room. They'd been…slashed? Torn apart? "No," Claire whispered. Dammit, those clothes were all she had! Fury had her shoving past Noah.

He grabbed her and wrapped his arms around her stomach. "Don't! The bastard could still be in here." He pushed her back once more. Then he stalked forward. He yanked open the closet. Checked the bathroom.

Claire stood in the doorway. The room was wrecked. The mirror was shattered. Chunks of glass littered the floor. The overturned mattress slumped against the small nightstand.

My things...they're all —

Her gaze fell on the floor. On the picture frame that had been smashed. Claire rushed forward and grabbed it. Broken glass bit into her fingers.

Her family stared back up at her. *Her mom.* Claire had her mom's blonde hair. *Her dad.* Claire had his blue eyes. Her parents were both smiling. And Claire — Claire was standing next to her sister, Sara.

Claire had been fifteen years old then.

She'd been happy.

"Claire!"

Her head snapped up at Noah's call. Her hold tightened on the frame.

He stalked toward her. "You were supposed to stay in the hall."

She shook her head. "He's not here anymore."

"Dammit, you're bleeding."

"It's just a cut." Her voice sounded so hollow. "Nothing to-to worry about."

"Christ, Claire, there's plenty to *worry* about. Some asshole broke into your room. Destroyed your things. And now you're hurt."

A small wound, nothing more. She'd suffered plenty worse. But he took the frame from her and led her into the matchbox-sized bathroom. He put her hand under the rush of water in the sink. "Here," Noah said, "let's push up your sleeves..."

Because she was still so shocked by the savagery in her room, it took Claire a moment too long to react to his words.

He pushed up her sleeves.

Claire glanced down. Saw the white scars on each wrist. "No!" She jerked away from him but Claire knew it was too late. He'd seen those marks. "I'm fine." Her voice was stronger now. She whirled to face Noah. "*I'm fine.*"

His gaze held hers.

"I need the frame. The picture." Her voice was softer now. "Nothing else matters." It couldn't matter. It was all gone.

She brushed past him.

"*What in the hell happened here?*" At that bellow, Claire looked toward the doorway. The Hamlet's Hotel manager — a man with thinning hair and small, dark eyes — glared at her. "Did you have a party? We don't allow —"

Noah was across that room in an instant. He grabbed the manager and shoved him up against the thin wall of the room. "Does it look like a damn party?"

The manager's small eyes got very big.

"Someone broke into her room because the security at your hotel is shit." Noah's voice vibrated with fury. "He got in here, and he wrecked Ms. Kramer's things. If she'd been here, he could have *hurt* her."

"I-I know you," the manager gasped out as his eyes widened with recognition. "You're Noah York!"

In this town, most people knew him. Or, knew *of* Noah.

"Call the police," Noah snarled at him. "Call them now. I'm sure they have this place's address memorized." He let the guy go. The man stumbled away.

Noah focused on Claire once more. She held the frame in her hands. He rolled back his shoulders and demanded, "Has this ever happened to you before?"

Having her place trashed? Unfortunately, it had. Claire nodded.

His jaw hardened. "How many times?"

"It hasn't happened since I lived at home, back in Alabama." She never let her southern drawl slip out. She'd worked hard to lose her past.

But the past wouldn't let go.

"At first, people blamed me," Claire confessed quietly. At first? That was a lie. Claire knew that too many still blamed her for what happened down in Alabama. "The house was trashed a few times back then." Goosebumps were on her arms. "This — this was just a break-in." It *couldn't* be related to her past. "The thieves must have realized I'd taken my purse, that nothing valuable was left behind, so they trashed the place."

His eyes glittered.

"It was just a break-in," Claire repeated, willing herself to believe those words. "Like you said, the police have this address memorized. Crimes happen here all the time."

"I don't want you ever coming back here," he gritted out the words.

She looked around the room. "There's no reason to come back. Not anymore." But it looked as if she'd be starting her new job with just the clothes on her back.

And with the memory of her past rushing through her mind.

***

He watched as the police came. They would find no clues in that dank, little hotel room. Nothing that could be tied back to him.

He never left clues behind.

Claire was there. Broken Claire Kramer. She stood in front of the Hamlet, clutching tight to her photo.

Nothing was left of Claire's family. They were all bones in the ground. She was alone.

Except...*who is that guy with her?*

Because there was a man near Claire. A man who let his body brush against hers. A man who wrapped his arms around Claire's shoulders even as the man seemed to bark orders to the cops.

No, no, no! Claire didn't get to turn to another. That wasn't how this worked.

And Claire...Claire didn't *like* to be touched.

Only that man was touching her.

That man was also loading Claire into the back of a big, dark limo.

What in the hell?

Rage pulsed within him. He'd made sure that Claire was at the end of her rope. He'd pushed and pushed her. She should have been falling apart then.

Just like she did before.

No white knight was supposed to ride to Claire's rescue. That damn well wouldn't happen. Claire Kramer deserved to be punished for her crimes.

And no matter what, he would see to it that she *was* punished. She'd suffer, just as Claire had made others suffer.

Punishing Claire was his job, and he was very, very good at that job.

CHAPTER TWO

The knock at her door woke Claire the next morning. She rolled over, pushing away the memory of blood and death and gunshots, and a quick glance at the bedside clock showed her that it was six a.m.

Claire had slept in a hotel robe last night. There hadn't exactly been tons of options for her. So as she rose from the bed, Claire secured the robe once more and hurried toward that demanding knock.

She glanced through the peep-hole and saw Noah standing on the other side of the door.

He wasn't alone.

Her hand automatically flew up to try and smooth down her hair. She had to look like hell. She had to—

"Open the door, Claire."

How had he known that she was standing there?

Claire opened the door. Noah immediately pushed his way inside. "Bring in all the clothes. Put them in her closet."

Two men hurried in after him. They were both wearing York Towers jackets, with the distinctive YT emblem, and both men were also carrying armfuls of bags.

The names displayed on those bags told her that the items inside had come with a very hefty price tag.

"Noah, what did you do?"

He stood close to her. Not touching, but still making her too aware of the warmth that always clung to him. His gaze was on the frame near her bed. She…liked to keep it close.

After a moment, while the other men got busy unpacking those bags, Noah turned back to glance at her. "You look good in the morning."

What?

"No makeup. Just soft lips. Wide eyes." His voice was low, carrying only to her ears. "And you even have a little sprinkle of freckles across your nose. Your makeup hid that from me before."

Claire shook her head. "Who are those men?"

"Franco and Paul both work in the concierge department here at the hotel. They've got plenty of connections in this town, and they used those connections to help me out."

Only they weren't helping Noah. They were helping her. "How did they know my size?"

The clothes they were unpacking — *unreal.*

"I knew your size. Don't forget…" And his voice dropped even more. "I did have the chance to get up close and personal with you in Chicago."

Up close and personal? She'd been punching him! But he'd been holding her tight. "I thought you were — you were some mugger. I was scared —"

"So you attacked." He nodded. "But when you did, I was able to get a pretty good feel for your body."

She suspected the guy was an expert when it came to getting a "feel" for a woman's body.

"The shoes will be here soon," Noah murmured. "Don't worry. I didn't forget them."

Franco and Paul nodded toward her, then they slipped out the door.

"The only thing I didn't get picked up…" Noah's voice was stronger now that they were alone. "I didn't want them getting your underwear."

Her cheeks had to be flaming.

"I'll take care of that today," he added.

"No!" That response was a horrified squeak from her. "I can take care of that myself!" There was no way she wanted him buying her bras. Her panties. *Anything* sexual.

She paced away from him and stared at the now full closet. "I can't pay for this." She also couldn't pay for the underwear that she needed. Shame burned through her. She'd tried to stay at those other jobs. Tried to save money, but each time she'd been forced to move and start again, her bank account had depleted more and more.

Until nothing was left.

"Consider it an advance on your salary." He didn't even sound a little concerned.

Probably because he had money to burn. She didn't. She also had pride. Her hands tightened around the robe's belt as she glanced at him. "You have to deduct every penny from my paycheck."

He rolled one shoulder in a careless shrug. "It's really a business expenditure, you know."

Bull.

Another knock sounded at the door.

Noah advance toward the door as he told her, "Where I go, you will go. You needed clothing that would—"

"Let me fit in your circle?" Claire finished and her pride sure felt like it took a hit then.

He paused at the door. "You already fit me, Claire." He opened the door. Franco and Paul were already back—and loaded down with shoe boxes this time.

While they unloaded the shoes, Noah returned to Claire's side. "The police have nothing," he said, voice softer once again. "They think it was just a random break-in at the Hamlet."

"I-I'm sure it was." She needed to believe that.

"Claire…How can I help you, when you're so determined to keep your past locked away?"

She forced herself to meet his gaze. "You already know what happened to me. I saw that manila file on your desk. That file told you what college I went to, so I'm sure whatever investigator you hired also told you all about what happened when I was sixteen."

He didn't speak again until Franco and Paul were headed toward the door.

"Thank you," Claire told them as she stepped forward. "Thank you so much—"

Paul, a red-haired man with dark green eyes, waved away her thanks. "Ma'am, when the boss tells us to jump, we do. And considering some of the crazy things we've had to do for him…" Paul laughed. "Taking care of his new assistant was a pleasure."

"Yes," Franco agreed, smiling. Franco appeared to be in his early twenties, and his skin was a deep coffee cream. "Nothing like the time he had us get rid of that dead body."

"*What?*"

Franco laughed. "Sorry. Couldn't resist." He gave her a little wave. "I'm sure we'll be seeing you very soon."

Then he and Paul were gone.

Claire faced Noah. "I should go use those new clothes and get dressed." She gave a firm nod of her head and turned away to—

"Running, Claire?"

"Walking," she said without looking back at him. "Walking very slowly."

She'd taken about four steps when he said, "Trace Weston."

The name had her pausing.

Trace Weston was a billionaire, a man with a dangerous reputation—and the man who'd saved her sanity once upon a time.

Claire's sister had worked for Trace. Sara had been his assistant for several years before she'd been brutally murdered in Chicago.

Claire cleared her throat. "If you had Trace Weston investigate me, then I'm sure you discovered all of my dirty little secrets. Weston Securities is the best firm in the U.S."

"You don't have dirty secrets."

Yes, she did. Everyone did. Hers were bloody and dirty and dark.

"You know, so I don't have to tell you." She needed to get dressed. The clothing almost seemed to be armor that she had to don in order to deal with him.

"There's plenty for you to tell me. One day, you will."

He sounded so certain. So confident.

Claire found herself whirling toward him. For years, she'd been the good one. The quiet one. The one who never tried to step a foot out of line.

But I still lose everyone who gets close to me. "Only if you tell me your secrets, Noah. Because I know you have them. You and Trace…your *military* past. You both pretend to be such good, upstanding members of society, but there's more to you both, right? Secrets that some people would kill to know."

His lips twisted. "Touché."

Her breath heaved out. "I'm going to get dressed. Wait outside the suite."

He blinked.

What? Had no one ever given the guy an order before? *Money can't buy everything, Noah York.*

"I'll go," he said with a nod, "because we need to get ready for our flight."

"Flight?" she echoed.

"York Towers is a world-wide operation, you know that. I rarely stay in one city too long."

She pulled at the sleeves of her robe, making sure her wrists were covered. "Where are we going?"

"This time, it's just a short trip to D.C."

Claire could feel all of the blood leaving her face. *D.C.* "Claire?"

"I'll be ready in twenty minutes," she promised him.

He's not in D.C. any more. He's long gone. I'll be safe there.

"You don't have to—"

"Outside," she said again. Then she headed for her closet and the clothes that he'd bought for her. She heard him walk away.

Heard the soft click of the door shut behind him.

And then she heard a whisper from her past. The voice of Ethan Harrison's father, Senator Colby Harrison.

You little bitch. I know you made my boy kill. You did this. I'll make you pay. No matter how long it takes, you'll pay.

And all of his rage had come at her *before* he'd lost his senate seat due to the scandal. After that, he'd blamed her, hated her, even more.

But Colby Harrison isn't in Washington, D.C. I'll be safe with Noah.

Her hands were shaking when she reached for the clothes.

***

Noah yanked out his phone as he paced in front of Claire's suite. He didn't give a damn what time it was. His buddy owed him.

The phone rang once. Twice. Then—

"Dammit, Noah," Trace Weston growled, "you know I'm on my honeymoon, right?"

Yeah, he did. Lucky bastard. Two weeks ago, Trace's fiancée, Skye, had confessed that she didn't want to have a big wedding that would just be fodder for the gossip pages. Instead, she'd asked Trace to run away with her. To elope.

And since Trace would do anything for Skye…

They'd gotten married in Paris.

"I need your agents in New York to look into a break-in for me." He kept his eyes on Claire's suite door.

"Uh, then *call* the office there, man. Don't just—"

"It's about Claire Kramer, and I only want your best men on the case."

Silence. Then… "Is she all right?"

"She's with me."

"That doesn't answer the question."

Noah yanked a hand through his hair. "The SOB who killed her parents is still locked up in an Alabama prison."

"I made sure of that." Grim satisfaction coated Trace's words.

Noah knew that Claire's sister Sara had used her connection to Trace in order to get his help. He'd used his power to convince the parole board that Ethan Harrison shouldn't be walking outside of those prison gates anytime soon.

"Someone broke into Claire's hotel room at the Hamlet yesterday. Slashed her clothes. Destroyed every damn thing there."

"The Hamlet? What the hell was she doing there? Noah, I thought you said you were watching—"

"I've got her now," Noah growled into the phone. "I want your men to see if they can find out who broke into her room. The cops aren't looking hard. The Hamlet gets robbed every other day. It's just business as usual at that place." But the knot in his gut told him that the destruction in Claire's room hadn't *just* been the result of a robbery gone wrong.

Noah never ignored his instincts. They'd kept him alive too many times in the past, and they'd put his enemies in the ground.

"I'll get my men on it," Trace said, voice flat. "And if I find out anything—"

"You call me right away." He knew he could count on Trace.

"Will do."

"And, hey, one more thing, buddy…"

"What is it?" Worry deepened Trace's voice.

"Give that pretty bride of yours a big kiss for me."

"Screw off," Trace muttered and hung up the phone.

Noah's lips tilted as he kept staring at Claire's door.

Trace had loved his Skye for over ten years. Loved her, but nearly lost her to a crazed stalker.

Once upon a time, Noah had thought that Trace's single-minded love for Skye made the other man weak.

Now he knew…

It makes him lucky.

***

She'd never been to D.C. Claire had actually made a point of staying out of the area.

She hadn't wanted to attract any unwanted attention.

But as Noah's private jet touched down in D.C., tension settled heavily over Claire's shoulders.

First trip to D.C. and my first time to fly in a private jet.

Noah had talked to her all during the flight. Business only. He'd gone over a listing of his most profitable hotels, hinted at his plans for expansion, told her the PR work that needed to be done…

And he'd kept her mind off the fear that wanted to snake through her.

"What's that look for?" Noah asked as he unbuckled his seatbelt. Time for them to go.

She fumbled and managed to unhook her belt, too. "I, uh, I'm just curious about the city." Such a lie.

"You haven't been here before?" He seemed surprised. Since globe-hopping was no doubt a habit for him, it probably was surprising.

"Most people don't get to jet off whenever they want," she said as she fought to keep her voice light. "Besides, I…I was busy."

"You mean you didn't want to come here." He stood, blocking the exit. Trapping her, but not touching her. "You don't need to lie to me."

Right.

"I didn't want to come here." Her hair slipped forward and fell over her left eye.

Before she could brush the blonde locks back, Noah's hand moved. His fingers pushed the hair back and lingered on her cheek. "But you came for me."

Her heart was beating faster. "I came for *me*." Because she wouldn't let fear lead her life. "Colby Harrison isn't here." She wasn't going to dance around this issue. Noah had his neat file, after all, so why hide the truth? "He lost his position two terms back."

And she hadn't seen the man in eight years.

"When you worry…" His fingers slipped from her cheek and his index finger moved to lightly tap her lower lip. "You have a tendency to bite this lip."

Her breath caught in her lungs.

His finger caressed her lip. "Don't do that. Don't hurt yourself."

"I-I wasn't…" She barely breathed the words against his touch.

But…when she spoke, she…she licked his finger.

It was an accident. She hadn't meant to do that. Not at all. Had she?

His pupils expanded, swallowing the gold. "*Claire…*" Need, lust, deepened her name.

She backed away. Tried to. But there was nowhere for her to go. The seat was behind her. He was in front of her.

His hand fell to his side. Fisted. "Don't tease."

"I didn't mean—"

"I want you every fucking time I see you."

Her eyes widened.

"But I'm trying to give you what you want."

Claire wasn't even sure what she wanted.

To be safe?

No, no, there had to be more to life than safety.

"You have to ask, remember?" His voice was so deep. So dark. So tempting. "Just ask." He turned away. "Let's get the hell off this plane before I forget that part."

When his back was to her, Claire finally managed to suck in a deep breath. "I should tell you something."

But then the pilot strode from the cockpit. Claire immediately clamped her lips shut. She sure wasn't about to make this particular reveal in front of anyone but Noah.

Claire didn't speak again until they'd cleared the airport and were in the back of yet another limo. Noah and his limos. At this point, she figured that wherever he went, a car would be waiting.

As the car drove, she found herself leaning closer to the window as she tried to get a glimpse of the city.

"It will be a while before you see anything out here."

She kept looking. Everything here was new to her.

"The privacy shield is up." And the deep longing, the lust, was gone from his voice. Noah seemed back to business now. "Finish what you were saying to me on the plane."

Making sure that she did not bite her lip, Claire turned toward him. "I can't give you what you want."

"Don't be so sure of that..."

Claire shook her head, hard. "Hot sex. Pleasure."

"That's *exactly* what I had in mind."

He wasn't understanding her. "That's not for me."

A faint line appeared between his brows. "Claire, if there's one thing you're made for, it's pleasure."

But pleasure just brought more pain. "I don't have lovers."

Silence. His stare seemed to measure her. After what had to be at least two minutes of extremely awkward silence, he said, "You *don't* as in...you don't have one now?"

"I don't have one now. I haven't had one in nine years." She didn't let emotion leak into her voice. There was no emotion. She was simply stating a fact. "I don't let men get close to me. So you and I...it's not going to happen." She glanced away from him. There. She'd done it. Now Noah wouldn't touch her again. And she wouldn't feel the longing that his touch stirred. A longing for something Claire knew she wasn't meant to have.

"He should be dead."

Those cold, biting words had her gaze flying back to his.

"The only lover you had? That bastard who tried to destroy you?" Noah growled the words. "He should be rotting in the ground."

"H-he's in a cell—"

"Prison is too easy for Ethan Harrison."

His eyes...his voice...Claire shifted nervously. "You aren't who you pretend to be."

He smiled then, and the sight chilled her. "No, Claire, I'm not. I'm a man who knows too much about death and dealing out bloody justice."

"Why?" The question slipped from her. She hadn't meant to ask, but—

"Why do I think Ethan should be dead? Because he's a monster. No amount of rehabilitation is going to fix what's wrong with him. If he ever gets out—"

I'm a dead woman.

Claire already knew exactly what would happen to her if Ethan Harrison ever got out of prison. "That's not what I was asking." She took a breath and pushed on. "Why do you even care what happens in my life? You once said that you owed me a debt, but…we both know you don't, not really. So why do I even matter at all to you? You're *Noah York*." He'd been on the cover of a dozen magazines that she'd passed in the airport. "And I'm…I'm no one."

He leaned closer, but he didn't touch her.

She was…disappointed? No, surely not.

I am.

"You're someone to me."

She had to look away from him again. His gaze seemed to see too deeply into her.

His fingers caught her chin. He turned her head back so that she had to stare into his eyes. "Your sister died in Chicago because she was pulled into Trace's battle. You lost her, and I wish every day that hadn't happened."

So did Claire. "Sara was all I had left." The one person who'd believed in Claire, no matter what accusations were tossed around in their small town.

"I damn well do owe you, Claire, but that's not why I have my *interest* in you."

She waited.

"I want you." Flat. Almost angry. "More than I can remember wanting any other woman."

"Y-you've had dozens of lovers—" Claire began.

"Yes, dozens." He released her chin. "But for the last three months, when I close my eyes, I only see you."

Claire swiped her damp palms on her new, black pants. "I can't compete with them." The guy dated super models, heiresses, and—

"There's no damn competition." He gave a hard, negative shake of his head. "I told you, I've never wanted anyone as much as I want you."

"But...*why?*"

"Because I find you sexy as hell. I look at you, and I ache."

Her breath came faster.

His gaze was on her mouth. "And I have the feeling that when I do finally taste you, you just might addict me."

Helplessly, Claire shook her head. "I can't give you...what you need."

"We'll see about that, Claire." He inclined his head. "You might want to look out the window now. You don't want to miss what's coming..."

She turned back to the window, dazed. D.C. rose before her, but in her mind, she saw a pair of glittering, golden eyes. Eyes that shone with desire.

A desire that she'd felt, too. She hadn't wanted any man, not in so long. She'd been in cold storage but...

He was warming her again. And making her want things that were too dangerous for her to ever have.

***

At eight p.m., Noah walked into Claire's temporary D.C. office. They'd been in meetings all day. Talking with contractors, working with marketing staff. They'd barely stopped for lunch.

Claire had surprised him. He'd known that she was smart. After all, the woman had graduated at the top of her class, but she was also damn savvy when it came to the inner workings of the hotel business. And the woman sure had a gift for tact.

Noah wasn't always so tactful. When he'd been ready to tear into the contractors, Claire had carefully interceded. Charmed.

She was sure charming him.

She was also not even aware that he was in the room with her. Claire was crouched over the laptop that he'd given her earlier, her fingers tapping furiously across the keys.

It was rare that a woman could ignore him.

But then, Claire *was* a very rare woman.

So he just crossed his arms over his chest and watched her. A small furrow was between her brows—a sign of her focus, he was certain. Her cheeks were pale, her lips bare of color. But Claire didn't need makeup to shine. She was already so close to perfect that he ached just looking at her.

I don't have lovers… I don't have one now. I haven't had one in nine years.

He'd taken that revelation like a punch to the gut. Claire truly was made for pleasure, and by locking herself off from the world, she was just giving that SOB Ethan Harrison more power over her.

Claire deserved pleasure. Noah was going to see that she got it.

Claire glanced up then. She saw him—and jumped.

"Sorry," Noah murmured as he straightened. "Didn't mean to scare you."

Claire surged to her feet. "Then you shouldn't skulk in doorways."

Skulk? He smiled at her. "You looked focused. I was waiting for the right time to interrupt."

Her eyes narrowed, and he knew she was trying to decide if she believed his story or not.

Since it was a lie, he let his smile stretch a bit more. He hadn't announced his presence because he'd just enjoyed watching her. "You need to wrap things up for the night."

She pushed back her hair. "Ah, right…just give me—"

"We're going out for dinner," Noah added. Then, so she wouldn't be so nervous, he said, "I want to check out the competition in town." He'd just bought one of the historic hotels in D.C. – the hotel they were inside of right then. His crew was updating the hotel's interior, while still working to keep the ambiance and the character that the clientele would love. He wanted to add a roof-top restaurant to the hotel, though. A new place that would be the talk of the town. He already had a celebrity chef lined up for the new venue.

So while he didn't *technically* need to check out the competition, he did want to take Claire to dinner.

Their first date. Even if she didn't know it.

Claire nodded. "I'll change and meet you in the lobby."

Sounded like one fine plan to him. He wondered what the odds were that she'd put on the sleek, black dress that had been purchased for her. One that dipped low in the back and would reveal Claire's long legs.

She approached him slowly. Cautiously.

Noah realized that he was blocking the door.

If he didn't move, Claire would have to brush against him as she passed.

I want her to get used to my touch.

He also wanted her to make the next move.

He slid to the side.

But Claire…she still brushed against him as she passed.

That's it, Claire. Touch me. Do it all you want.

He turned, watching her as she left the little office. Hell, yes. Claire had been made for pleasure.

And soon, he'd give her so much pleasure that she screamed.

***

Noah was in the lobby, talking with the hotel manager, when the elevator doors slid open and Claire walked out.

She was wearing the black dress. It clung to every curve that she had.

And her legs…sweet hell, her legs seemed to go on forever. Her feet were clad in high, black heels. Fuck-me heels.

She'd put on lipstick. Slid color on her cheeks. Pulled her hair back into a little twist.

She also had black ribbon tied around her wrists. Sexy, silky ribbon that made Noah think of Claire…

Tied to his bed.

"Ah, Mr. York?" The manager, Chuck Collins, cleared his throat. "You were, um, you were telling me about the construction upstairs—"

He couldn't remember a damn thing that he'd been saying to Chuck. "Carry on with your work." He nodded curtly to the guy.

"But Mr. York—"

Noah stalked toward Claire. The woman looked good enough to eat. How was he supposed to keep his hands off her?

She put *her* hands in front of her dress. At that angle, it almost looked as if her wrists were bound together with the ribbon.

Noah swallowed. The woman had no clue what she was doing to him.

"Sorry it took so long," Claire told him with a slightly nervous edge in her voice. "I had to, um…improvise a few things."

He reached for her hand. Noah had to do it. That ribbon was driving him insane. How could something so simple be so sexy?

He lifted her hand. Turned her wrist and realized—

She's not wearing this to be sexy. She's using the ribbon to hide her scars.

"I improvise if I wear something without sleeves," Claire said, her voice so low it was almost a whisper. "It's just…people might ask questions, and I didn't want to embarrass you."

A growl rumbled in his throat. "You would never embarrass me." He didn't let her hand go. He knew exactly how Claire had gotten those scars on her wrists. His Claire had broken once.

Because of Ethan Harrison.

Noah would make sure that she never broke again.

Her lips started to curl. He waited for her smile to come. For her dimples to flash. He—

"*Claire Kramer!*" The snarl cut across the hotel's lobby. The tall, arching ceiling in the historic hotel seemed to make the cry echo all around the space.

Noah turned at the cry, frowning at the fury he heard in those words.

An older man had just entered the lobby. His gray hair had thinned, his shoulders hunched, but a feverish intensity lit his eyes. Eyes that were locked on Claire.

"I'd know you anywhere," the man snapped.

He advanced on Claire.

The hell, *no.*

Noah stepped in front of Claire even as he heard her gasp behind him.

"Mr. Harrison, *no!*" This cry came from the man who was hurrying to grab the older guy's arm. A brown-haired fellow wearing a three piece suit. Probably in his late twenties, with one of those All-American faces.

But *Harrison* shook off the man's hold. "You damn bitch!" He yelled at Claire. "You should be in prison! Not my boy! You should be—"

"You need to close your mouth," Noah said, his own voice lethally soft. "Before I close it for you." His hands were clenched, and he wanted to drive his fist into the old man's jaw.

He knew he was looking at *ex*-Senator Colby Harrison. He'd seen photos of the guy, but those photos had been during the man's time in office. Harrison hadn't aged so well. Age spots and thick lines marked his face, and the stench of booze clung to the man.

Colby Harrison wasn't a D.C. power player any longer. This jerk was about to find his ass kicked into the street.

"I'm sorry," the man with Harrison muttered. "He got a call that she was here, and I couldn't stop him—"

Harrison made a mistake then. He tried to lunge around Noah and actually touch Claire.

Huge mistake.

Noah shoved the bastard back. "You don't touch her. You don't even *talk* to her again, understand?"

Colby Harrison blinked as he stumbled back a bit more. His gaze was full of rage and hate. "You know what she did?" He shook his head then yelled, "*She ruined my boy's life! Twisted him! Made him —* "

"From what I hear," Noah's voice was still low, but grating with fury. "Your Ethan was a twisted bastard all along. *You* knew that. Instead of getting him help, you just covered up for the asshole." He closed in on Colby Harrison. Stood toe-to-toe with the guy. "I know who you are. The question is…do you know *I* am?"

The ex-senator frowned at him.

"Noah York," the other guy whispered from behind Colby. "He owns this place. Now, boss, come on, we need to get out of here."

Colby's shouts had attracted too much attention. That just wouldn't do. Not only because Noah just didn't allow shit like this in his hotels but because—

Claire can't be upset.

"If you don't get the hell out of here in the next five seconds," Noah told him, holding Colby's stare, "then I'll have my men throw you out." He smiled and knew the sight would be grim. "Or maybe I'll just do that part myself. Because I don't give a shit how old you are or who you *used* to be. When I look at you, I just see garbage that needs to be tossed away."

Colby sucked in a sharp breath. "She should've lost her freedom. Just like *him!*" He tried to crane his neck and see Claire. "She seduced him. Made him kill. That woman is *evil!*"

Noah was done. He grabbed the guy's shoulders and pushed him toward the door.

"You can't do this!" Colby yelled. "I'm a senator! I've got powerful friends in this town!"

Two members of the hotel security team rushed toward Noah. He didn't let go of Colby. He wanted the pleasure of tossing the bastard into the street himself.

"Knew this would happen," the younger man said as he hurried behind them. "Knew it…"

Noah didn't stop until he was on the sidewalk in front of his hotel. He still had a tight grip on Colby's shoulders. "I don't care who your friends are. You come near Claire again, and no one will be able to save you." He leaned in close because he wanted to make sure Colby understood exactly what he was saying. "You so much as look her way, and I'll destroy you."

Then he dropped his hold. Colby stared up at him, fear flickering in his gaze. Good. The guy had gotten the message.

"I'm, um, sorry," the dark-haired fellow began.

Noah whirled on him. "Who are you?"

"Vincent Finch. I'm the senator's…I'm his manager."

What the hell ever. "Keep him away, Finch, or go down with him."

Noah turned on his heel and marched back into the hotel. Claire stood just a few feet in front of the elevator, exactly where she'd been moments before. Her head was down. When he looked closely, he could see that she was trembling.

Screw this.

He didn't want Claire cowering from anyone or anything. People in the lobby were whispering as they gazed at her. He was pretty sure he'd even caught sight of a reporter with a camera. Gossip and D.C. — the two were always locked together.

Noah didn't hesitate. He stalked right up to her. *"Claire."*

Her head snapped up. "I-I'm sorry —"

He pulled her into his arms and kissed her.

CHAPTER THREE

Shock froze Claire. Noah's arms were around her, he had her pressed tightly to his body, and his mouth—

His mouth claimed hers.

Her lips had been parted when he kissed her. His tongue slipped inside her mouth. There was nothing hesitant about the way Noah kissed her. He just...took.

And ignited her.

Her hands rose. Curled around his shoulders. She should push him back. She should do something, anything but—

Pull him closer.

Kiss him back.

Fear and shame knotted within her, fighting with a tide of hot desire that caught her by surprise.

Noah's hands were on her hips. Holding her so tightly and he was—

Pushing her into the elevator. Still kissing her, but guiding her movements.

She heard the elevator ding, and Claire pulled away from Noah. For a moment, she stared up at him, lost.

"Will that be all, sir?" The question came from the man standing near the elevator doors. He had his hand up and was holding the elevator open. *Chuck Collins.* Claire had met the hotel manager earlier. As she stared at him, Chuck cleared his throat and asked again, "Will that be all?"

Noah glanced over at him. "Not quite." His words were low and lethal. "That asshole never comes into the hotel again."

Chuck nodded. "Understood." Then he dropped his hand and the elevator doors slid closed.

Claire was still in Noah's arms. Still shocked and lost and aching in a way she shouldn't be.

"You can...you can let me go," Claire managed to say.

Noah shook his head. His eyes were on her mouth. "I knew one taste wouldn't be enough."

It wasn't enough for her, either. Noah tasted good. Very good. Good like the kind of wine Claire had when she saved her money and splurged. Not that she'd done any splurging, not in the last year. Like the wine, he also made her a little drunk.

"Ask me to kiss you again, Claire."

He wanted to keep kissing her? After what had just happened in that lobby?

"Let me go." She pushed against his chest. The elevator was rising, and she didn't even remember Noah hitting the button on the control panel. But she knew where they were headed.

The top floor, of course. What she was thinking of as *his* floor.

The faint lines around his eyes deepened, but Noah let her go.

Claire rubbed her arms, chilled without him. "He shouldn't have been here. I'm so sorry—"

"Apologize again, and I swear, Claire, you'll push me too far."

Her breath caught.

He nodded. "Good. Here's the deal. Colby Harrison is your past, got it? He doesn't matter. What he says...*doesn't matter.*"

"But all of those people...they saw. They heard." They'd all been staring at her. When she'd lived in Alabama, she hadn't even been able to walk down the aisle at the grocery store without people stopping to stare and whisper.

Did you hear...that's the girl...she seduced that poor boy...made him crazy...

Got him to kill her folks…

Claire shook her head as she tried to make those voices vanish. They'd haunted her for too long.

"I don't care about those people."

"It's your business. Your hotel. You *should* care." She'd been so worried about doing something to tarnish his image. And now…

"Scandal sells, baby, or haven't you realized that?"

Claire flinched. She hated scandal. She wanted…secrecy.

The elevator doors opened.

"So much for dinner," she muttered.

He caught her hand. Brushed his fingers over the ribbon on her right wrist. She'd learned to be creative over the years. When people saw the scars there, well, there was no mistaking them. You got scars on your wrist-those long, thin scars — from one act.

Claire had wanted to die when she was sixteen. When she stood at her parents' graves, when it seemed that the whole world hated her, she'd wanted to escape.

To be with my mom and dad again.

People had spray painted her home. Written words like "whore" and "killer" on her windows. Senator Harrison had done a massive job on the local media. He'd worked so hard to convince everyone that his son was just the poor, misled boy.

And Claire was the evil seductress.

He'd told her, time and again, that she should be the one to suffer. The one to be punished.

I just wanted to escape.

The scars would always be there. She covered them so she didn't have to see the curiosity, the pity, in the eyes of strangers.

"Come back to me."

Claire blinked and focused on Noah.

He had lifted a dark eyebrow. "I told you, the past is over." Anger pumped in his words. He pulled her toward his room. Not just a room. A suite. One as big as the place he had in New York.

He opened the door. Kept his hold on her and pulled her over the threshold. When the door closed behind them, Claire exhaled slowly as relief hit her.

Safe.

"He's the reason, isn't he?" Noah asked her. "The reason you lose your other jobs. The reason you move around the country so much."

Claire nodded. Her gaze was on the D.C. skyline. She'd wanted to walk through the city at night.

But Harrison is out there.

"He...I think he hires someone, a detective maybe, to watch me. Each time when I feel like I might have a life, Colby Harrison comes in. Reveals my past. Gets me fired." An endless cycle.

"He won't be a problem any longer." Noah's voice was grim.

Claire glanced over her shoulder at him.

"He's done, Claire. *Done.* He won't ever get near you again." He yanked a hand through his hair. "Nine years? Jesus, you put up with this for nine years? Why didn't you get a restraining order against him? Why didn't you—"

"He's never physically hurt me." There were so many other ways to hurt. Like when she'd been nineteen and her grandfather had been struck down by a heart attack. She'd flown back home to bury him. And at the funeral, Colby Harrison had been there...telling everyone that the whore was back in town.

"*Never again,*" Noah vowed.

She wished it could be that simple. "Noah, he's not going to stop. Not until I'm dead or-or he is."

Noah held her gaze. Nodded. "He's done," he said again, simply.

A chill skated over Claire's spine.

His stare drifted over her face. Down her body. Lingered on her legs. "I was supposed to wine and dine you tonight."

She'd never been wined and dined.

His golden eyes lifted. Locked on her mouth. "I knew one taste would do it for me. Claire, sweet Claire, you taste like candy."

She could still taste him.

"No lover? Not in nine years?" He stood about five feet away from her.

Claire shook her head. "The people in the lobby—"

"I told you, what they saw doesn't matter."

"They saw you kiss me. The other—the other York Towers employees. They'll all think—"

He took a step toward her. "That I'm fucking you."

"Yes."

He took another stop. "I told you, I don't fuck my employees."

He had said that but… "You kissed me."

Another step. "Nothing would have stopped me from kissing you then."

He hadn't turned from her in shock or disgust. Hadn't been embarrassed. After everything, he'd…wanted her. "You don't think I did it? You don't think I seduced Ethan Harrison into killing for me?"

"No."

Her lips trembled. They'd crossed a line downstairs. She knew that. She also knew exactly what she had to do.

They saw us kiss. I can't keep working for him now. Coming to Noah…taking the job…it was a mistake. One desperation had led her to make.

And perhaps she was about to make another mistake. But Claire found she didn't care.

"I want to kiss you again," Noah told her.

He took another step toward her.

So little space separated them. Claire shook her head.

Noah's face hardened.

"I want more," she told him, then Claire pulled in a deep breath, grabbed tight to her courage and asked, "Will you fuck me?"

***

"You shouldn't have gone to the hotel," Vincent murmured. "Th-that was a mistake, sir."

"The mistake was made years ago," Colby snapped back at him. "When that girl wasn't charged along with my son." Sure, Ethan had been troubled. He'd been a little wild, but he'd never *killed*.

Not until he'd gotten involved with Claire Kramer. A little cheap piece of ass who'd destroyed Colby's world.

Vincent shifted uncomfortably beside Colby. They were in the back of a cab, heading to their hotel. Once, Colby had only ridden in limos. He'd had the D.C. folks jumping to do his bidding.

But he'd lost his congressional seat after the trial.

Nearly lost his fortune in the legal battles over the years.

He *would* have lost it all, if it hadn't been for his other son. Austin has saved him.

Austin was the only good thing he had left.

Because Claire took my life away.

"Uh, sir, I read the newspaper articles. Ethan tried to kill Claire—"

The bastard *dared* to say that to him? "Because he couldn't live with what she'd made him do! Ethan told me the truth. He couldn't stand what she'd done, how she'd used him, and he was just trying to stop her from hurting anyone else."

Claire Kramer. Not some sweet innocent girl. She was a lying, manipulative whore who'd destroyed his boy.

It was a good thing Colby's wife hadn't lived to see the tragedy that hit his son. But Lily had died when Ethan was just three years old. She'd slipped from Colby's life too soon. His perfect Lily—*gone*.

Lily was in the ground, but Claire Kramer was still walking around, living the high life. That was so unfair.

His hands were shaking. His gut twisting. He yanked out his phone. Vincent was a damn idiot. He didn't understand anything.

Colby's call was answered on the second ring. "You were right," Colby said, the words heaving out of him. "She was here. *York* brought her here. The bastard is probably screwing her."

Because Claire always used her body to get just what she wanted.

The tremor in his hands got worse as his rage swelled. "It can't go on any longer," Colby said. "I'm going to make sure she *suffers.*"

As his boy suffered, every damn day in that prison cell.

Ethan had nothing.

Claire deserved the same fate.

***

Noah's hand lifted and curved around Claire's chin. "You need to be very sure. There will be no going back."

There wasn't any place for her to go back to.

"I want to be with you." Her words were the truth. She wanted him for tonight because tomorrow, well, then she'd begin running again.

A new city.

A new job.

Maybe this time, it would take Colby Harrison longer to find her.

Maybe.

He leaned toward her. "I'm going to make you scream for me."

She shook her head. She wasn't the screaming type. Ethan had fumbled with her in the dark, and it had hurt, but she knew there had to be more to sex than rough touches. Others found pleasure in the act. She would, too.

I want the pleasure.

But Claire didn't think she'd scream. Not even for a lover like Noah.

"Yes, I will." His lips pressed to hers.

Her eyes closed. She leaned into him.

His tongue glided over her lips. Into her mouth. Noah knew how to use his tongue so well. He wasn't wet or rough. He was…savoring her.

She wanted to devour him.

His hands slid over her shoulders. Touched the straps of her dress.

Then the dress was sliding down to pool at her feet.

And he was kissing his way along the line of her jaw. Down her throat. Over the pulse that raced so frantically. His tongue licked over her skin. She felt the light score of his teeth on her.

Claire gasped.

"Like that?"

She liked everything that he was doing.

"What I like…" Noah muttered, desire heavy in his voice. "I like the fact that you didn't wear a bra. Claire, I like that *a lot.*"

A bra wouldn't have fit under the bodice of that dress and—

He eased away from her. Stared down at her. The lights in the suite were on, shining all around them. There was no darkness.

There was only Noah.

"So perfect." He lifted his hand. Caressed her right breast. Her nipples were hard. Aching. And his touch sent a surge of arousal straight to her sex.

I'm wet for him. Already.

She reached out to Noah. "I need you now." Her fingers fumbled with his belt. "Noah, we can—"

"No." He caught her hands. "Not yet." He pushed her hands back to her sides. "I'm just getting started with you."

Sex with Ethan had been fast. So quick. In the back of a car or—

"*Claire.*"

Her lashes lifted.

"Claire, I'm going to give you so much pleasure you won't ever think of anyone else." Then he lifted her into his arms. The move surprised her and she grabbed tightly to him.

But he didn't carry her far. Just a few steps. Closer to the window. To the big, leather couch that waited right beside that glass.

He spread her out on the couch. She started to cover her breasts, but he caught her wrists. Lifted them above her head. "Don't move them." He swallowed. His gaze burned her. "You look sexy that way."

She'd been hurt badly in Chicago, and she bore the scar from that attack, but Noah didn't seem to see it at all as he gazed at her. Noah didn't seem to pay much attention to any of her scars.

I'm the one who can't see past them.

But Claire shoved her doubts away right then. She was going to have this moment with him. No matter what...*I'll have this.*

She still had on her black panties. Panties that *she'd* picked up back in New York before their flight had left. And she wore her heels. Heels that were higher than anything she'd worn before.

Noah bent his head. His lips closed around her breast. He licked. Sucked.

Claire arched against him. She wanted to grab onto him and hold tightly, but she didn't move her hands. She kept them above her head, fisted.

His fingers worked her other breast. Lightly tugging at the nipple. Stroking her. Her hips arched again, helplessly. She felt so empty, and she wanted Noah to fill her. She wanted him to thrust deep inside of her.

Then she could pretend that she was just like every other woman. Having sex with her lover. Enjoying pleasure.

"With me, Claire."

His hand slid over the plane of her stomach. Down, down his fingers went until he was at the edge of her panties.

Her eyes were on his hand.

"If I pull these off, they'll just get stuck on your shoes," he murmured. "So…"

He ripped her panties. Tore them in two and tossed the scraps away.

"That's what I wanted." His fingers slid between her folds. "Ah, baby, you're so ready for me."

He positioned his body between her legs. He'd thrust into her soon, she was sure of it. He'd—

He slid a finger into her.

Claire jerked toward him.

"So tight. You're going to drive me out of my mind."

He was already driving her out of hers.

"But you have to be burning up. You have to need me more than breath." He withdrew his finger. Moved her legs farther apart. The couch was massive, so there was easily room for them both on it and he was—he was—

Noah put his mouth on her.

Claire flinched. She hadn't expected that move. Her hands flew down to his shoulders.

"No, Claire," the words growled against the most sensitive part of her body. "Hands up."

Then his tongue, that wonderful, wicked tongue of his, stroked her. Slid over her. Slid *into* her.

Her hands flew back up and locked around one of the pillows on the couch. Her hips were arching, so he grabbed them and held them tightly. And he kept tasting her. Licking her. Kissing her. Taking her breath away as she gasped.

Every muscle in her body seemed to tense. Claire heard herself crying out Noah's name.

Her release was close. She could feel it. No roughness. No fast groping.

This was sex. This was what it should be like. Hot. Consuming.

His tongue thrust into her.

Claire screamed when the climax hit her. Her eyes squeezed shut, and her body bucked beneath him. The pleasure rolled through her, seeming to crest again and again, and Claire shuddered with the powerful release.

"That's a good start."

Her eyelashes lifted. Her breath heaved out.

"I like it when you scream for me, Claire." He put on protection. Settled right back between her legs. "Let's see if you can do it again."

He drove into her. His hands lifted and pinned hers in place. His eyes locked with hers.

He filled her so completely. Stretching every inch of her, and Claire froze, caught between pleasure and pain.

"I wanted to fuck you from the first moment we met."

She tried to suck in a deep breath.

"You feel so good."

He still had his clothes on. She was naked. In only her heels, and he was fully dressed.

That knowledge made her feel vulnerable, exposed and—

"Will you scream for me again?" He withdrew.

She wanted him back inside, as deep as he could go. Her legs flew up and locked around his hips.

"So…damn…good."

He thrust into her again.

Withdrew.

She met him, thrust for thrust. The rhythm became wild, so hard. He was in her so deep.

No pain.

Only more pleasure.

So much pleasure that the whole world seemed to explode. She wasn't sure if she screamed or not. She only knew that after years of being cold, it felt as if she were in an inferno.

One that swept her up, hollowed her out, and left her aching for more…more pleasure.

More…of Noah.

His hold tightened on her. He drove into her again. Her sex was contracting around him, aftershocks from her release.

"Nothing like this…never like this…" He heaved into her. Tensed.

She was staring into his eyes when he came, and Claire actually saw his gaze go blind with pleasure.

"Claire!" He kissed her. "Mine…" Noah whispered against her lips.

His hands still held hers pinned. She was spread beneath him. Filled with him.

Surrounded by him.

Mine.

***

Claire woke when she heard the squeak of the bedroom door. Noah had carried her to the bedroom after he'd given her that mind-numbing, world-altering orgasm.

He hadn't undressed. He'd put her in the bed. Held her.

She'd fallen asleep with his arms around her.

Only now he was…leaving?

"Noah?" She sat up, pulling the sheet with her as she glanced over at the bedside clock. The numbers glowed, showing her that it was close to midnight.

He was a shadow in the doorway. "Go back to sleep, Claire. I just have a little business to attend to."

"Wh-what kind of business?" Business at midnight?

"I have to meet with the manager. We need to upgrade the security here."

Because of her.

The sheets felt cool against her body. *I'm still naked.*

"Harrison won't ever be let in this place again, and I want to make sure every staff member knows that. Chuck is waiting for me now."

Chuck would know — as would everyone else who'd seen them enter the elevator — that they'd slept together.

I don't fuck my employees.

"Thank you," Claire softly said.

"You don't need to thank me, baby. If I'd realized that SOB was in the city, hell, I never would've let him get within thirty feet of you."

What had brought the man back to D.C.? She'd thought Colby stayed close to his place in Alabama these days.

"Get some sleep," Noah told her from his position near the bedroom door. "I'll be back soon."

She climbed from the bed. The lush carpeting swallowed the sound of her steps as she went to him in the darkness.

"Claire?"

Her hand lifted. Pressed to his chest. She would've liked to see him naked. His shoulders were so wide. So built. He probably had a six pack.

She swallowed. "Thank you," she said again, and she rose onto her toes. Her lips skimmed the hard line of his jaw.

But then his fingers sank into her hair. He tilted her head back. Took her mouth. Kissed her long and deep.

Her nipples tightened as they pressed into his chest.

"If you really want to thank me," Noah rasped when his head lifted, "you'll stay in that bed and be ready for me when I come back." He let her go. "I *will* be back soon, Claire."

She believed him.

She stood there, in the darkness, and a few moments later, she heard the sound of the suite's main door closing.

Her body was so sensitive. He'd touched her— everywhere. Claimed her. Marked her.

Taught her about pleasure.

Claire knew she wouldn't have much time, so she dressed quickly. She yanked her hands through her hair. Rushed to the smaller room she'd been given when they checked in.

She grabbed her bag. Wrote him a note. Because she suspected that he would look for her, and she didn't want Noah to worry.

She also didn't want to throw her troubles onto his doorstep. He'd been too good to her. He didn't deserve to be yanked down into her hell.

Her note was simple. Short.

Then Claire rode the elevator down to the lobby. Even at midnight, there were still plenty of people milling around the hotel. She didn't see Noah or Chuck, so she dashed across the lobby and hurried outside.

She paused to talk with the bellman, just for a moment. When he offered to get her a taxi, Claire refused. Why waste the money? Claire turned away and marched down the sidewalk.

And she didn't look back.

***

A hard knock pounded against the hotel room door.

Colby Harrison jerked at the sound. Who the hell would be coming to see him at this hour?

Muttering, he climbed from the bed. He'd just gotten to sleep a few moments ago.

He shuffled toward the door.

The knocking came again. Harder. Almost…desperate.

Colby weaved a bit as he reached out for the knob. He'd been drinking. The drinks helped him. They always did. Without them, he couldn't sleep at all.

When he tried to sleep, he thought about Ethan. Poor Ethan. Wasting away in that prison.

He squinted as he tried to see through the peephole on the door. He couldn't see a damn thing.

A rough knock had the door shaking.

Furious now, Colby jerked open the door. "What the hell do you—"

His visitor's hand flew away from the door. Had that hand been over the peephole?

Colby frowned. "I sure as hell didn't expect to see you here—"

A gun was shoved into his face.

Terror flooded through Colby as he stumbled back. "Y-you can't do this!"

Laughter. Then… "I can do anything." The door was kicked shut. They were sealed together in that room.

The gun's barrel was too long. *A silencer.* Colby licked his bone-dry lips. Tried to think. "I didn't mean—"

The bullet blasted through his head before he could finish.

"I know exactly what you meant."

Colby's knees hit the floor.

"At least I didn't make you beg."

Colby slammed face first into the carpet.

CHAPTER FOUR

"Claire?" Noah opened the suite's door, frowning as he called her name. He'd been gone longer than he'd planned, but there hadn't been any help for that delay.

He'd had to be careful and not rush his return to her.

"Claire?"

She didn't answer him. Noah figured Claire was probably asleep. He strode into the bedroom, but the bed was empty. The covers had been carefully arranged, re-made, and Claire was gone.

No.

He spun on his heel and nearly ran from that suite. When they'd checked in, Claire had been given a separate room, and he was in front of that room moments later. He had a key, and he opened the door, not bothering with a knock. He was too pissed for a knock. The woman didn't get to just run out of his bed in the middle of the night.

Her room was smaller than his, and in an instant, he knew she wasn't there. The bed hadn't been touched. Her bag was gone.

Hell, no.

The woman wasn't about to pull one of her disappearing acts on him. Not when he could still taste her on his tongue.

Not when I want more.

Then he saw the note. Folded, right in the middle of her pillow.

He scooped it up and instantly recognized the hotel stationary. He should, he'd picked that shit out.

A flowing, feminine handwriting told him...

Thank you, Noah. You taught me more about pleasure than I ever expected.

And she'd made him hungry for more.

Noah balled up the note and shoved it into his pocket. *We're not finished yet, Claire.*

Three minutes later, he was storming outside of the hotel. He turned to the bellman. He knew the guy — Blayne — had started at the hotel just a few months back. "Claire Kramer."

Blayne swallowed nervously and straightened his suit.

"Blonde hair, five foot ten. Slender. She would have left here alone, probably within the last two hours."

The bellman nodded. "I saw her. She was in a big hurry. Only stopped to talk with me for a few moments."

"Which taxi company did she use?" Because he could call them. Track her down.

"She didn't use a taxi, sir. I offered to get her one but…" Blayne pointed down the street. "She just started walking that way."

Noah glared down that street.

It's not that easy, Claire.

He started walking.

***

Vincent Finch stared down at the senator's body. He'd called the cops less than fifteen minutes ago, and they were already on the scene and trying to push him out of the room.

"You found him just like this?" The detective asked. The detective was a woman, barely five feet tall, with coffee cream skin. Her partner was a blond male, and the guy towered behind her.

Vincent nodded. "I…I came in to my room late." Because he'd been trying to pick up the waitress who worked at the bar across the street. "H-his door was open. I thought something was wrong and—" He broke off, gagging a bit, because he'd seen the spray left behind when the bullet sank into Colby's head.

His brain.

"And you said the victim was Colby Harrison?" The female detective pushed. "Why do I know that name?" she murmured, as if to herself.

"He used to be a senator." Vincent swallowed. He could smell the blood. "From Alabama."

The detective—she'd introduced herself as Gwen Lazlo—scribbled down that bit of information.

"I'm guessing a senator could have a lot of enemies in D.C." This came from the detective's blond partner. Vincent couldn't remember the man's name.

After he swiped a hand over his mouth, Vincent eased out a slow breath. "There was an…incident earlier tonight." And Vincent knew that he had to tell them the rest.

"What kind of incident?" the male demanded.

The screaming match would be in the news. Vincent had caught sight of the reporter at York Towers. "A woman from his past," he muttered. "Her name's Claire Kramer. She's in town. She and the senator…they had words tonight." Though now that he thought about it, he wasn't sure that Claire had actually spoken to the senator at all during that tense exchange.

"She an ex-lover?" Detective Lazlo asked as her eyebrows rose.

Vincent shook his head. "She was involved with his son, Ethan." He turned away from the hotel room. He didn't want to look in there anymore. So Vincent stared down at his hands. "Ethan went to jail for killing Claire's parents."

The blond whistled.

"Sonofabitch," Gwen Lazlo muttered. "*That's* why I remember the guy's name."

There was more. *Say it.* "On my…on my way into the hotel…before I found the body…" His hands clenched. *I'd always felt a bit sorry for her.* "I thought I saw Claire outside." He looked up and found the blond watching him.

The blond detective asked, "You think she might have killed the guy?"

Vincent held his gaze. "Claire's parents were both shot in the head. Just like the senator was tonight. And Claire...Claire hated Colby Harrison." *With good reason. I hated the old bastard, too.* "I don't know if she killed him, I just know...Claire is a very distinctive woman. You don't forget her once you see her." Maybe he'd been wrong to feel any sympathy for her. "She was outside of the hotel. She was here." *Don't look back at that room.* "And now Harrison is dead."

***

Claire sat on the stone steps, her arms curled around her up-drawn knees. The Lincoln Memorial was behind her, glowing in all its glory. In the distance, she could see the Washington Monument, reaching straight up into the dark sky.

Despite the fact that it was close to 4 a.m., Claire wasn't the only one hanging out near the Lincoln Memorial. So many people were there. Walking. Talking. Taking their pictures.

Plenty of people.

So why did she feel so alone?

"I figured I'd find you here."

At that deep, familiar voice, Claire's head turned and she saw Noah, walking up the steps toward her. She scrambled to her feet.

He kept coming. Slowly. Stalking up those stairs.

Her heart was racing in her chest now. He wasn't supposed to come after her.

Noah didn't stop his advance, not until he was right in front of her. "Why did you run from me?"

She shook her head.

"You liked being with me. I know a woman's body. I could feel your pleasure."

A lump rose in her throat, and it took Claire two attempts to actually speak. "I screamed for you," she whispered, not wanting anyone but him to hear her words. "I-I...never expected that."

"Then why leave me?" His words were harder. Sharper.

Claire squared her shoulders. Her bag was at her feet. "Because you don't fuck your employees."

He kept staring at her.

"You fucked me, so I'm not your employee any longer. I thought it would be…easier…if you came back and I wasn't there."

"It wasn't easy." He bent and grabbed her bag. "Where the hell were you going?"

"Some place new," she told him, her voice still soft. "Some place—"

"Where you hoped Harrison wouldn't find you? Forget him. He's done. He'll never bother you again."

If only she could believe that.

One of his hands easily held her bag while his other hand brushed over her cheek. "Do you seriously not realize just how much power I have? I can bury the man. I *will* bury him. You don't have to fear him again."

Hope was fragile as it tried to rise in her heart. She wanted to believe him but…

We still fucked. Noah had told her that they couldn't work together if things got personal. She had to move on.

"Do you want to leave me?" Noah asked her as his body seemed to surround hers. "If you do, Claire, if you really want to go, I'll let you get on my jet, and I'll have it take you any place you want." His hand fell from her skin.

I want his touch back.

"But I don't want you to go." His voice was a deep rumble. "I want you with me. In my bed. Screaming my name again. One night wasn't enough for me."

It hadn't been enough for her, either.

He stepped back. "*Your* choice, baby. Always yours. Stay or go, but you won't get to cut out on me in the middle of the night again. If you stay, then you're mine."

"My job—"

"I'll work it out. I'm the boss, and that means I can do anything." His eyes glinted. "Even break my own rules. For you...*I'd break any rule.*"

He lifted his hand. Offered it to her, palm up.

She wanted to take his hand. So badly. So very badly.

"What's it going to be? Do you want to be with me? Or..."

Are you gone?

The question hung between them.

Claire had no one. Nothing. The clothes in the bag were really Noah's. If she left, where would she go?

Do I even want to leave him?

Her hand reached for his. His fingers were a little rough, callused on the tips.

She liked the roughness of his hands. She liked to touch him.

"I want to stay with you."

His fingers curled around hers. "Remember that." Then he bent and kissed her. She leaned into him, because right then, Claire thought that maybe, just maybe, she could have a chance.

Everyone else could live and love.

Why not her?

***

Noah shut the door of the suite.

I've got her. She won't leave again.

Claire glanced back at him. She tucked a lock of blonde hair behind her ear. Her gaze was nervous. Hesitant.

Did she know just what he wanted to do with her? To her?

Fucking Claire Kramer had been incredible. And he planned to do it again and again.

"I won't be easy this time." He felt it was only fair to warn her.

Her eyelids flickered.

She didn't realize just how furious he'd been when he returned to find her gone. Women didn't slip away from his bed in the middle of the night, acting as if screwing him was somehow shameful. They stayed. They begged for more. But...

I never want Claire to beg.

He didn't want her to beg for anything.

"I don't remember ever asking you to be easy," Claire said, surprising him. She turned to face him fully. She was wearing a snug pair of jeans and a loose top.

She looked even sexier than she'd been in that black dress.

"It's going to be hard. It's going to be fast." *Fair warning, Claire.* They were lucky they'd made it up the elevator. He'd thought about taking her there, but then he'd remembered the security cameras installed there. He didn't want anyone else seeing Claire's passion. "And it's going to be right here."

He yanked his shirt off and tossed it to the floor. His hands went to his belt. To the snap of his jeans.

Claire's gaze was on his chest. Her blue stare...*heated.*

His cock jerked, swelling even more as it pushed against the zipper of his jeans.

Claire walked toward him. Her eyes were on his chest. "I wondered..." She licked her lips.

Sweet hell. Lick me.

"I wanted to touch you before," she confessed.

Wait, hold the hell up. Claire had *wanted* to touch him? His heart was jack-hammering in his chest.

Her hand rose, hovering above his shoulder. Then, while he barely breathed, her fingers lowered and skimmed over his flesh. Lightly, carefully.

"You're always so warm." Her voice was husky. Pure sin. "I like that." Her fingers slipped down.

His body wasn't perfect. Far from it. Scars snaked across his chest. Some from wounds he'd gotten while he was enlisted, and the newest came from the attack he'd survived in Chicago.

The world might think he led the easy life.

They thought wrong.

"I knew there was more to you," Claire said as her head bent. "You're not just the businessman."

Hell, no, he wasn't.

Her lips brushed over the scar on his shoulder. Then the one that was too near his heart. The bullet that had nearly ended him.

His muscles stiffened.

Claire slid down his body. Her mouth skimmed over the scar that wrapped around his side. Then she went even lower.

Her knees dropped to the carpet.

Fuck me.

"Baby, as much as I like where you're going, I can't wait." Her mouth on him…*there'd be no control then.*

He didn't want to hurt Claire. He was far too close to the edge.

He pulled her back to her feet. Stripped her in seconds.

"But—"

"Here, Claire. *Now.*"

Then he put her against the door. "Are you on the pill?"

Claire shook her head.

"Don't *move*," he growled out the order.

She didn't.

In seconds, he was back. He wanted to go bare with her. To drive deep and feel her hot grip all around him. And he would…

Soon.

But this time, he'd use care.

He lifted her up against that door frame. "Wrap your legs around me."

She did.

"Hold tight."

She did.

And he thrust into her as hard and deep as he could go.

Just as Noah had known…the feel of her sensual grip pushed him right over the edge. There was no holding back this time. No slow build. No sensual foreplay.

He thrust, and he took.

And he wanted *everything* that Claire had to give.

She was arching against him. Squeezing him with her tight little sheath. She was so tight it was almost as if she were a virgin.

She's mine.

He lifted her up, easily controlling the motions of her body. Then he pulled her back down as he thrust again. He made sure his cock slid over her clit, and Claire gasped.

Then she moaned.

He did that same move again and again. He was so wild for her, so desperate. He pinned her to the door. Thrust deep. Loved it when her nails scraped over his skin.

He put his mouth on her throat. He could feel the frantic beat of her pulse beneath his lips. Her scent surrounded him.

When she came, it was *his* name that she cried out.

He erupted right after her.

Noah's breath sawed out of his lungs as the release pounded through him. It seemed to never end, and her sex was squeezing his cock and damn near making his eyes roll back into his head.

Finally, *finally,* his heart rate started to slow down. He was still holding her against the door, and he hoped he hadn't scared her. He'd be better next time. He'd be —

"I like that," Claire whispered. "Can we do it again?"

Hell, *yes.*

He kissed her.

***

Noah glanced at the clock. "Come on, Claire, we need to go. The jet's waiting on us." The sooner he got her back to New York, the better he would feel.

The bathroom door opened. "I'm ready." She was wearing all black — the woman just looked good in black. Black pants. Black top. Those sexy shoes he loved.

Get her on the plane, then fuck her. Those were his immediate priorities.

He grabbed her bag. "Let's go."

She nodded and hurried to keep up with him. He didn't want to tell her why they needed to rush. Claire would just worry. She'd been in the bathroom when he got the phone call that tipped him off about the visitors coming their way, so she didn't know what was happening.

I'll tell her…later.

When he got her in the elevator, he pulled Claire into his arms. He kissed her long and deep. The woman still tasted like candy to him.

But he forced himself to pull back a few seconds later. The doors slid open. He locked his fingers with hers. *Claire.* He finally had her just where he needed her to be.

They stepped into the lobby. Hurried toward the hotel's main doors.

From the corner of his eye, he saw a couple talking with Chuck. The woman was small, attractive, with light brown skin and a haircut that skimmed her jaw. A blond male was at her side. Tall. Wide shoulders.

Something about them put Noah on alert.

His fingers tightened around Claire's. They were almost to the doors.

"Mr. York?" The voice calling to him belonged to the blond male.

Noah kept walking.

Claire stopped.

Dammit. When she stopped, he had to stop, too.

"Mr. York? I'm Detective Lane Scott. I've got some questions for you."

Claire still wasn't moving. Because of that, Noah had to turn and fully face the cops — he was sure the woman was a cop, too.

"What's happening?" Claire asked as she edged closer to Noah.

Then the man and woman were right before them. The guy's gaze slid to Claire. "You're Claire Kramer."

Claire nodded.

The woman with Lane Scott asked, "Want to tell us where you were last night?"

Noah stepped in front of Claire. "What's this about?"

The woman's dark eyes cut his way. "I'm Detective Gwen Lazlo. Lane and I work the D.C. homicide division."

"Good to know," Noah murmured. "But we've got a plane to catch."

"Senator Colby Harrison was murdered last night," Gwen said. When she made this reveal, she'd made a point of maneuvering to the side so that she had a line-of-sight with Claire.

"*What?*" Claire gasped.

"Um…" That non-committal sound came from Lane. "Someone shot the guy — right in the head — last night between one and three a.m." Lane paused as his gaze swept over Claire. "Where were you then, Ms. Kramer?"

Noah turned back to Claire. She'd gone ashen. Her eyes were too wide.

"In the…in the head?" Claire whispered.

Just like her parents.

Because he'd read the autopsy reports on them. He'd *needed* to read them, had to learn as much as he could, after he'd met Claire.

"It's all right," Noah told her and he made sure that his voice was calm. "Look at me, Claire. *Look at me.*"

Her gaze met his.

"It's all right," he repeated. They had to be very careful here. If Claire hadn't left last night, his staff would have been able to vouch for her.

I didn't count on her leaving.

That had sure wrecked his plans.

Claire nodded slowly.

"I don't know that it *is* all right," Lane drawled.

Noah glanced back at him. The blond was scratching his jaw.

"I mean, a man is dead. Half of his head was blown away and — "

Noah heard Claire's sharp inhalation of breath. His jaw clenched. "Be *very* careful how you proceed, Detective," Noah warned him. "You don't want to make any enemies today."

Lane's eyes widened. "You threatening me?"

Noah had to laugh. "Threats are useless. Why bother with them? I make promises."

Lane glanced at his partner.

"Ms. Kramer hasn't answered our question," Gwen said, voice tight. "We need to know her whereabouts. It's come to our attention that she and the victim had an…altercation last night."

"Bullshit," Noah snapped before Claire could speak. "I'm the one who had an altercation with the drunken idiot. He came into *my* hotel and insulted my guest, so I threw his ass out." He flashed his teeth in a hard grin. "End of altercation."

"But Ms. Kramer—" Gwen pressed.

"I didn't kill him," Claire said. She eased to Noah's side. Stared at the detective. "That's what you really want to know, isn't it? If I killed him?" Claire shook her head. "I didn't."

Gwen pursed her lips as she assessed Claire. "A woman fitting your description was seen at the senator's hotel, right around the time of his death. Actually, the senator's manager, Vincent Finch, didn't just say she fit your description. He's sure that she *was* you."

"He's wrong," Noah said flatly. "And there are plenty of blonde's in this city."

"But there aren't that many who would probably take a savage satisfaction in blowing out Senator Harrison's brains," Gwen said. Her voice was low, and her eyes were still on Claire. "After what happened to you, I could see where you'd want payback. Your boyfriend killed your parents. Maybe you just got around to evening up that score."

"I didn't kill him," Claire said, voice soft.

"Why don't you come down to the station and answer a few questions for us?" Lane asked her, and the jerk was trying for a solicitous tone. The man must think Noah was an idiot.

You aren't getting Claire any place near your station.

"We have a plane to catch," Noah said.

Lane shook his head. "We have an active murder investigation, you can't just leave—"

"I can. We will." Noah cocked his head to the right. "We'll be in New York for the next few days. If you want to reach me or Claire, you can contact my attorney." He rattled off the name and number of his lawyer. The lawyer in question was a lady who would chew up and spit out anyone who ever came after Noah.

Then he rolled back his shoulders in what he hoped appeared to be a careless shrug. "Now, I'm sure you have plenty of work to do. After all, there's a killer out there for you to find."

He took Claire's elbow and walked with her toward the doors.

"Ms. Kramer?" Gwen called out.

And, of course, Claire glanced back.

Noah sighed.

"I'm curious…are you glad he's dead? Because, in your place, I would be."

Noah had to give Gwen credit. The woman was very skilled at the good cop role.

"Yes," Claire whispered. "I'm glad." Then she walked through the door. Noah made sure that she didn't have the chance to stop again.

***

"Well, well…" Lane exhaled as Noah York and Claire Kramer left the hotel. "That went pretty much as I'd thought."

Yeah, it had gone nowhere.

Gwen rubbed the back of her neck. Tension was thick there, knotting the muscles. She'd been awake for almost twenty hours, and she needed to crash.

Unfortunately, every time she closed her eyes, she saw Colby Harrison's body.

"You think she did it?" Lane asked as his arm brushed against hers.

Gwen looked over at him. He'd been her partner for a year.

Her lover for six months.

"If I'd been her, I would've probably killed him," Lane added. "I mean, shit, you read the file on her. The fellow's son went full-on stalker over the woman. He had a gun to her head when the cops arrived. Everyone there knew just what he'd done, but then the *Senator* started spinning that bull about Claire being the mastermind—"

Gwen's sigh cut through his words. "Men. You see a pretty face, and you forget the danger."

He blinked at her. Then he leaned in close. His lips brushed her ear as he whispered, "You're the only pretty face I see."

Gwen wouldn't let her reaction to his words show. She'd learned to be very careful with Lane. With everyone. "I'm saying I think there is more to Claire Kramer than meets the eye."

Lane ran a hand through his hair, tousling the short locks. "Despite what he said, I'm betting that Noah York is going to put an *army* of lawyers in our path, not just one lady, if we go after Claire Kramer again."

Lawyers didn't scare Gwen. "Then we just have to be sure that when we go after her, we have enough evidence to knock our way right through that army." And she knew just where they had to start with that evidence. "Let's go get Vincent Finch. I want him brought into the station." She had plenty of other questions to ask the guy.

If Claire Kramer had killed the senator, Gwen wasn't about to give the woman a free pass. She might feel bad for what Claire had been through—

But you don't get to kill in my town.

***

The plane was in the air. Noah exhaled slowly. He'd wanted to get away before the cops stopped them, but…well, *we're still clear.*

Claire was beside him. She wasn't looking at him, though. Her gaze was locked on the window.

The pilot was up front. They were alone in the back. Secure. So he waited, knowing that sooner or later, Claire would turn to him.

Five minutes later, she did.

"Do you think I killed him?" Claire asked as her delicate eyebrows arched.

Noah shook his head.

"Why not?" She seemed confused. "I don't have an alibi. I don't—"

"You misunderstand me, Claire." He caught her chin. For this part, he needed her to look directly into his eyes. "I don't *care* if you killed him."

Her lips parted.

"But I will make sure that no matter what else happens, those cops stay away from you."

"I didn't do it!"

He kept staring into her eyes. "Were you at his hotel?" *Say no.* It would be so much easier to cover up if she just—

"I was." Her gaze lowered. Her long lashes shielded her eyes. "I asked the bellman at our hotel where the senator had gone. He-he'd been there when the taxi driver got the destination." She eased out a soft sigh. "I thought about talking to the senator alone. Asking him to pl-please stop. To just leave me alone."

Anger surged within him. *She shouldn't beg.*

Then Claire's lashes lifted. Something new was in her eyes. A spark. Anger of her own. "Then I realized he'd just like it if I went to him, pleading. He wasn't going to stop harassing me. There was no point in me talking to him. The bastard was going to hound me for the rest of his life." Her breath eased out slowly. "I'm glad he's dead. That should make me feel bad, but it doesn't."

It didn't make Noah feel bad. During his life, he'd seen plenty of death. Before he'd started York Towers, he'd been a soldier, one too good at killing. He'd gotten a spot on an elite military team.

He and Trace Weston had run that team. Their job had been to rescue high-level prisoners who'd been captured by U.S. enemies. Collateral damage had been a way of life.

His fingers stroked down her neck.

Collateral damage.

After he'd ended his last tour, Noah had kept working with Trace. They'd gone independent. There were still individuals who'd needed their help. Powerful men and women who'd gotten caught in the wrong place, at the wrong time.

Some of their clients had been extremely grateful.

One had been so grateful that he'd given Noah his first hotel.

And Noah had walked away from the bloodshed. From the battles. From the death.

For her, I'd walk back.

For Claire, he was coming to realize that he might do just about anything.

Even kill.

***

"There he is," Gwen said as she pointed across the street.

Vincent Finch had just left his hotel.

"Let's get him." Lane let out a loud whistle.

Finch glanced up at the sound. They'd called him and told the guy they'd be coming back to pick him up.

Finch hurried toward the cross walk.

The light changed. Finch didn't stop walking. He ran into the street.

An engine revved.

Gwen's eyes widened. "Finch, *stop!*"

A black SUV shot forward. It slammed right into Finch. The guy's body flew into the air, twisted, then hit the concrete.

The vehicle kept driving. It raced away with a squeal of its tires. She heard Lane calling for back-up. Gwen ran across the street.

Blood, oh, jeez, blood was everywhere.

Finch was face-up on the concrete. His neck was twisted. His eyes—closed.

"Finch?" Gwen put her hand to his throat.

No pulse.

Their only witness was dead in the street.

CHAPTER FIVE

"I have to leave town," Noah said as he paced toward Claire.

Shocked, she could only shake her head. "We just got back *in* town an hour ago." They'd made it to York Towers less than ten minutes before.

"This can't wait," Noah said.

Claire was shaken. *Senator Harrison is dead.* She wanted Noah to stay with her. She didn't want to be alone and— "I can come with you," she offered and hoped that she didn't sound desperate. She sure felt that way.

He shook his head. "Not this time."

"Where are you going?" *What was happening?*

"Vegas," he said flatly. "I'll be back by tomorrow." He started packing. Claire just watched him, totally lost.

After everything that had just happened, he was going to fly away and leave her?

"Drake Archer is going to keep an eye on you while I'm gone."

Claire stiffened. "I don't need anyone to 'keep an eye' on me." And she sure didn't need Drake to be that guy.

She'd met Drake in Chicago, right around the time she'd met Noah. Drake had been involved in that nightmare situation, too. Like Noah, Drake was caught in the tangled web of Trace Weston's past. Claire didn't exactly know what those three men had done when they were in the military, but they'd made plenty of deadly enemies.

They're all dangerous. She understood that. Danger clung to Noah as surely as it clung to Drake and Trace.

But she wasn't afraid when she was with Noah. Drake, on the other hand, made her nervous.

"Someone trashed your hotel room here, did you forget about that?" Noah had his bag filled. Talk about a record-breaking packing job. If he kept running off so much, she wondered why he didn't always have a bag at the ready.

"I didn't forget about that," Claire snapped back. "But I hardly think that will be an issue here at *York Towers*. I hope you have better security than what they've got at the Hamlet."

His lips twisted and a gleam appeared in his eyes. "We do, baby. But when word of Harrison's death hits the media, you could get dragged into the mud. I want to make sure no reporters get close to you while I'm gone."

"You think it's all going to get stirred up again, don't you?" That was what she feared.

"I think reporters like juicy stories. The gorier, the better." His voice was grim. The gleam had vanished from his eyes.

Claire looked away from him. "So I just sit here and twiddle my thumbs while you rush off and tend to your business?" Since she didn't have a job anymore, what else was she —

"No, Claire, you stay here and you get to work learning more about my company and the staff at York Towers."

Her gaze flew back to him. "But, you said — "

"The rules are different with you." He strode toward her. Dropped the bag. Wrapped his hands around her shoulders. "*Everything* is different with you."

And everything felt different with him.

Noah kissed her. It was a rough, hard kiss, and she liked it. Claire was discovering that she liked quite a bit…with him.

"I'll be back soon."

"Don't leave." No, had she just said that? *It's Harrison's death. Everything is stirred up. The memories are so strong right now.*

"I have to do this." He let her go. "I'll be back for you, baby."

Then he just…walked away.

Left her.

Claire stayed in their bedroom. *No, his bedroom. His suite.* She looked down at her hands. At the scars on her wrists.

She thought about life.

About death.

And about what it would feel like to kill.

***

When the limo door shut behind him, Noah pulled out his phone. He'd already called Drake Archer earlier, before he'd even left D.C., so this phone call was for Trace Weston. Noah knew that he could count on both Trace and Drake to have his back.

"I heard," Trace said when he answered the phone. "The senator's dead." A pause. "Shouldn't you be celebrating?"

Noah didn't answer that particular question. "I know you've got pull down in Alabama." The same pull that Trace had used a while back when he'd made sure Ethan Harrison didn't get paroled. "Use that pull for me now. I want in to see the SOB."

"You're not serious." Trace's voice hardened as he demanded, "*Tell* me that you're not serious."

"Claire's mine now, so yes, I'm fucking serious." He had to see Ethan Harrison with his own eyes.

"Right now? Jesus, his old man isn't even cold yet and —"

"Something is happening. I know it. Claire's room gets trashed, the senator dies — *just the way her parents died* — that's no damn coincidence." His breath heaved out. "I don't want Claire in danger, and this whole tangled mess leads back to Ethan Harrison. He needs to know that Claire is off-limits. Now and forever."

"He's in jail, man. He can't get to her. You just need to settle down —"

The hell he did. "Like you settled down when Skye was in trouble? Did you *settle down* then, Trace? Or did you do what damn well had to be done?"

Trace had killed to protect Skye. If anyone could understand what Noah was doing, it should be Trace. *Maybe he won't have my back after all.*

Silence hummed over the line. "You can't kill him while he's in prison. That's too much, even for you."

Noah felt his lips curl. "I'm not planning to kill him in prison. I'm just going to deliver a message to him." One that had to be personally delivered.

Trace sighed. "I'll get you in."

"I knew you would."

"But I'm going on record as saying that this is a *mistake*, Noah. A huge mistake." Trace's voice hardened. "This isn't like you. Drake's the crazy-ass one. You're more controlled, you're—"

He thought about the faint scars on Claire's wrists. "I'm not controlled when it comes to her."

Then he ended the call. His hands fisted, and he planned.

***

It was nearing sunset when Noah passed through the gates of the Holman Correctional Facility in Atmore, Alabama.

The guards were waiting for him, and they took him straight to the warden's office.

Warden Jeremiah Quill was sweating when he shook Noah's hand. "This is…highly unusual."

Noah didn't care how unusual it seemed. "I'm sure inmates get visitors every day." He made sure to meet the Warden's stare directly as he said, "I'm just another visitor."

The warden's eyes darted away from him. *How much pressure had Trace put on the guy?* "Ethan Harrison is waiting for you in one of our holding rooms." He led Noah down the hallway.

Prison bars were to the right.

To the left.

"Is Ethan Harrison kept in general population?" Noah asked, curious.

"No." The warden glanced back at him. "His father wouldn't allow that."

"His father's dead now."

The warden lowered his voice, "But Harrison's great-uncle is the governor. You don't quite seem to understand how things work down here."

He was getting a crystal clear view.

The warden stopped in front of a heavy, metal door. "He's inside. A guard's there, too."

Noah lifted a brow. "Is the guard supposed to be for his protection or my own?"

The warden swallowed. "It's protocol."

It sounded to Noah as if protocol got screwed a lot down here.

The warden opened the door.

Noah stalked inside. Ethan Harrison was cuffed to an old table. He wore a bright, orange jump suit.

Nine years ago, the guy had been a fit, blond teen. Noah had seen Ethan's pictures when he'd explored Claire's past. He'd wondered how Ethan had fared in prison.

It looked like the guy had been on a vacation.

Ethan's face was tan. His hair even blonder. His shoulders were wide. He appeared fit—and, worst of all, the bastard was smiling.

"I know who you are," Ethan said as he inclined his head toward Noah.

"Good for you."

Ethan leaned forward. He never even glanced at the warden. "Did Claire send you to see me?"

Noah hated to hear her name come from that jerk's mouth.

"I miss Claire." Ethan's smile stretched. "But I have her pictures to keep me company."

Noah tensed.

"They help me to get through the days. And the nights."

Noah pulled out the chair across from Ethan. "You've had someone watching Claire."

"My father liked to keep track of her." Ethan's eyes gleamed with what looked like amusement. "Did you hear? He died last night. Someone shot him." Ethan raised his cuffed hands and tapped his forehead. "Right in the head."

"Your father had a private investigator tracking her?" Noah kept his focus. This was important. He wouldn't let the other man bait him. Noah's rage built, but he held it back. "And he sent you the information that the PI gathered."

Ethan tilted his head. He smiled at Noah. That smile was getting on Noah's nerves. "Claire will tease and she will flirt," Ethan said, "but she won't sleep with you." He shrugged. "She can't. Claire knows she belongs to me."

"Your father had someone watching her in New York." Noah was trying to put all the pieces together. "He told you that Claire was with me."

"I get to make one phone call a day." Now Ethan glanced at the warden. "Even get to use his office. Thanks, Warden. I'll be sure to let my great-uncle know just how well you treat me. Bet there will be some kind of bonus coming your way soon."

Noah wanted to drive his fist into the guy's face.

"I used that phone call last night. Talked to my father. He seemed to think you and Claire were together." Ethan shook his head. "But he was wrong."

"Your father was wrong about a lot of things."

Ethan's smile dimmed.

"He thought you were the poor, misled boy, didn't he?"

"He thought I was obsessed. Claire's the type of woman that can obsess a man." Ethan's gaze turned calculating. "But that's why you're here, right? Claire's obsessed you."

It was Noah's turn to smile. "I can see you for what you are. I'm not some drunken old man."

Ethan's mouth tightened. "A man obsessed will do anything for the woman he loves, and I do love my Claire."

No, he didn't. He was a twisted jerk who needed to forget Claire. But that wasn't happening. Noah knew that with absolute certainty now. "You're never getting out of this place."

"Because my parole was revoked?" Ethan's brows climbed. "I only got fifteen years for the murders. I've served nine already. Six more years...*Hello, Claire.*"

The hell that would happen.

"And you know...with my father dying...I wonder if I'll even get a special circumstances waiver..." Ethan's stare darted to the warden once more. "With guards, of course, I might get to attend my beloved father's funeral."

Sonofabitch.

"So I will get out. One way or another."

Noah had wanted to see Ethan Harrison for himself. To talk to him. Sometimes, monsters weren't as bad as you thought.

Sometimes, they were.

He can't ever get near Claire again.

"Claire has stayed true to me all these years," Ethan murmured. "And I'll always be true to her. I did exactly what she wanted, and she'll never forget that."

"Still trying to spin that line of bull?" Noah asked Ethan, and he shook his head in disgust. "I told you, I'm not your drunken old man. Claire didn't get you to kill her parents."

"Are you so sure about that?" Ethan laughed. "Even Claire's closest friends weren't sure. Claire...she has secrets. A darkness inside. With her, what you see isn't what you get."

Noah flattened his hands on the table. "There will be no more investigators who follow Claire. No one will watch her. No one will report to you."

Ethan laughed again.

"If I see anyone even *trying* to watch her, they'll have to deal with me."

"The big, bad, hotel owner." Ethan shuddered. "How terrifying...oh, wait, I've been locked up with murderers and rapists for *nine years*. You don't scare me. Nothing scares me anymore." And his façade dropped right then.

The humor, the mockery — vanished.

Evil remained.

"Claire owes me," Ethan snarled. Spittle flew from his mouth. "And the bitch will pay me back *everything*."

"I'm giving you fair warning," Noah gritted out as his back teeth clenched. "A warning that needed to be delivered in person." And he didn't care if the guard was listening or if the warden overheard his words. Noah leaned forward. "You don't know the man I used to be."

Ethan's brows furrowed.

"That man would have killed you the instant he walked into this room," Noah said flatly.

"The guard—"

"I would've been across the table. I would have snapped your neck before you even had the breath to scream."

Ethan swallowed.

"You forget Claire Kramer. You forget her now. Or the next time we meet…" Noah smiled at him. A smile that held a grim promise. "You'll be a dead man."

Then he rose and walked toward the door.

The warden followed him out, and the guy was sweating even more. Jeremiah ran a shaking hand over his face.

"I want to see his cell," Noah told the warden.

Jeremiah hesitated.

Noah just kept staring back at him.

A quick nod, then Jeremiah was leading the way for him. Noah wondered what sort of pressure Trace had applied in order to get the warden so compliant. Had it been cash? Or another, darker motivation?

Trace has a way of finding out everyone's secrets…and using those secrets against his enemies.

Noah walked past dozens of cells. After about five minutes, Jeremiah stopped near a cell that was separate from the others. A nearby guard opened the door.

Noah slipped inside. The place was about five feet by nine feet. The cell contained a toilet. A bed.

A dozen pictures of Claire were on a back, stone wall. Fucking *recent* pictures judging by Claire's hair. One…he leaned forward. *Sonofabitch…*One was of Claire at her sister's funeral. He recognized the dress that she wore in that shot.

Noah spun to confront the warden. "She was his victim," he snarled. "He put a gun to her head. He was going to *kill* her."

Jeremiah backed up a step. "His father—"

"Is going to be rotting in the ground soon."

"The governor—"

Noah whirled back around. He ripped those pictures from the wall. "No more." Rage had a haze covering his gaze. "He doesn't see her. If *any* more pictures find their way to him, you'll have more than the governor to worry about." He tore the pictures into pieces. Marched toward the warden. "You'll have me. And when it comes to the biggest threat you need to fear, Warden, it's not the governor because I can buy and sell him ten times over."

The warden glanced nervously around the room. "He…he's probably going to get out." His voice was low, carrying just to Noah's ears. "For the funeral. He was right. There won't be anything I can do to stop it if the order comes down…"

Noah's fury burned even hotter. "If that happens, you call me. Understand?"

The warden's gaze dropped to the torn pictures scattered on the floor. "I know what he is," Jeremiah said. "And if I had my way, he'd stay locked up forever." His eyes lifted. Held Noah's. "If he ever gets free, he will kill that woman."

"No," Noah swore, "he won't."

***

"All right, Claire…" The rumbling masculine voice was followed by a light rap on the office door. "It's quitting time for the night."

Claire glanced up and found herself staring into Drake Archer's green gaze. She'd been aware of him covertly checking on her during the day. He hadn't actually spoken to her until now.

Since the guy had a tendency to unnerve her, she'd appreciated his silence.

Claire shut down her computer. Well, Noah's computer. She was in his office, in his suite, and she'd spent the day pouring over marketing plans for the hotel in D.C. She wanted to prove to Noah that she could be useful to him.

And not just as a bed partner.

Drake stepped into the room. The light glinted off his dark, blond hair.

Claire tensed.

"Why do you do that?" Drake asked her, frowning. "I'm not going to bite."

She wasn't sure she believed that.

She'd met Drake and Noah back in Chicago. Actually, her first image of Drake was rather twisted. Stained in blood. One thing remained clear to her, though.

Drake Archer is dangerous.

"It's not the first time an old friend has asked me to keep an eye on his girl," Drake added with a roll of his broad shoulders. "And Skye doesn't jump when I get within ten feet of her."

She rose to her feet. "I'm not Skye."

His gaze slid over her. "True, but this is the same city she used to love. This is the place where I watched her." His head tilted a little to the left as he seemed to savor a memory. "Skye was one hell of a dancer."

Claire had actually seen Skye once on stage. He was right—Skye was phenomenal.

"You remind me of her," Drake added as he kept studying her. "Something about the eyes. No, the fear in your eyes."

Warily, she eased around the desk.

"What are you afraid of, Claire Kramer?" Drake murmured. His voice was low, rumbling. His face was all hard lines and angles. Danger. When she looked at Drake, she thought of darkness and of the threats that waited in the night.

Some women might like that wild edge that clung to him. It just made her nervous.

What are you afraid of? His question had made her tense. "Don't you know?" Claire asked him. Noah did. Trace did. Surely Drake had been told about her past, too.

But Drake shook his head. "Some. Not all. Your past is your own." His lips twisted. "I sure as hell don't want anyone looking at my past. It's bloody and full of death."

"So is mine."

The silence stretched between them.

"Then why don't we just screw the talk about the past and just focus on the present?" Drake suggested. "And in the present, you sure have my boy Noah twisted up."

She did?

Was that good or bad?

"Noah's not like me and Trace. He holds himself back. He's damn smart. He knows that a woman can destroy a man faster than anything else on earth."

Drake sounded as if he were speaking from personal experience. "I'm not looking to destroy Noah."

"Good." His smile flashed. "Because then I'd have to destroy you, and I think I rather like you."

He'd just threatened her. Claire's fingers curled tightly around the edge of the desk.

"I don't have a lot of friends in this world," Drake continued. "Noah is one of the few people who has always stood by me, no matter what screwed up shit I did."

Just as Noah was standing by her?

"But don't let his appearance fool you, sweetheart."

Sweetheart. Helplessly, Claire shivered. Only one other man had called her by that endearment.

"Noah is a hell of a lot more dangerous than most people believe. I've always thought that, if someone were to wreck that perfect control of his, Noah York might just be the deadliest man I've ever met."

"Why…" She pulled in a deep breath. "Why are you trying to warn me away from him?"

"Because I think you might be the one to wreck that perfect control." He crossed the room until he stood just two feet away from her. Not touching her, thank goodness, but still too close. "He doesn't keep them, you know."

Now she was lost. "Keep what?"

"His women. He sleeps with them, gets the lust out of his system, then he lets them go. He doesn't like to have the same lover twice in a row."

Her heart seemed to freeze in her chest. Noah had been with her, and as soon as they'd returned to New York, he'd rushed out of town. *Away from me?*

"He usually pushes his lovers aside, but here you are, all snug in his suite, and he has me playing guard duty for you." He gave a low whistle. "That's new, and it's dangerous."

He was wrong. "I'm not a threat to Noah."

"Aren't you?"

She shook her head.

"Good. Because, as I said, I like you."

Then what did he tell to the women he *didn't* like?

"Even if you do have that injured, delicate bird thing happening." He waved his hand at her. "Do something about that, would you?"

She could only blink. "I'm not an injured bird." Now that was just insulting.

He smiled. "That's better. You had some bite in those words."

Her eyes narrowed. "I'm in the suite. Completely safe for the night." She'd been safe all day. "I think you can probably leave now."

"Why would I leave the suite? I just ordered room service for us. The room service menu in this place is damn good. Noah made sure of that."

Uh, yes, Claire had realized that quickly.

"Come on. It will be here any moment…" Then he turned his back and took about four steps before he hesitated and said, "I promise, I won't bite. Noah's already marked you as his. I know how to keep my hands to myself." After that little announcement, he kept walking.

She didn't follow him.

Noah's already marked you as his.

She rubbed her chilled arms.

***

Noah opened the door to his suite and slipped inside the dark interior to—

"Three a.m., hoss…sure didn't expect to see you come dragging in at this hour."

A light flipped on near the couch. The illumination spilled on Drake's features. The guy was lounging against the cushions, looking quite at home. *Too* at home.

"What the hell are you doing in my suite?" Noah demanded. Since he'd known that Drake was in New York, he'd gotten the guy to keep an eye on Claire.

Not spend the night in the same suite with her.

Drake grinned. When Drake grinned, it made Noah nervous.

"I was getting to know your Claire," Drake said. "That woman likes her secrets, doesn't she?"

Claire…she has secrets. A darkness inside. With her, what you see isn't what you get.

Noah shut the door behind him. "What do you mean?"

"I mean getting the woman to talk with me was like pulling teeth." He shook his head and stayed sprawled on the couch. "I don't think she cares much for me."

"Usually you don't have a problem charming the ladies."

"No." Drake glanced toward the shut bedroom door. "But I don't think she's one for charmers."

Noah dropped his bag. He was so tired his bones ached, but he'd been determined to get back to Claire as fast as possible.

"Want to tell me about your mystery trip?"

Now Noah was the once glancing toward the bedroom door. "Is she asleep?"

"She's been that way for a few hours now. Tried to get her drunk with some wine," Drake confessed. "Didn't work. The woman didn't even touch her glass."

Noah's eyes narrowed. "We need to be clear on something." He'd thought it was obvious when he asked Drake to watch Claire. "You don't fuck with her, understand?"

Drake laughed softly. "But you do."

"Only me." He tossed aside his jacket. "Claire is—"

"A broken bird, a woman who needs your protection." Now Drake was mocking.

"No," Noah snarled. That sure wasn't what he saw when he looked at Claire. "She's a survivor. She's been through hell, and I want to make sure she never has to suffer again."

Drake seemed to absorb that. "And you'll do anything to keep her safe, is that it?"

"Yes," he rasped.

"Oh, how the mighty have fallen." Now Drake rose and paced toward Noah. "I don't give out advice often, but for you, I'll make an exception. Seeing as how we go back so far...and you're one of the few people who can—"

"Actually stand your psychotic ass?"

"Understand me," Drake muttered. He heaved out a sigh. "You were smarter than Trace and I were. You didn't get wrapped up in a woman. You kept your distance. You played it safe."

Noah waited.

"You need to keep playing it safe. Opening yourself up to a woman like Claire, that is a big mistake. She'll rip your world apart, man."

Noah didn't speak.

"When Trace almost lost Skye, you saw what it did to him." Drake's face hardened as worry glinted in his eyes. "Do you really want that shit to happen to you?"

His back teeth had clenched so hard they ached. "I have no intention of losing Claire."

"Aw, hell, it's already too late for you, isn't it?"

It had been too late for Noah the moment he'd met Claire — and she'd taken a swing at him in that Chicago alley.

"What are you doing?" Now real concern was in Drake's voice. "Don't let her push you too far."

But how far *was* too far?

"Reporters were at the Towers most of the day, trying to get to her. They even asked me if she was involved in the death of a certain Senator Colby Harrison." Drake's brows rose. "Seems he died in D.C., right during your recent little visit there with the tempting Claire."

Noah fired another fast glance at the bedroom door. "When she was sixteen, Claire's boyfriend killed her parents. He put a gun to Claire's head, and he was going to kill her, too."

"*What?*"

"That boyfriend was Ethan Harrison, Senator Harrison's younger son. Instead of just admitting that he had one screwed-up kid, the senator tried to paint Claire as a seductress who'd led the boy down the wrong path."

Drake rocked back on his heels. "She said her past was blood and death."

"It is." Her future *wouldn't* be. "The senator harassed her for years, and now she's free of him."

Drake absorbed that, then muttered, "Free, right at the same time you two hook up."

Noah didn't let his expression change. "Sometimes, that's how fate works."

"Don't be cute, Noah...*did you do it?*"

"If I had, then I wouldn't be so worried about keeping a watch on Claire." He did *not* want Claire overhearing this conversation. "Before she moved in here at the Towers, someone trashed her hotel room at the Hamlet. That asshole Ethan Harrison, he's been watching her—*from prison.* He's got a PI on her. Ethan had photos of her, recent damn photos, all over his cell."

"So that's where you went on your little trip."

"I needed to see him with my own eyes. Needed to talk to him."

Drake assessed him. "You were measuring your enemy."

It was the way they'd worked when they were in the military. *Know your enemy. Learn his weaknesses. Exploit them. Take out that enemy.*

"He's as obsessed with her now as he was nine years ago." Actually, the guy might even be more obsessed. Time should have made the bastard let her go.

The bedroom door squeaked open. "Noah?" Claire slipped out of the darkness and into the light of the main room. A smile swept over her face. The smile that he loved. The one that started with her lips, that flashed her dimples, and made her eyes shine.

Every muscle in his body locked down.

"I don't think he's the only one obsessed," Drake said, voice low. "I'm telling you...watch yourself. Because you're headed for an implosion." Then Drake raised his voice as he drawled, "I'll be seeing you again soon, Claire Kramer."

Then he left them.

Noah drank in the sight of Claire.

"How was your trip?" Claire asked him as she crept toward him. A few seconds later, she stood in front of him. Her hands lifted, then hesitated.

He didn't want Claire to hesitate when it came to touching him. He started to reach for her, but Noah locked his muscles down. He wanted the next move to be hers.

After a moment, she pressed herself against him. Hugged him. It only lasted a moment, but he felt the impact of that embrace rock through his whole body.

"I'm glad you're back." Her words were faint as she drew back. She put her hands behind her. Stared up at him with those big blues that always seemed to make him a little weak.

I missed you, Claire.

When he'd never missed anyone, not until her.

This wasn't about just repaying some debt anymore. Wasn't about trying to fix the hole in Claire's life that her sister's death had left behind.

It was about more.

"Did you finish your business?" Claire asked him.

He put his hand on her cheek. Like touching silk. "Not yet," he told her. "But I will, soon."

Her breath caught as she stared up at him. "Noah?"

"I need you." So badly that his whole body seemed to be burning. He hadn't been able to get back to her fast enough. She'd been the only thing he could think about on the flight home.

She wore a dark robe. Her hands lifted. Unbelted that robe. It fell at her feet.

Claire took his hand. She led him back to the bedroom. The woman had no idea just how close to pouncing on her he truly was.

He should be careful with her. After their last time together, she was probably sore.

"I want you." Her voice was pure sin, like a stroke right over his aroused cock.

His control was shredding. Every second with her ripped it a bit more.

"I want to give you pleasure," Claire told him as she stared up into his eyes. "Teach me how?"

Right then, he couldn't. He could only push her back onto the bed. Part her thighs. See the perfect pink flesh that waited. "This gives me pleasure." He put his mouth on her and feasted.

She bucked beneath him. Arched. Her taste drove him insane.

Get her ready. Take her.

When her nails raked down his back, Noah rose. He positioned his cock right at the entrance to her body. He'd put on a condom, pausing just those few seconds — *one day I'll have all of her* — and he drove deep into her.

Only then, *only then,* the frantic tension left his body. The fear. The fury. The lethal combination that seeing Ethan Harrison had roused within him.

Claire will tease and she will flirt, but she won't sleep with you…She can't. Claire knows she belongs to me.

Ethan was so wrong.

Noah thrust harder into Claire. She whispered his name. Her sex squeezed around him. So hot and tight and wet. Perfect for him.

She climaxed, crying out and her sex clenched him even tighter.

Noah's thrusts became faster then. Deeper. The bed shook beneath them. The headboard thudded into the wall. He didn't care.

Nothing could have stopped him at that moment.

He plunged into her. Lost sight of everything but Claire.

And when he came, he roared her name.

Mine. Always.

Noah would do anything necessary in order to protect what was his.

***

They'd taken Claire away.

Ethan Harrison paced the length of his cell, rage pouring through his veins. All of his pictures were gone. The pictures that let him see Claire. That let him feel her.

Those pictures were important.

He needed them.

I need Claire.

That bastard Noah York didn't scare him. After what he'd survived in prison, nothing scared him.

His father had thought that he kept Ethan safe from the other inmates. But when the lights went out, when the guards turned their backs...you had to protect yourself. He'd gotten very good at protecting himself.

And now...his father was dead.

The funeral would be in a few days. That gave him so little time.

It was a good thing he'd been plotting his escape for nine years. All of the plans were already in place. Soon...very soon...

I'll see you again, Claire.

And it wouldn't just be a thin photograph that he touched. He'd have the real deal in his arms once again.

No one will take you from me.

CHAPTER SIX

"They're burying the senator today."

When Noah made that announcement, Claire's fingers stilled over the computer keyboard. She'd been staying with him at York Towers for the last few days. Sleeping in his bed at night, working by his side during the day.

Drake had vanished.

The reporters had stayed close.

But not as close as Noah.

Noah cleared his throat and said, "And they're letting Ethan go to the funeral."

She looked up. They weren't in the suite now. Instead, they were working in one of the offices downstairs. They'd spent the morning going over blueprints for the Washington restaurant addition. Talking marketing. PR. Noah wanted to open the roof-top restaurant with a bang on New Year's Eve. Throw a huge party and—

"*Claire.*"

She swallowed and focused on him. She'd already known that Ethan was being allowed to attend the funeral.

"You're wearing a mask, Claire. *Talk* to me." He caught her hands. Pulled Claire to her feet.

"What do you want me to say?" There wasn't *anything* to say. She wasn't going to pretend some sort of grief for the senator's death. It was wrong, but she felt relief now that he was being buried.

He can't hurt me anymore.

"I want you to talk to me." The words were hard, but his hands were light on her. "Claire, it's me. I won't judge anything you say. Just...*talk to me.*"

"I'm scared." There. She'd said it.

His hold tightened on her.

"I saw on the news that the Alabama governor was granting some sort of special release for Ethan." A temporary hardship release or some other kind of bull. "I don't like knowing that he's out there, free, not even for a second." She wanted him locked away behind as many bars as possible.

"He won't touch you."

His gruff words sounded like a vow, but Noah didn't understand. "That's what my parents told me, too." She pulled away from him. Headed to the nearby window. Stared out at the city. "They told me I'd be safe. That Ethan wouldn't hurt me again. That I could just walk away from him."

Behind her, Noah swore.

"I wasn't safe. Even with a restraining order on him, he came after me. He killed them, and he found me."

He'd told her that when he first found her on the dock. Been so proud.

"He watched me in that courtroom. Watched me like he owned me." She'd been sixteen. So terrified. "And when I left the courthouse each day, there'd be people outside, yelling at me. Calling me so many names. There'd be spray paint on my house. People were believing his story. I thought..." This was the part that twisted her insides, but saying it out loud...*I have to do it.* "I thought Ethan was going to get away with what he'd done."

Noah's hands wrapped around her shoulders. He turned her around and forced Claire to face him. "He didn't."

"I thought he was, though, and I knew if he got free, he'd come after me." She looked down at her wrists. Covered by her long sleeves. Always covered so carefully. "So I took the razor." A hard smile lifted her lips. "I made sure I cut myself just the right way, and I waited to die in the same house that my parents had died in."

His hold on her was bruising.

"I know it was weak," she said, voice husky, "but I was sixteen, and so scared, and death was better than having to see him again."

He yanked her against his chest. She could feel the mad drumming of his heart.

His scent wrapped around her. His arms held her close. She felt safe there, in his embrace. Once, she'd thought that she'd never be safe.

"You won't see him again," Noah promised her. "He's going back to jail."

But one day, Ethan would get out, for good. In five years, eight months, and seven days. Yes, she knew exactly how much time he had left to serve.

"Sara found you, didn't she?" Noah asked her.

Claire pulled away from him, just a little bit. "She came home early." Her big sister. Older by four years. "She saved me. She got there in time." Her lips trembled as she thought of Sara's recent death…and how she'd just been minutes too late to save the one person in this world that she loved. "I couldn't do the same for her."

Claire had lost everyone that she loved.

So much pain. Sometimes, she felt as if it were choking her.

His lips brushed against her forehead. "We're getting the fuck out of here," he said.

Claire blinked. "What?"

"I've got a place in the Hamptons. We're going to the beach. You're going to drink wine with me, and you're going to relax on that beach—even if it is getting a bit cold now—and you're not going to think about death, Senator Harrison, or that asshole Ethan." He tipped up her chin. "You're only going to think about me. Got it? Me…and you…and the way we can make each other feel."

"But…the Washington hotel, the restaurant—"

"Will still be there when we come back. We're leaving, Claire. Because you're alive, I'm alive, and the rest of the world can just screw off."

***

He hated funerals. Particularly this funeral.

The overdone mourning. All the fake tears. The talk about the "good" man that had been taken too soon.

Such bullshit.

Drake Archer shifted beneath the hanging branches of the old oak tree. Spanish moss clung to the sprawling branches, and the moss blew lightly in the faint breeze.

It was a packed funeral, but Drake had expected nothing less. Old senators, law enforcement personnel, reporters…and, of course, just the curious had turned out for this event.

It's like a freaking circus show.

Noah hadn't asked Drake to attend the funeral. After he'd left New York, Drake had actually planned to just head back to Biloxi, but the funeral in Fairview had been too close for him to pass up. Maybe he was just curious, too.

Or maybe I'm a suspicious bastard, and I wanted to see Ethan Harrison with my own eyes.

Because the guy was there. Not wearing prison orange, but instead dressed in a black suit. Drake sure never would've guessed that man had spent the last nine years in a cell.

It turned out there were actually two Harrison boys. Ethan Harrison, and his older brother, Austin. Ethan was the black sheep, but the brother who currently sat beside him on the front row, right next to the casket, well, it seemed Austin Harrison was supposed to be the savior of the family.

He was an attorney, some big corporate deal. Drake had done a little digging, and he'd discovered that Austin was the one who'd kept the family afloat for so many years. After the senator had crashed and burned, it had been Austin who made sure the family never lost their position in Alabama society.

They'd kept their mansion. Kept their power.

Drake shifted again, moving to get a better view of the brothers. His eyes narrowed. Ethan was staring at the grave. He was...smiling?

"Are you a friend of Senator Harrison's?" A soft voice asked him. "Or are you family?"

He turned his head and saw a petite beauty with light brown skin standing close by. "I'm neither," he told her.

She tilted her head. The woman's shoulders were straight. Her hair fell just to her chin. She was dressed simply but stylishly in black pants and a matching blouse. Her gaze held his, then slid to the mourners, as if assessing them.

His instincts kicked into gear. The way she was watching the crowd...

Cop. Or a private investigator. He could usually spot them easily.

Even when said cop came in the form of such a pretty package.

"Don't bother," she said, not glancing back at him. "I'm taken."

Drake felt a grin curl his lips. "I was just admiring."

"Um." Her gaze was on Ethan Harrison. "Well, Mr. Neither, if you aren't a friend or family member, then want to tell me why you're at the funeral?"

"I was just passing through. It's not every day that a senator gets buried." He kept his eyes on her. "And what's a cop with a northern accent doing down here in Alabama?"

"I'm the cop who found the senator's body in D.C."

"So why aren't you *in* D.C. right now?"

Her gaze came back to his. "Because I'm trying to find a killer, Mr. Archer."

Ah, he wasn't Mr. Neither any longer. The lady had known exactly who he was all along. Interesting. "It would seem then you're a pretty good cop."

"You're a friend of Noah York's," she said. Once more, her gaze turned to sweep the crowd. "Did he send you down here to watch the funeral…or to watch Ethan Harrison?"

"Neither."

He thought her lips curled a bit at that answer. "Like I said, I'm just passing through," Drake told her.

This time, she turned to face him. "Your friend could be a killer."

There was no *could be* about it.

"You wouldn't protect a killer, would you?"

I'd protect Noah York any day. "Once upon a time," he said as he remembered days better left in the past, "Noah pulled me out of hell. A man doesn't forget things like that."

Because he could've died in a frigid prison, if Trace and Noah hadn't fought so hard for him. They'd been willing to die in order to save him. No, he'd never forget what they'd done.

His gaze slid back to the funeral.

Drake knew that, if he had to, *he'd* kill in order to protect Noah. Because he would not just stand back and watch his friend crash and burn.

***

The funeral was over.

Ethan Harrison tried not to smile as he stared at the grave. His father was gone.

Good fucking riddance.

The mourners kept looking at him. They were driving him insane. There were so many whispers and curious stares. He hunched his shoulders. Looked at the ground. And tried to act like this wasn't one of the best moments of his life.

I'll be getting away soon.

His brother tried to brush by him. Ethan grabbed Austin's shoulder. "We need to talk." He steered his brother to the relative privacy of a nearby mausoleum. The guards stayed close, about ten feet away, so Ethan dropped his voice when he said, "You haven't come to see me, *brother*."

He and Austin had the same eyes. Same green color. Same shape. And right then, Austin's eyes were bright with fury. "Why the hell would I come and see you?"

"Because we're family!" That should be plenty of reason. "You don't lock family away and forget about them."

"You do if the family is anything like you." Austin glared at him, the disgust plain to see on his face. That was Austin all right. Always looking down his nose at him. Always acting like he was so much better than Ethan.

You're not.

"Everything that happened is on you," Austin snarled at him. "If you'd just left that girl alone—"

"Claire."

Austin's eyelids jerked. "You should have left her alone."

Austin had always been the perfect one. The quarterback. The valedictorian. The every-fucking-thing. "You saw her first," Ethan recalled.

"What?"

"In the diner, *you* saw her first." He could remember this so well. "I wouldn't have noticed Claire at all, if you hadn't been staring at her so hard. Hell, you even said…'I'm gonna ask her out.' I just beat you to the punch."

Austin's jaw dropped in surprise, and he surged toward Ethan. "*That's* why you hooked up with Claire Kramer? Because you thought I wanted her?"

Ethan just smiled at him. *You did want her, brother. I saw it in your eyes.*

Austin sucked in a deep breath. Then he smiled, too. And laughed. "You're such an idiot, Ethan. I hope you enjoyed your afternoon of freedom, because it's over. They're waiting to take you back to jail." His voice dropped to a low whisper. "And guess what happens when you get back? Your preferential treatment ends. No more being separated from the others. Welcome to general pop."

Was that supposed to scare him?

"Dad's gone. And I'm not as blind as he was. *Everything* will change for you now. You did the crime, and you'll suffer for it."

Ethan glanced away from Austin's glittering eyes. "One thing I always wondered…" His stare lingered a moment on the casket. *Rot, old man. Rot.* "Did he hit you, too? Or did he just save that shit for me?"

Silence. Maybe that was his answer.

"Your big brother is supposed to protect you. How come you never helped me?" Ethan asked him. Then, because maybe he didn't want to hear the miserable lie that Austin would spout, Ethan walked away from him.

The whispers were louder as he headed back to the patrol car. The black and white car was parked near the edge of the lot, close to a thick patch of trees. Those trees backed up to a little bayou. He'd taken Claire to that bayou once.

He'd taken her virginity there. They'd been in the back of his car then.

"Time to go," one of the guards said as he stepped to Ethan's side. Bo. Bo Dunnelly.

The other guy was Marcel Reed.

They'd been good enough, for cops.

Marcel opened one of the car's back doors. Ethan knew the reporters close by had been waiting for this shot. The picture of him being loaded back up for jail.

The cops didn't cuff him.

He'd counted on that.

So he waved to the crowd. He sucked in a deep breath of that free air. And he remembered Claire.

He slid into the car.

Marcel and Bo headed toward the front of the vehicle. They climbed inside.

"Damn, son," Marcel said as he settled into the front seat of the car. "That was sure a lot of folks to see your dad off."

Yes, it had been. "He always liked a good show." The old bastard had cared so much about what everyone thought.

Too bad no one had realized what an abusive prick he was.

***

The show was over. Drake strode past the grave. He glanced toward the patrol car. Ethan Harrison had just been loaded up in there and—

The force of the explosion threw Drake back about five feet. He nearly landed right *in* that damn grave.

Drake jumped up as fast as he could, then stared with narrowed eyes at the sight before him.

The patrol car was a ball of flames. People were screaming, running, and Ethan Harrison...

He was burning.

The little cop ran toward the car. Damn foolish mistake. Amateur hour. He grabbed her, jerked her back and—

Another explosion sent the flames surging even higher.

"There are men in there!" The cop screamed. "Two officers, I saw them load Ethan in—"

And all he could see was fire now. "They're dead." Someone had wanted to take out Ethan Harrison and the cops had just become collateral damage.

The heat from the flames lanced over his skin.

***

When his phone rang, Noah thought about ignoring the call. He would have, if the ring hadn't been the distinct tone that told him Drake Archer was on the other end of the line.

"Shouldn't you be gambling some place?" Noah asked when he took the call. Drake owned a series of casinos along the Mississippi Coast, and Noah had thought that his friend would be getting right back to business.

Noah and Claire had just arrived at his house in the Hamptons. Claire was walking along the beach. He intended to join her there in the next sixty seconds.

"Can't talk long," Drake said, the words low. "I'll tell you more later, but...*Ethan Harrison is dead.*"

Noah wasn't sure he'd just heard correctly. "What?"

"I was at the senator's funeral..."

Why the hell had Drake been there?

"Everything was fine until Ethan Harrison got loaded back into a patrol car. Someone put a bomb in the car. *Everything* and *everyone* in that car are gone."

Noah stared down at the beach. "You're sure he's dead?"

"Unless the man can walk through fire, hell yes, he's gone."

Good.

"Be careful," Drake warned him, "there's a cop here. A woman from D.C. She's asking a lot of questions about you."

"I'm always careful." *Claire was free.*

"I'll see what I can find out from the authorities down here. But, shit, Weston's the one who is good at investigating things, not me." There was the murmur of voices in the background. "Got to go." The line went dead.

Noah kept staring down at the beach. Claire had turned and was walking toward him. She wasn't smiling, but she didn't look as frightened as she'd appeared back in the city.

He moved to the edge of his deck. The wind tousled Claire's hair as she climbed up the steps. Her gaze darted to his phone. "Is everything okay?"

Just tell her. "Ethan Harrison is dead."

She stopped.

"Drake was at the senator's funeral." *Why?* "A bomb was put in the car, and he's...Ethan is gone, Claire."

Her breath heaved out, and Claire hunched over, clutching her stomach.

"Claire!" He ran to her. Put his hands on her arms.

She looked up at him. Tears streamed down her cheeks. "He's dead?"

"Yes." If Drake had said the man was gone...*he was gone.*

Noah didn't mention that when it came to demolitions, Drake was an expert. He'd always been the one to set the detonations for their team.

And Drake just happened to be at the funeral? Shit, but this could get bad, fast.

"Ethan won't ever come after me," Claire whispered. She was crying and smiling, and breaking the heart that Noah didn't think he still had. "He's gone!"

Then she threw her arms around Noah and held him tight. He held her just as tightly.

Ethan Harrison might be gone, but things weren't over. Not yet.

The senator's dead. Harrison's dead. Would that be the end of the killings? Or were things just getting started?

He pulled her closer. Noah didn't know what was happening. Someone had just saved him one hell of a lot of trouble though. Because Noah had already put a plan in motion to eliminate Ethan.

Claire looked up at him. "I don't have to be afraid any longer."

He nodded. He didn't tell Claire what he was thinking. What would be the point?

Maybe he was wrong.

The senator...Ethan...their deaths might not touch Claire at all.

His fingers slid down her back.

He was the only one touching her, and anyone who wanted to hurt Claire would have to go through him.

***

"Will you take me out on your boat?" Claire asked. Her stomach was in knots. It had been that way, pretty much all day long. The knots had gotten even worse when she found out the news about Ethan's death.

He's dead. Dead. He can't hurt me. He can't find me. I'm finally safe.

Noah was cooking dinner for her. Such a normal, domestic task, and one that she *never* would've pictured Noah York performing. The guy always seemed to have an army of chefs at his beck and call.

But out there, it was just him. Just her.

Exactly as he'd promised.

He glanced up at her. "My boat?"

She blinked. He'd just sounded so wooden. "Yes, I, um, I saw the boat down by the dock. I thought—I thought you might want to go out." When she'd been younger, she'd loved heading out on the water with her grandfather. She'd always felt so free then.

His stare turned toward the window. Darkness had fallen, so he wouldn't be able to see the boat. "I don't usually take anyone out with me."

Her cheeks burned. "I-I'm sorry. I didn't mean to—" She stopped because Claire didn't know what to say. They were lovers, but according to Drake, it was just some sort of temporary situation. She was bumbling around, and trying to make plans and do things because—

I feel free.

Noah put down the knife he'd been holding. He headed for her. His face was so hard. So tight.

Nervousness pushed through Claire. She'd done something wrong. "Forget I said anything." The moment was thick with tension, and she just wanted to go back to the way they'd been before.

"You really don't know about my past, do you?"

She shook her head.

His gaze held hers. "Some women…they make plans for me."

"Plans?"

"They learn everything they can about my life. Then they use what they know to try and win me over."

"I'm not trying to win you." It hurt that he thought she was just trying to manipulate him.

"No." His lips tightened. "You tried to run from me."

Because she'd thought it was best.

"Dinner can wait," he said. He reached for her fingers. Threaded his with hers. "I know about your hell. Maybe it's time you knew about mine." And he led her out onto the balcony. Then down the wooden steps.

Her bare feet curled in the sand. The wind blew off the water, sending her t-shirt fluttering around her body. There was a chill on the wind that sent goosebumps rising along her arms.

The moon was out. Heavy and full in the sky. The big boat was docked nearby.

"I was thirteen when they died," he said. "They were the only parents I ever knew." He released her hand. "My real folks gave me up when I was a kid. But Mac and Kylie…they loved me so much." A pause. "Probably the same way your parents loved you."

She'd never thought about Noah's family before. Why not? The guy *had* to be connected to others. He wasn't just—

"My dad loved to get out on the water. He started teaching me how to steer when I was barely tall enough to reach his waist. We'd go out on that water. Stay for hours."

"I-I loved the water, too," Claire whispered, needing to say something. There was an echo of pain in Noah's voice, and she wanted to soothe him. "I always felt free out on the water." But she sure hadn't been out on a boat like this one. She'd gone out on a little fishing boat—one with a small motor or she'd just used paddles.

"The water's beautiful," Noah said and his gaze turned toward the waves. "And it's dangerous."

The waves crashed into the beach.

"Sometimes it reminds me of you."

He thought she was dangerous? Claire shook her head, then realized he couldn't see the movement. "I'm not dangerous to you." She'd never hurt him. He'd been one of the few people to actually help her. To care.

"You're more dangerous than you know." The wind took that soft reply, twisted it, and Claire wasn't sure he'd even said those words.

Then he turned his back on the water and faced her. "A storm came up. One of those freak storms that *shouldn't* have happened. It sent our boat rolling. We lost the sail—hell, we lost everything."

Goosebumps rose on her arms. "Noah…" Claire didn't want to hear the end of this story. She wanted to picture him happy. She wanted him to introduce her to Mac and Kylie.

"I wasn't strong enough. I couldn't keep my dad afloat. He'd gotten hit in the head with the mast, and he was bleeding. I *couldn't keep him afloat.*"

She wrapped her arms around him. "I don't want to go out on the water," Claire whispered. *You don't have to tell me anymore. Stop, Noah, just stop.* Because it hurt him to share this story. She could feel the pain vibrating through him.

"I couldn't save my mother, either. I tried. So damn hard. I treaded water with her for hours, but when the Coast Guard finally found us…" He wasn't holding her back. Just standing stiffly in her embrace. "She was dead."

In his arms.

Claire squeezed her eyes shut, but the image was there, burning brightly in her mind.

Sometimes, she forgot—*I'm not the only one who has lost.* Her own pain was so thick. It had blinded her. *I should've seen his pain sooner.* Noah had been so busy helping her, but she'd done nothing for him.

"I don't take anyone else out on the water with me because I never want to be in that situation again."

Holding someone he loved and watching that person slip away?

"I get sea sick," she lied, talking quickly and still holding him tightly. "I hate being out on the water."

He pushed her back. Stared down at her.

"Let's go back inside," she said. Her voice was husky with tears that she wanted to shed, for him.

"The water reminds me of them," he told her. "I hate it, and I love it." He shook his head. "I'll never let it take anyone else from me again."

Was that why he had this place here? A place that was both haven and hell? A place he'd brought her to? "How many…" She cleared her throat. "How many other women have been here?"

"Just you, Claire. Just you."

Drake's words whispered through her mind. *He doesn't keep them, you know…He sleeps with them, gets the lust out of his system, then he lets them go. He doesn't like to have the same lover twice in a row.*

"Why me?" Claire asked him.

"Fuck if I know."

She blinked. Well, that wasn't exactly some romantic confession. She started to ease back from him.

But then *he* was holding tight to *her*. "I just know that I need you close. Sometimes, I think if I can't see you, if I can't touch you—" He broke off, and his head jerked to the left.

His body tensed as he stared into the darkness.

Jeez, but she didn't want the guy to stop talking. "Noah? What were you saying?" *Keep saying it.*

"We're not alone." Then he pushed her back and ran toward the sand dunes.

Shocked, Claire stared after him for a few seconds before understanding kicked in—it sure kicked in hard when she saw the dark shadow rise from the sand dunes and start running away.

Only Noah wasn't letting that shadow get far.

Claire raced after Noah. The sand flew beneath her feet.

Noah tackled the shadow. *A man.* They hit the sand with a thudding impact that she heard even over the waves. Then Noah spun the guy over. *"Who the hell are you?"*

Breath heaving, Claire rushed to his side.

"Get off me!" The guy shouted. He tried to swing at Noah. A terrible mistake. The swing missed.

Noah's fist drove down. He didn't miss. He hit the man in the face. Once. Twice. Powerful blows that were brutal with their intensity.

"Try again…" Noah snarled. His fist was poised over the man's face. "Who. Are. You?"

"P-private investigator!" Then, he snarled, "Shit, you broke my nose!"

"I'm about to break a whole lot more than that," Noah told him. She'd never heard Noah's voice sound that way. Lethal.

Deadly.

Chilling.

Claire tried to peer at the private investigator's face. She could see the round curve of his cheek. The high forehead. The thinning hair. The moonlight was strong as it shone down on them.

"Who are you working for?" Noah asked him. His hand was still poised to punch.

"Screw off!"

Noah's fist plunged down again.

"Noah!" Claire lunged forward. She grabbed his arm. "Stop!"

"Shit!" The PI cried. There was a dark shadow streaking down his face. Blood. Definitely blood. "I'm going to sue your ass! This is assault!"

Claire tried to drag Noah off the guy. He didn't move.

"This is private property, dumbass," Noah bit out. "And you took the first swing." Then Noah shoved his hand into the guy's pockets.

"Wait, stop, what—"

Noah rose, and he had what looked like a wallet in his hand. "Guessing your ID is in here."

The man stumbled to his feet. He put his hand to his nose, obviously trying to stop that blood flow.

Claire stood there, her frantic breaths still shaking her chest, shocked by the violence that had erupted so suddenly.

"Harrison sent you," Noah said flatly.

The guy's shoulders jerked.

"The senator's dead," Claire said. It didn't make sense that this guy would be here if he'd been hired by Colby Harrison to—

"Not the senator." Noah's voice was sharp. "Ethan. You were the one sending him the pictures of Claire, weren't you?"

Pictures? Her goosebumps got worse.

"In case you haven't heard, Ethan Harrison is dead, too," Noah announced and it sounded like there was…satisfaction in those words.

The man backed up. "What?"

"Why don't you try and call your employer? You're going find out that your services aren't needed. No one's left to pay you." The waves crashed behind them. "And after you do that, you need to get out of this area as fast as you can." He advanced on the guy.

The PI darted back.

Claire couldn't move.

"Because I'll give you one warning. Only one. If you *ever* come near Claire again, it will be the last mistake you make."

Noah's sudden eruption of violence…the deadly intensity that clung to him…

It made Claire think too much of her past.

Ethan had erupted into violence so quickly. So often.

Noah isn't Ethan.

"Get the hell out of here," Noah ordered.

"Give me back my ID and I—"

"You don't get anything back. I'll be turning this over to Weston Securities. They'll learn every detail I need to know about you."

"Th-there's no need—"

"Yes, there is, because if you don't stay away from me and Claire, I'll be the one lurking in the shadows near *your* door. And you'll see what it's like to be hunted."

The man turned then and he ran, disappearing into the darkness.

Noah stared after him. One hand was clenched around the wallet he'd taken. The other hand was fisted at his side.

The waves kept pounding against the shore.

"How do you know...about the pictures?" Claire asked.

Noah glanced over his shoulder at her.

It felt as if someone had punched *her*. "You said Ethan had pictures of me. That *he'd* been the one to hire that guy...how do you know all that, Noah?"

"It doesn't matter." He stalked toward her. Shoved the wallet into his back pocket.

She stood her ground when she wanted to flee.

Noah isn't Ethan.

She'd never been afraid of Noah before.

She'd also...never seen him attack a man before. One instant, he'd been sharing his past with her.

The next...he'd been punching a man with lethal fury.

Now he seemed so contained. So *controlled*.

"It matters to me," Claire said as she lifted her chin and forced her shoulders to stay straight. "How did you know that?" Maybe he'd just been guessing. Just been—

"Because Ethan looked me in the eyes, and the bastard *told* me that he had someone watching you."

Her heart was racing in her chest, pounding louder than those waves.

"And I went to his cell. I saw the pictures that he had of you."

Claire shook her head. This wasn't happening. "When?"

"I saw him yesterday." Flat.

The day before Ethan died?

"Noah…" Fear was there now. Fear and enough dread to choke her. "What did you do?"

CHAPTER SEVEN

Claire was afraid of him.

Sonofabitch. She wasn't supposed to fear him. He was the one who wanted to protect her. To help her.

But when Noah took a step toward Claire, she backed away from him.

"Did you kill him?"

He could hear her fear.

"Did you kill him?" Claire asked again. Her voice was shaking.

His eyes narrowed on her. "Why does it even matter? You know you're glad that he's gone."

Claire spun from him then. She *ran* from him.

He hadn't meant to send her fleeing. "Claire!"

She didn't slow down at his call. She just ran faster. Why? Because she thought that she was running from a killer?

That's exactly what I am.

No matter how many fancy suits he put on. No matter how many hotels he opened. No matter how many charity balls he hosted…Noah couldn't hide the truth.

At his core, he was a killer.

That's what I'll always be.

And he wasn't letting Claire run away. Noah rushed after Claire. "Stop!"

She was fast. He was faster. He grabbed her arm and spun her around to face him.

Claire hit him.

Noah hadn't expected Claire to drive her fist at him—she had one hell of a hook—and he let her go.

She didn't run then. She stood, staring up at him, her chest heaving, and the moonlight showed the horror on her face. "Noah, I'm sorry, I—" She shook her head. Her hand fell to her side. "What's happening? What are we doing?"

"We should go inside." He fought to keep his voice level, his control in place. If the PI came back, Noah didn't want the guy overhearing anything else that he and Claire said.

Claire glanced toward his beach house. The lights were on and glowing brightly. He stepped toward her.

Claire flinched.

He held up his hands. "Let's go inside and talk." Claire was at the edge of her control. He could see it.

I did this to her.

He wanted to wrap her in his arms, but he couldn't. Not yet.

Her head nodded jerkily, and she hurried to his house. He noticed she made sure to keep a careful distance between them. When they were inside, he secured the door.

"It all seemed so perfect before," she murmured, her eyes on the table in the kitchen. On the plates that were still there. Their half-made dinner waited steps away. "I don't...I don't get perfect, though. I should've known that."

Hell, no, he wasn't perfect. He never would be.

Claire squared her shoulders. "There was no trip to Vegas."

"No, there wasn't."

"You lied to me." Pain whispered through her words. "I thought I could trust you."

"You can."

Her eyes lifted to meet his. "You went down to Alabama."

He nodded. "Trace got me in to see Harrison."

"Ethan." Her whisper was stark.

He forced himself to take a long, deep breath. That breath didn't calm him worth a damn. "The senator was dead, but I needed to make sure that Ethan understood exactly where he stood with you. With us."

Her eyes closed. "Did you kill him?"

"I didn't set the bomb in that car." He could say that with absolute honesty.

After a tense moment, her eyes opened. Her confused gaze was on him. "I'm just a woman you had sex with. Drake says there are plenty of us."

There was only one Claire.

"Why would you go all the way down there? Why would you—"

He *had* to touch her. Noah wrapped his arms around her shoulders. "You're not like anyone else. You never could be."

Her breath caught.

"I went down there because I needed to see him. He's the bastard who ruined your life. The one who put the fear and the shadows in your eyes."

When her eyes widened, he nodded grimly. "Yeah, baby, it's still there. It's always there. You look out at the world as if you're just waiting for people to strike out at you. You're beautiful…and you're scared, so scared. *He* did that to you." His hands slid down her arms. Down, down to her wrists. His fingers curled over the scars. "He did that," Noah repeated.

"I did it," Claire fired back, her words surprisingly strong. "I let him into my life. I'm the one who picked up the razor, I'm the—"

"*Stop it!*" His fury erupted.

Claire tried to pull away. He wouldn't let her.

"He's a sick, twisted freak. He locked onto you, and he was going to do anything and everything in order to keep you with him."

"He was in jail," Claire said with a shake of her head. "He couldn't—"

"He had photos of you all over his cell." He hadn't intended to tell her, and if that asshole PI hadn't shown up…*She never would have known.* "He was as obsessed with you as ever. He had plans, Claire." *Plans that won't ever happen.* "He was counting down the days until he would be free, and then he would've come for you again." Noah knew that Ethan would have killed her.

His fingers were caressing the skin along her wrists. Claire wasn't speaking. She was so stiff and still.

"I wasn't going to let Ethan hurt you. I went down there to tell him, to let him know that you weren't alone. If he came after you…he'd find me in his path, and I would kill him then."

Her lips trembled. "How can you talk about taking someone's life so easily?"

"Because Ethan Harrison wasn't a man. He was a monster that needed to be put down."

She tugged against his hold.

"*I didn't do it, Claire.*" But he would've. And maybe that was what she feared the most. What he was capable of doing. Noah let her go. "I didn't kill him, but that's just because someone else beat me to the punch. If he'd come after you, if he'd tried to hurt you…" It was better for her to see him exactly as he was. No lies. No masks. "I would have killed him in an instant."

She stood before him. Her eyes too wide. Her face too pale. "I don't want you to be like him."

Fury poured through his blood. "I'm *not.*"

"I knew he had a darkness inside, I knew it from the very beginning, but I wanted him anyway."

"Claire…"

"You have a darkness, too. I can feel it. I want you, Noah, more than I've wanted anyone, but you scare me, too." Her hand raked through her hair.

"I know." But she'd wanted him despite her fear.

And he just—wanted her.

"More than that…" She licked her lips. "I'm scared of the way I feel with you. Like the control I have, the life I've got…I could lose it all."

"I'm not going to let you lose anything." Why couldn't she see that he wanted to protect her? To help her? "I didn't kill him," Noah said again. "But I would kill to keep you safe." He backed away from her. "I want you. And you need to decide...you *have* to decide, if you want me, too." The rest had to be said so he forced himself to add, "You have to decide if you want me more than you fear me." Noah took another step back.

Claire wrapped her arms around her stomach.

"And when you do decide, you come find me."

Then, before he gave into the primal urge to touch her, to take her, to *make* her see what they had...Noah turned away from Claire. He went upstairs to his bedroom. The rage he felt had his hands shaking.

Claire shouldn't have learned about his trip to Alabama. He'd screwed up. He'd be more careful next time.

He yanked out the wallet he'd taken from the PI. Scanned the information inside. And, two minutes later, Noah had Trace on the phone. "Are your agents still working the break-in at the Hamlet?" Noah demanded when Trace came on the line. Claire's stay at the Hamlet...it seemed so far away, but it had just been days ago when he'd discovered her trashed room.

"*Another middle of the night call...*" Trace growled. "Shit, man, keep normal hours and —"

"Ethan Harrison is dead."

That shut Trace up.

"The car he was in exploded today."

"You *sure* he was in it?"

"Drake was there. He's the one who confirmed the kill."

The faint sound of rustling and then the click of a door eased over the line. "What the hell is going on?" Trace demanded. "First the senator, and now the bastard Ethan?"

"I don't know what's happening. I want you to find out." Trace had a slew of agents at his beck and call. "Start your hunt with a private investigator, a man named Sloan Hall."

"And why should I start with him?"

"Because the Harrisons were paying him to watch Claire, and the SOB was just here at my place in the Hamptons. If I see him again..."

"Got it," Trace said. Silence stretched over the line, then Trace cleared his throat. "Noah, you don't sound quite like yourself."

Noah glanced down. There was a faint tremor in his fingers. "Did Skye ever look at you as if you were the monster she should fear?"

"Uh, look, Claire's been through a lot and..."

"And that's a no, right? Because the woman you want *isn't* supposed to look at you that way. She isn't supposed to be afraid of you." His left hand fisted.

"Skye *isn't* Claire. After what she's been through, Claire has to be afraid—"

"I don't want her afraid of me." But he knew that people didn't always get what they wanted. Especially...

When she has a reason to be afraid.

"I'm taking over this case," Trace told him. "I'm coming in personally to handle it. Not just my agents. *Me.* I'll be on the next flight to New York."

"No. You stay with Skye, I—"

"I'm coming in," Trace said again. "I don't like this scene. First Senator Harrison, then his son? It reeks of a set-up. Kill the senator..."

"In order to get a shot at the son." Noah had thought the same thing.

"It's personal." Trace sighed. "And an attack against Ethan Harrison isn't personal without it being connected to Claire Kramer."

That was what Noah feared.

"You need to keep her close." Trace's voice had hardened. "Dammit, man, I *owe* her, too, and I don't want anything happening to Claire—"

The door opened behind Noah. He turned.

Claire was there, standing on the threshold of the room.

"Nothing will," he swore.

Nothing…but what she wanted to happen.

***

Sloan Hall swiped at the blood that kept gushing from his nose. He'd never expected Noah York to come after him like that. Suits weren't supposed to attack.

They were supposed to run.

He yanked out his phone. His bloody fingers smeared across the screen as he dialed his client.

Ethan Harrison is dead?

Shit, this couldn't be happening.

But…Ethan wasn't the one who paid his bills.

The phone was answered on the second ring. "This isn't a good time."

Sloan recognized the boss's voice immediately.

"Yeah, well, I hear that's because your brother's dead," Sloan said, words coming fast because he was afraid the guy was about to hang up.

Austin Harrison had never seemed to care much for him. Austin had paid him, but only because he'd been ordered to do so. *The senator had run that family with a drunken fist.*

"Word travels fast…" Austin murmured. "I figured the news shows would run with the story. They always enjoyed my family's pain."

"Wasn't the news." The blood wouldn't stop coming. "It was Noah York."

Silence. Then… "You're still on the job?"

If the job was Claire Kramer… "Not anymore. As of twenty minutes ago, I'm done, got it? The bastard attacked me!" He put his left hand to his nose. That shit hurt. He might have to go see a doc.

"Where are you?"

"The freaking Hamptons, and guess what? I hate the place. Claire's screwing her rich psycho, he's muttering about his parents dying on a boat, and I'm just wondering how much you're gonna be paying me for my pain and suffering." *Make this work. Salvage something, Sloan.* "Because if I have to do it, I'll go to the media. I'll let them know just how messed up the Harrison family became. Stalking that woman, getting all those pictures…day and night."

There was a murmur of voices in the background. What was happening? It sounded as if Austin had a dozen people around him.

Sloan's hold on the phone tightened. Had Austin just said, "detective" just then? Hell, had he *already* been replaced?

"I have to go," Austin told him. The guy sounded way too curt.

"What you have to do is deal with me!" Sloan was getting desperate. And his nose kept throbbing and bleeding.

"I will. I'll see you, very soon."

The bastard hung up on him.

Sloan glared down at the phone. "You'd better," he snarled. "Because I haven't been paid enough for this shit."

***

"Mr. Harrison?" Gwen Lazlo said as she cocked her head and waited for the guy to end his phone call. "I'd really appreciate a few minutes of your time."

Austin Harrison slowly turned toward her. There was no grief on his face. If anything, she'd say the guy showed signs of…relief.

His gaze—a glittering green—drifted over her. "I'm sorry, Detective Lazlo. For a man like me, business doesn't seem to stop, not even for death."

She barely controlled an eye roll. "Look, I don't have jurisdiction down here but—"

"No, you don't." His stare drifted behind her. They were in his house. Some fancy southern mansion with too many white columns, and people were milling all over the place. "I believe Sheriff Brady will be in charge of the investigation."

"In charge of the investigation into your brother's death, yes," Gwen said, her voice sharp. *And that investigation is going to take forever. Nothing was left of that car, those two poor cops, or of Ethan Harrison.* "But I'm still lead on your father's case, and I have a few questions that I must ask you."

He blinked at her. "My father…" His laugh was rough. "Strange, isn't it? I almost forgot about him. I just—I keep seeing the flames. Ethan was trying to talk to me, I wanted to get away from him, and then…he was just gone."

She'd always sucked at dealing with grieving families. This guy wasn't exactly grieving, though. She wasn't one hundred percent sure what he was. "Did your father have any enemies?"

"Plenty of them." He rubbed the back of his neck. "He was an asshole."

So she'd heard, but Gwen pressed on with her questions. "Any enemies that might want him dead? That might want him *and* Ethan dead?"

"Ethan was in jail. He couldn't hurt anyone in jail." His hand dropped. "I wasn't a good brother."

This was not helping her investigation. "I need names. I need to know who would want your father to die like that—a shot to the head and—"

"Claire Kramer." Her name was a sigh from Austin. "She's the one who'd want him dead. Who'd want them both dead, but Claire doesn't have the power to pull off something like this."

Gwen wasn't so certain of that. *Claire's new lover has plenty of power.* "When was the last time you spoke with Claire?"

He laughed. "I haven't spoken with her, not in years, but I know what they did." His jaw tightened. "I know what they both did to Claire, and if anyone would've wanted to see my father and my brother rotting, it would be her."

***

Her knees were shaking. Her stomach seemed to be tied in knots, and Claire was absolutely determined not to let Noah see her fear.

He tossed aside the phone that he'd held. His golden gaze locked on her.

"I am afraid of you," Claire told him because she thought the words needed to be said.

His lips thinned. "Tell me something I didn't know."

A spark of anger ignited within her. "How can I not be afraid? You attacked that PI. You—you told me that you'd kill Ethan—"

"Like you hadn't thought about killing him yourself? Come on, Claire. It's just us. I won't judge you for the darkness inside you."

The darkness inside you. So he did see it. She'd wondered about that. Keeping her eyes on his, Claire admitted, "Only every day."

His head cocked as he studied her.

"But if I killed Ethan, then wouldn't I become just like him?" And that was the root of Claire's terror. Ethan had been so drawn to her because he'd said they were the same. Mirror images, deep inside. She didn't want to be the same as Ethan.

She didn't want to kill. To destroy.

Claire never wanted to become so obsessed with one person that she let everything else slip away.

She couldn't quite read Noah's expression. Claire took a tentative step forward. "What's the difference between love and obsession?" That one question had haunted her for so long.

Noah didn't answer her.

"Have you ever been in love, Noah?"

He opened his mouth to speak, but Claire laughed, realizing what she'd just foolishly asked. "Of course, you haven't. You're the man with a new lover every night. You don't want to love."

"Love leads to pain," Noah said.

Claire nodded. "I was told once that you were in love when you needed someone so much that you couldn't bear to think of the world without that person, that you couldn't *live* without that person being near." She wet her too-dry lips. "I think that's obsession. A need that dominates you. Consumes you. A need for one other person. A need that makes you do...*anything*...to possess that person."

He was as still as a statue before her.

"Ethan thought he loved me, but I don't believe Ethan could love." Time to confess all. "I don't think I can love, either." She'd just been getting by, in a void, for so long. Watching the world. Hiding from herself.

From everyone.

"Do you think you can love?" Claire asked him.

His eyes glittered. "Do you want me to say that I love you?"

"No." Because she wouldn't believe him if he did. "You don't. You want to fuck me. I think you want to protect me, because you and Trace—" The slightly bitter laughter slipped from her again. "You both hold yourselves responsible for Sara's death. You're trying to make amends somehow to me."

"I do want to protect you."

But you don't love me.

"I'm asking if you *can* love, Noah." And it was so important to her. "Love or obsession...what is life about to you?"

His gaze slid from hers. "I think there's a thin line between love and obsession."

Her breath whispered out.

"I already feel obsessed with you," he said, his voice gravel-rough, "but you know that, don't you?"

Yes.

"I won't ever hurt you," Noah told her. The words were stark. "I need you to believe that."

Not her. She didn't think he would physically hurt her, but what about someone else? She'd been so wrong about a lover before. Trusting Noah completely seemed an impossible task.

"I'm *not* like Ethan Harrison. Anything that happens between you and me...it happens because it is what you *want* to happen. It's about what you *need*."

She needed him. She needed to feel like any other woman. "I didn't date again after Ethan. Didn't go to prom or any parties in college. I stayed as far away from men as I could get." She was trying to explain, and Claire was afraid he just wouldn't understand her. "*I don't know how to do this.* I don't know if what I'm feeling for you is normal and—" *Right.* She swallowed and finished, "Or if it's wrong." Claire had whispered like the shameful secret it was.

Her eyes lowered. She was staring at the lush carpet, and she saw his legs moving toward her.

"Ethan told me that I was just like him. That *I* consumed him. And at first, I felt like he consumed me, too." There was so much pain in those memories. "I feel the same way with you."

His fingers slid under her chin. He forced her head to lift, but her gaze darted over his shoulder.

"Look at me," he ordered.

Slowly, afraid to see his gaze, afraid of what would be *in* his gaze, she did.

"How do you feel when you're with me? Tell me...*exactly*."

"I want to let go."

A furrow appeared between his brows.

"I want to stop playing it safe. I want to not care what happens beyond the pleasure that you can give me and the pleasure I can give you."

That furrow smoothed away. His eyes heated.

"I want to let go," she said again as their eyes held. "I want to burn instead of always being cold. I want to claw your back. I want to buck against your hips. I want to scream."

"All you have to do is ask."

It wasn't that simple. "I have no control. I lose myself when we're together, and I-I just want more and more." More of his heat. More of the pleasure. More of the pretense that she wasn't broken beyond repair.

"Ask, Claire," he growled out that command.

"Can any obsession be healthy?" Because she felt obsessed with him. "Do they all have to end in fear and darkness?"

"I'm not him."

He and Ethan looked different. Night and day. But that same, dark intensity was there, just beneath the skin.

Only Noah isn't twisted.

His eyes blazed right through her. Saw right through her.

In that moment, Claire thought she could see through him, too. Past the veneer of the polished businessman. Right to his core. Darkness and light, all tangled together. Not perfect. Not evil. Not good.

"Ask," he whispered. His expression was stark.

"I want to be with you again," she said. Maybe it was just for tonight. Maybe what they had together would last longer. But she wasn't going to think of a future then.

She refused to think of the past.

"Make love to me?" No, no, that was wrong. It wasn't about love. Obsession wasn't love. She was sure of that. She got obsession. She didn't get love.

He pulled her into his arms. Kissed her deep and hard, and the chill slid from her skin. The hands that had been so brutal on the PI were gentle against her. There was so much power in his body, but he kept it ruthlessly restrained when he was with her.

He kept his control.

For me?

His hands slid over her back. Caressing. Seeming to scorch her through the t-shirt. Then he yanked that t-shirt up. He tossed it across the room. Her bra followed it.

Her breasts were so sensitive they ached. The nipples were tight and flushed. Noah lifted her up, and he took one nipple into his mouth.

She felt arousal flood her sex. His strength was such a turn-on. That much power, leashed.

Controlled. In that moment, Claire realized that she didn't need control. Noah had it.

And she had him.

He carried her toward the bed. That big, sprawling bed that was perfect for sex. A sturdy, wrought-iron bed. He hadn't taken another lover there. He'd told her she was the only one to come to this place.

He put her on the bed. Pulled away her jeans and underwear. "I could devour you," he said as his gaze slid down her body. The gold of his eyes turned molten when he stared at the juncture between her legs.

His hands went to the snap of his jeans.

Claire rose then, pushing up quickly. "I *need* to taste you." Her fingers tangled with his. "I want to." He was all about her asking so she did. "Can I taste you?"

"Claire…" There was a sensual warning in her name.

That warning just aroused her more. "I've never…" Her fingers pulled from his. Her knees sank into the mattress. "I've never done this, and I want to taste you. I want you to be the first."

"The only." His voice had deepened and hardened with possession.

Claire eased down his zipper. The hiss seemed so loud in the silence of the room.

He put his hands behind his back. "Take me," he told her.

Her heart pounded in a double-time rhythm. Excitement and nervousness both surged through her as she slid off the bed. Her knees brushed over the carpet as she knelt before him.

His aroused flesh sprang toward her. Long and full. Hard and hot. She stroked him at first, her touch tentative. She wasn't sure what he'd like, and this was important—giving him as much pleasure as he'd given her was vitally important.

His hands were still behind his back.

He wasn't touching her. She was the one touching. The one with power?

Claire leaned forward. Her lips skimmed over his erection, and his cock jerked beneath her mouth.

"Take me in…" Noah growled out the sensual command.

Claire's lips parted. She took the head of his cock into her mouth. She licked. Sucked. Savored. Slowly, still so hesitant, she began to move. To take more. To find a rhythm that had him groaning.

And had her arousal deepening.

She liked the way he tasted. Liked the way he hardened impossibly more beneath her mouth and she—

Claire was on her back in the bed.

Noah was over her. He had her wrists pinned to the bed. Damn but that man had moved *fast*.

He stared at her, locked his gaze with her—and *took* her. He filled her, every inch, and she gasped as the pleasure surged through her.

Her legs curled around his. She arched up against him.

He plunged. Fast. Hard. Deep.

Claire wanted to match his rhythm, but…he felt so *good*. Every thrust sent his cock gliding right over her clit, and the sensation was incredible. Powerful and hot.

His grip tightened around her wrists. "I can feel you…feel everything…" Noah groaned the words. "Should stop…tell me to stop."

No, she never wanted him to stop. "More."

He thrust even harder. Deeper.

She could feel all of him.

All.

Noah was trying to pull away.

No condom.

She didn't want to lose him. Didn't want to lose that moment. "I'm clean," she whispered. No diseases. No lovers, not until him.

"So…am I." Noah thrust again.

Claire was lost. She shattered beneath him as the pleasure slammed through her. Not some gentle wave. An avalanche that stole her breath and had her quaking.

And Noah was there. He thrust into her once more, the hot surge of his climax filling her, and her legs locked tightly around his hips. She held him as fiercely as she could.

In that moment, Claire realized that she'd crossed a line. For her, there'd be no going back.

She'd lived in the darkness for years, and now, finally, she could see the light.

***

Gwen Lazlo was bone-tired when she shoved open the door to her apartment and dropped her bag on the floor. Her flight had landed in D.C. less than an hour ago, and the sun still hadn't risen above the sky.

She stumbled forward in the darkness. She wanted to crash in bed. Bed was the goal. Bed was—

Warm hands slid around her stomach and she was pulled back against a rock-hard chest.

"Have I mentioned," Lane's voice rumbled in her ear, "how much I hate it when you're gone?"

Her body melted against his. "Maybe a time or two." She turned in his arms. The lights were still off, and she liked that. In the dark, he wouldn't be able to tell how happy she was to see him.

When did I get so attached? Gwen made it a habit not to get too close to anyone or anything, but Lane had snuck right past her defenses. "Let yourself in again, huh?"

"You have seriously got to change those locks." His lips brushed over her neck. "Anyone could get in here."

Her lips curved. That was Lane. He could always make her smile, even after her last hellish twenty-four hours. Her fingers curled around his shoulders. "Tell me that you made some headway on our case."

"Um, not a damn bit." He kissed her neck. "No one saw anything else at the senator's hotel, and the car from the hit and run turned out to be stolen. It was wiped clean, no prints." His mouth lifted from her skin.

Her breath rushed out. She wanted that mouth back on her.

"But at least I wasn't ten feet away from a car explosion." Now his words roughened. "Do you know how much that shit scared me when I found out what happened?"

"It was a targeted attack." Her fingers tightened on his shoulders. "Just aimed at taking out Ethan Harrison." And the two poor cops who'd been with him.

Lane grunted. "We know how easy it is for innocents to get caught in the crossfire."

Yes, she'd seen that too many times.

"Someone's cleaning house," Lane mused.

She nodded, then realized he couldn't see the move. "Yes."

"You think it's York? Because if it is…it's gonna be real hard pinning anything on him."

Because he was such a power player. But power players didn't intimidate her. Never had. Never would. "If it's him, we'll nail him."

"Damn straight." He lifted her into his arms, surprising her with his strength the way he always did—the way she loved. "But let's leave the killers alone for a while. Right now, I need you."

His mouth pressed to hers.

"*I missed you, Gwen.*"

Her heart ached at his words. She'd seen so many people killed in crimes of passion. Seen others nearly driven to the breaking point of sanity because they'd lost someone close.

But Gwen had never understood those powerful emotions, not until Lane.

Now she knew all too well how emotions could twist a person. They could blind you to a lover's faults. Make you desperate to do anything to protect your lover.

Even make you kill.

Is that what you did, Noah York? Did you kill for a lover?

Lane kissed Gwen again.

And she knew the stark truth...*I'd kill for him.*

***

Noah dreamed of death. Of a field covered in snow, and of the blood that stained that snow.

He dreamed of Claire. Claire with her deep, blue eyes and her blonde hair.

He tried to get to Claire. But she lifted her hands toward him, and blood dripped from her wrists.

"You did this," she whispered as tears slid down her cheeks. "Why?"

Noah shook his head. He wouldn't hurt Claire. Not ever. Things were going to be different with her. So different from the way they'd been before.

"You killed me," she told him as the blood dripped from her wrists. She was standing in the middle of the snow, and her blood dripped down from her wounds, falling slowly.

Then Claire fell, and Noah was too far away to catch her.

***

Noah jerked awake, his heart racing. Claire was by his side. She was breathing softly as she kept sleeping.

He ran a shaking hand over his face. He often dreamed of that damn, snow-covered field. He'd lost a friend on that field. Barely managed to get another away from the carnage.

But Claire...

You killed me.

He turned to look down at her. Her hand was near her face, positioned loosely on her pillow. Her hand rested, palm up, and with the early morning sunlight filtering through the window, he could see the scar on her wrist.

Noah swallowed and tried to shove the images from his mind. He wasn't going to hurt Claire. He wanted to protect her.

Protecting Claire helped him to atone for the sins of his past.

And...

I just want her safe.

He bent his head and pressed a kiss to the scar along her wrist.

I will keep you safe. No matter what.

CHAPTER EIGHT

"We should talk about it," Noah said carefully. He'd been hesitant to broach this subject before, but they were nearly back in the city, and he had to man up and face facts.

I lost control with her.

"It?" Claire echoed. He could feel her stare on him, but Noah kept looking at the road. "What is 'it' exactly?"

His teeth clenched. "No protection," Noah gritted out. "You know I didn't use a condom last night."

"Oh. That."

His gaze snapped to her. The woman sure didn't sound concerned.

"I told you I was safe," Claire told him with a shrug. "There hasn't been anyone for me in years."

And he *never* went without protection. Well, he hadn't. Until her. "I'm talking about the risk of pregnancy, Claire."

"You don't have to worry about that."

"Uh, yeah, I do. I was the guy fucking you last night." He forced his gaze back to the road. "So if you get pregnant, we'll—"

"You don't have to worry," Claire said again, cutting through his words before he'd been able to finish his sentence. And that finish would've included…

We'll get married.

The idea had come to him as he'd stood on the balcony, watching the sun rise. After his nightmare, sleep had been an impossibility. He'd had plenty of time with his thoughts.

His thoughts had focused on her.

"Are you on the pill? Some sort of contraception—"

"I don't need anything." Her voice was totally devoid of emotion. "I can't have kids, okay? So, again, you don't have to worry."

His hands tightened around the wheel as his knuckles whitened. "You can't have kids?"

"No…I…I was pregnant before."

He slammed on the brakes. Car horns behind him blared. *What?* She'd been pregnant with Ethan Harrison's baby? That hadn't been in the reports he'd read.

Claire glanced at him. Her cheeks had paled. "That part didn't make the papers."

Or my reports.

The cars kept honking.

Noah started driving again. "No, it sure as shit didn't make them." His guts were twisted into knots. "What happened?"

"The pregnancy was one of the reasons my parents sent me away to my grandfather's fishing cabin. I'd found out I was pregnant, and I was trying to figure out what to do."

His heartbeat thundered in his ears.

"Then Ethan killed my parents. He nearly killed me, and I-I lost the baby after that. It was…the doctors said it was a tubal pregnancy. The baby died, and they saved me." Her breath rushed out. "And that was when I started to think that I shouldn't have been saved."

Fuck, fuck, *fuck.*

"The doctor said it would be unlikely that I could conceive again. They told me that I'd been lucky to have the first pregnancy…Lucky," she whispered and her voice rasped with pain. "How was I lucky if I'd lost the baby?"

"Claire…"

She cleared her throat. "I left the hospital as soon as I could. Sara knew, she always knew. The doctors had said that there was some surgery that could be done to increase my chances of conceiving again, but we didn't have money for that. We were barely surviving back then."

"I can get you any damn doctor you want." If there was a way for Claire to have a baby, if she—

"I lost one fallopian tube with that pregnancy. They said the other…it wasn't functioning the way it should. That's why my pregnancy chances were unlikely. Surgery might be able to help me, or it might not." Her fingers tapped against the window. "Back then, I figured it didn't matter. I wasn't planning to get close enough to another man to have his child."

You're close to me.

Her voice husky, Claire continued, "They told me the surgery might not work, anyway. That there was only a twenty percent chance of success."

But I can get you any doctor. The best in the world.

"I figured if I ever wanted kids, I could adopt them. There are plenty of kids out there that need homes. I could love a child just the same if he came from my body or if he didn't. Blood doesn't make family."

He'd stopped at a red light. Noah had to look at her again. His mother had told him something similar to that, when he'd first learned that he was adopted.

You're mine, Noah. Blood doesn't make you more or less my son.

"Noah?"

His breath rushed out. "Blood doesn't matter."

She looked relieved that he'd agreed with her.

"Hell, I know that more than anyone else." The light changed. He had to glance toward the road once again.

There was silence in the car. Then Claire asked, "Do you want kids, Noah?"

He'd never thought about them, not until he'd stood on that balcony this morning. Then he'd imagined a little girl. He hadn't seen that little girl clearly in his mind. He'd just had an image of Claire, smiling that full smile of hers—the one that flashed her dimples—as she bent to hug the child. "Maybe I do."

"Then I hope you have them," she told him, and she cleared her throat. When she spoke again, her voice was stronger as she said, "I hope you get everything that you want."

They eased into the valet line in front of his hotel. As the valet rushed toward them, Noah offered Claire a smile. "I fully intend to do just that."

You're what I want.

***

Someone was pounding at his door.

Sloan Hall groaned as he cracked open one eye. He'd been at the hospital last night — *damn broken nose* — then he'd gone out to drink his sorrows away.

Maybe mixing pain pills and booze hadn't been his best idea.

But it had sure felt good at the time.

Sunlight poured through the cheap blinds by his window. The light hurt his eyes and he swore as he headed toward the pounding.

Someone was being a dick.

He yanked open the door. "What the hell do you —" Sloan broke off when he got a look at the person on the other side of the door. "What are you doing here?"

His guest stepped forward.

Sloan hurried back.

And he started wishing that he hadn't had quite so many glasses of whiskey.

His guest shut the door. Then the guy's hand reached under the long, dark coat that he wore.

Fuck me, a gun!

Sloan tensed. His gaze locked on the weapon and the silencer attached to the end of it.

"No, man, no!" Sloan's voice was frantic. His own weapon was shoved under the sagging mattress a few feet away. If he moved fast enough, maybe he'd be able to grab it. "I-I was doing my job!"

"Your services aren't needed any longer."

He's going to kill me.

Sloan spun away, rushing for the bed. He'd go out fighting or he'd—

The bullet tore into the back of his head. It felt like someone had just swung a hammer into his head and then—

Nothing.

Sloan hit the floor.

***

Noah's phone rang just as he entered the elevator. He glanced down, but didn't recognize the number. "York," he said. His gaze was on Claire. They needed to talk more. He hated that he'd brought up the possibility of a pregnancy to her because now Claire looked shaken.

She's lost too much.

He wanted to give her everything.

"I know Claire Kramer's secrets." The voice was low, growling.

Noah frowned. "Who the hell is this?"

"We met last night. I had such a nice view of you and Claire."

Sloan. The guy's voice was so low that Noah had to strain in order to hear him.

The elevator rose.

"Look, dumbass," Noah snarled. "I thought I made myself clear when we—"

"Claire killed the senator, and I have proof. I was watching her. Always watching. Come to meet me, or I'll go to the cops." Laughter. Rough. Taunting. "I'll go to that pretty D.C. cop. She already thinks that Claire is guilty. It'll be so easy, and Claire will finally get just what she deserves."

Claire's eyes had flared with alarm. "Noah? Noah, what's happening?"

Noah shook his head. "Where. When."

"You've just bought a new building here in town, right? The old Claymire Hotel."

The building was completely empty right then. His crews would begin renovation work the next week.

"Meet me there at three, or, by four, I'll be on my way to D.C."

The caller hung up.

The elevator's doors slid open.

Claire touched his arm. "Noah, what's happening?"

He didn't speak, not there. He caught her hand and led her to his suite. When they were alone, when he was sure that no one could overhear, Noah said, "I have to know the truth."

"What truth?" Claire shook her head as confusion flashed across her face. "I've always told you the truth—"

"Did you kill the senator?"

Her eyes widened in surprise.

He didn't have a lot of time. *Protect her.* He pulled her closer. "Did you?"

"No!"

"Then why did that jerk PI just tell me that you did? He says that he has proof, Claire. Proof that can lock you up."

"I-I was at the senator's hotel, but I didn't go in. I didn't see him." Her voice shook. "I told you this already. You believe me, don't you?"

"I have to know the truth." His eyes never left hers. "If I don't know what I'm facing, I can't cover our tracks well enough."

Her breath caught. Understanding filled her eyes. "Oh, my God." She yanked away from him. "All this time…have you actually thought I killed him?"

Noah didn't speak.

"He was *shot* in the head! Just like my parents." She covered her mouth with her hand. Her gaze was stunned as it held his.

"He made your life hell. You wanting some revenge only seems natural."

Her hand fell away from her mouth. "Killing isn't natural for me. My parents were murdered. My sister was murdered. Violence has taken everyone from me." She gave a hard, negative shake of her head. "Trust me. Believe in me. I didn't do this."

Then what the hell kind of game was Sloan trying to play? "I want you to stay here. Don't leave the hotel until I get back." He turned for the door.

But Claire grabbed his arm. "Where are you going?"

"The PI wants to meet me. Says if I don't come, he'll turn over the proof of your guilt to that D.C. cop, Gwen Lazlo."

"There is no proof," she whispered as her fingers tightened around him. "He's lying to you."

"He's about to realize I'm not the kind of man you can jerk around." *Bad mistake, Sloan.* He tried to brush by her.

Claire didn't ease her hold. "If you're going, then so am I."

"No." He was definite. "You're not."

"This is my life we're talking about here! He's saying I'm a killer. *I* get to face the guy!" Her breath heaved out. Red stained her cheeks. "You aren't leaving me behind for this."

That was exactly what he planned to do.

"The last time you saw Sloan, you attacked the guy," Claire reminded him. Not that Noah needed the reminder. "Maybe this is some kind of payback plan he has. Get you alone, and then attack."

Bring it, asshole.

Claire's stubborn chin notched up. "I won't let you be hurt because you're trying to protect me."

Wait—*what?*

"That won't happen." Claire straightened her shoulders. "So either we both go, or you're going to have to tie me to a chair...because I will follow you."

This was the woman Drake had compared to a broken bird? Hell, *no.* There was so much more to Claire than just what met the eye.

"My life," Claire said again. "Don't shut me out. Noah, pl—"

He kissed her. Deep and hard. *I told her not to ever beg me.*

His tongue thrust into her mouth. He tasted her. He took.

Claire's fierce response stunned him. Her tongue met his. Her kiss was as frantic and feverish as his own.

A perfect match.

Noah lifted his head. Their breath panted out.

"Take me with you," Claire whispered.

If I have to hurt the guy, I didn't want you seeing that. I don't want you seeing…me.

But maybe it was time that he stopped hiding the man that he really was from Claire. Maybe it was time for her to see him for what he truly was.

Would she run then?

Or would Claire prove to be stronger than the others?

***

Noah stared up at the old hotel. The building was boarded up, and his crew had put a large, chain-link fence around the property's perimeter.

He didn't see anyone, but that didn't mean Sloan Hall wasn't already inside, waiting for him.

Claire's shoulder brushed against his. "So what's the plan here?"

He'd thought about getting back-up for the trip, but until he found out exactly what Sloan had to say, Noah hadn't wanted to involve anyone else.

Claire didn't kill the senator.

He believed that, but he also knew just how easy it was to frame someone for a crime. He wouldn't let Claire be pulled into a legal nightmare.

"The plan is that I go in—"

"*We,*" Claire corrected crisply.

Right. "We go in," he allowed, "and we find out what game this jerk is playing."

Cautiously, they approached the building. He saw that the wood near the entrance had been pried open. *Are you inside, Sloan?*

He climbed up the steps. Claire hurried with him.

Then his phone rang.

Noah hesitated. *Sloan?*

He yanked out the phone, but this time, he recognized the number of the screen. It was Trace Weston's personal line. "Not a good time," he growled to his friend when he answered the call.

"I'm staring at a dead body," Trace told him. "I just thought you might want to know about that."

"*What?*"

Claire was trying to peer into the darkness of the hotel.

"I made it to New York about three hours ago." Trace's voice held a hard edge. "My agents and I came out to have a little talk with Sloan Hall."

"I'm about to have my own talk with him," Noah snapped. *Dead body?* What the hell?

"That'll be hard," Trace murmured. "Seeing as how the guy is missing half his head."

All of the distant noise seemed to quiet right then. The car horns muted. The rush of traffic eased. Noah focused completely on Trace's voice. "The dead body? It's Sloan?"

"He's in some flea-hole of a hotel. My agents tracked him. Seems the guy had to visit the hospital last night for a broken nose."

"*How long has he been dead?*"

"Judging by the smell, at least a few damn hours."

Noah hadn't heard Sloan's voice clearly on the phone. The guy had been whispering. Trying to disguise his identity?

Claire was about to slip inside the small opening near the old door. "No!" He grabbed for her arm.

"Uh, what?" Trace asked. "What are you yelling about?"

Noah didn't answer him. Every instinct he had was screaming at him.

This meeting wasn't about blackmail. It wasn't about Claire's innocence or guilt.

It was about them being lured to this hotel. To this empty, abandoned spot.

"Claire, come on!" But he didn't wait for her to come. Noah wrapped his arm around her stomach, and he lifted her up against him. He ran, nearly falling down those stairs.

Get away. Get away. Get —

The explosion sent chunks of the old building spiraling into the air. The boards covering the windows shot out. Shards of glass rained down on Noah, and he tried to hunch his body over Claire's. But the blast had him flying through the air, too, and all he could do was hold her, as tightly as he could.

They hit the ground. Hard enough to rattle his bones. He felt blood sliding down his right arm, and a board slammed into his back.

Claire was beneath him. The flames from the explosion scorched his skin as he tried to keep covering her.

One explosion so far, but there could be more.

I have to get her out of here.

"Come on, Claire," Noah whispered. "We have to make a run for it."

Claire didn't respond. When he lifted her up, her head sagged back weakly. "Claire?"

Her eyes were closed. Blood trickled down the side of her head.

No!

He lifted her up and ran then, as fast as he could toward the fence that circled the property. Another explosion had the ground trembling beneath his feet, but Noah didn't stop. He kept going. Kept holding her as tightly as he could.

Then he was free as he slid through the opening in the chain-link fence. He rushed across the street. Traffic had stopped. People were screaming, running, but he barely saw any of them. They were just smoke covered blurs to him.

He put Claire down on the sidewalk. "Baby?"

Her eyes were still closed. He brushed back her hair. Blood was on his fingers, and it smeared across her cheek. But when he moved her hair, Noah saw the gash on her head. About an inch long, and already, the skin around that wound was turning a dark, bruised purple.

Sirens screamed in the distance. Help, coming in fast.

"Claire." He put his hand to her throat. Her pulse was steady. He checked for other injuries but only saw the gash on her head.

Be okay, baby. Be okay.

***

They hadn't gone in the building.

They'd been so close, but Noah had stopped just steps away from the entrance. He'd gotten that phone call, and the guy had started to pull Claire back.

He'd had to detonate then. There had been no choice.

A few steps. Noah had been so close to death.

But not as close as Claire.

As he watched, she was loaded into the back of an ambulance. Noah was with her. Standing so close. Jumping into the back of that emergency vehicle when she was pushed inside.

He'd wondered just how close Claire and Noah truly were. Now he realized…

Claire has got to Noah, too.

She had a real talent for drawing in her lovers. Winding men around her finger. Batting those blue eyes and getting them to do anything for her.

Lie.

Steal.

Kill.

But Claire wasn't going to twist him. Her days of playing games — those days were long over.

He'd missed her and Noah this time.

Next time, they wouldn't escape. He'd make sure of it.

***

Claire felt like she'd been hit by a truck. She opened her eyes slowly and winced at the pain. Her head throbbed and nausea rolled in her belly as the room before her came into focus—

And then that nausea just got a whole lot worse.

"A hospital," Claire whispered, surprised by the slightly hoarse sound of her own voice. "No, not—"

"It's okay." She turned her head at that deep voice. Noah was beside her bed. His fingers had curled around her wrist. "You're not alone."

He'd ditched his coat. He wore a white shirt, one that had flecks of blood over the sleeves. Actually, one sleeve was cut nearly to the shoulder, and she could see the outline of a white bandage on his arm.

The shirt was also stained gray—with soot? Ash?

"The hotel," Claire said as the memories pushed through her mind. "It caught on fire."

His lips tightened. "Two bombs were planted there."

Her heartbeat kicked up, and the machines near her bed began to beat even faster. "The PI tried to kill us?"

Noah shook his head. His face looked harder, the faint lines near his eyes deeper than before. "Sloan wasn't the one who set up that meeting."

The throbbing in her head got even worse. "But you said—"

"I thought I was talking to Sloan, but it turns out that guy was already dead when I got that phone call to set up our meeting."

She jerked beneath his hold.

"Easy," Noah murmured as his fingers kept stroking her. "You've got a concussion. You have to be careful."

The concussion would explain the jackhammer in her head. "How did he die?" Her voice was stronger. "What happened to him?"

Noah glanced away from her.

No, no, no—

"He was shot in the head."

Oh, God. "I have to get out of here." She tried to climb from the bed.

Noah pushed her back. "No, stop it!" He held her easily in the bed. "I can't let you hurt yourself."

"What is happening?" The machines were still beeping too loudly and fear had her whole body tensing. "The shot to the head...just like the senator, just like—"

"Your parents," he finished grimly. His hands were around her shoulders now. He eased her back into the hospital bed. "And the bomb...well, we both know a bomb just took out Ethan Harrison."

"Someone wanted us to go out that way, too." Bombs didn't just kill. They obliterated. "Why? Why is someone after me?" But then horror filled her. *"You."*

Noah frowned down at her.

"I-I wasn't the one called to that hotel. You were. You were the one who was—" Claire broke off, unable to say more.

You were the one who was going to die.

She tried to get out of the bed again.

He pushed her back against the pillow. "Claire, stop it!"

She couldn't stop. "I need to get away." She twisted beneath his hands. "No, you have to get away from me. It's happening again." But he wasn't letting her go. *"Leave, Noah, just leave!"*

Instead of leaving, he sat on the edge of the bed and pulled her into his arms. "You're okay."

This time, she was. He was. What about next time? "It's because of me," Claire managed to say.

Noah eased back just enough to peer down at her.

"You almost died...because of me." Because he'd gotten involved with her. He'd helped her.

I won't let him suffer because of me.

"It's not because of you." Intensity hardened each word. "Some bastard out there is playing some sort of sick game." He shook his head. "And he's playing with the wrong man."

This wasn't a game. "You need to stay away from me." He had to see that.

Everyone close to me dies.

"That's not happening," he said.

Then I have to stay away from you.

The door opened behind Noah then, swinging in with a soft swoosh of sound. Noah glanced toward the door, but he didn't release Claire. Claire followed his gaze.

She instantly recognized the man who stood in the doorway. Tall, with broad shoulders, the guy had a handsome, but hard face and glittering blue eyes.

*Trace Weston.*He'd been her sister's boss, and Sara had looked up to him so much.

Sara had also feared him.

"Claire?" The soft, feminine voice came from the woman beside Trace—his new wife, Skye. Skye hurried toward the bed. Her dark hair fell over her shoulders, and her pretty face reflected her concern. "Are you all right?"

No, Claire was pretty sure she might shatter into a million pieces at any moment. "Someone tried to kill us."

Noah slid from the bed.

Skye came closer. She started to touch Claire, then hesitated.

She knows I don't like to be touched. Skye understood Claire far better than any other woman had. Maybe it was because Skye had been through her own nightmare. Stalked, kidnapped, starved…Skye had managed to survive, but the horrific nightmare had marked her.

We're both marked. On the skin, and deep within.

Skye's hand hesitantly curved over Claire's shoulder. "You're safe now. Trace has two men guarding your hospital room door, and he's going to keep a guard on you until we can figure out what's happening."

Claire glanced toward the doorway. Noah was leading Trace back out of the room. "Noah?" Claire called.

He glanced back at her. "Don't worry, I'll be right outside."

There was something…different…in his eyes. A wildness. A fury.

It scared her.

The door shut softly behind him.

***

"She nearly died," Noah snarled as soon as he was out of that hospital room.

The two guards near her door glanced at him with wide eyes.

He glared at them.

Trace caught his shoulder and steered him toward the corner. "She didn't die. You got her out of there."

Noah yanked a hand through his hair. He couldn't cool the rage that burned him from the inside out. "Only because you called. If that phone had rung two minutes later, hell, even *one* minute later, we'd both be dead."

Trace crossed his arms over his chest. "Then I guess it's a good thing you answered your old friend's call."

Noah surged toward him. "I *won't* lose her."

Trace's eyebrows flew up. "Shit, who are you?"

"What?" Noah's hands fisted. He wasn't in the mood for any bull. Not even from Trace. "Man, don't push me, I don't—"

"You're losing your control right in front of me. This doesn't happen to the Noah York I know."

"Oh, yeah? Well, it's happening. Claire was in my arms, and she wasn't moving." He swung away from the guy. He wanted to drive his fist into the nearest wall. He did. When a nurse shrieked, he snarled, "I'll buy a new wing!"

Because he might be destroying this one.

Trace's hand settled on his shoulder once more. "Talk to me."

Noah whirled back toward him. "When that bastard had Skye, when you thought you'd lose her...*how did you stay sane?*"

Trace exhaled on a rough sigh. "Is it that bad?"

It was worse. Noah felt like he was ripping apart. "She was bleeding. I couldn't get her to open her eyes." That image would never get out of his head. "Fire was lighting the sky, glass was raining down, and Claire was too still."

Trace took a step back.

"I *won't* let her go," Noah said. He couldn't. "No one is going to hurt her again. I'll make sure of it. I'll find the SOB. I'll—"

"Watch what you say," Trace interjected, voice flat. A wave of his hand indicated the folks lurking close by.

Hell, half of the hospital seemed to be staring at them.

"And you aren't doing anything alone." Trace gave a grim nod. "Because you know I've got your back."

***

"I haven't seen you since the funeral," Skye said carefully. She gave Claire a faint smile. "And I was sure hoping when we met again, it would be under better circumstances."

Claire realized this hardly counted as "better" than anything. "I'm scared," she admitted. Confessing that truth to Skye wasn't hard. She'd only met Skye a few times, but Claire had never felt as if Skye judged her.

She knows what it's like to be helpless.

"What can I do?" Skye asked her.

"Help me to get away."

Skye's eyes flared. "You don't mean—"

"Noah could've died because of me. They're *all* dying because of me. The senator, Ethan, Sloan Hall—they were all tied to me." The senator who harassed her, the lover who nearly killed her, and the PI who stalked her. Their one common denominator—*it's me.* "Noah was the one who was supposed to go into that old hotel. He was the one being set up to die."

"And how will you leaving help him?" Skye shook her head. "It won't. It will just drive the guy crazy!"

"Or maybe it will take a target off his back."

Skye's breath caught. "And do what? Put that target straight on you?"

Maybe. Claire was sitting up on the bed now. She really wanted to make a run for it. "If I leave, if I change cities, then, yes, perhaps this guy will come after me and leave Noah alone."

A furrow appeared between Skye's brows. "Just how hard did you hit your head, Claire? Because I've got to say, that sounds like a real piss-poor idea to me."

Claire blinked at her in surprise.

"Noah isn't just going to let you walk away. I saw the way he looked at you."

"It's sex." The words sounded hollow. "Noah trades up his lovers all the time."

"Really? And how long have you been his lover?"

Just a few short days. Not long enough for him to really care, and certainly not long enough for him to put his life on the line for her.

"Claire, I can't help you run. That would just be putting you in danger."

Then she'd have to do it on her own. "You felt this way, didn't you?" Claire asked her.

Skye stared at her with a troubled gaze.

"You knew someone was out there, and you just wanted to get away."

Skye's mouth tightened. "Trace has the best security firm in the U.S. He's got agents working on this case now. He's going to find the person doing this. I know he will."

But how long would it take? And would the man hunting out there, *killing out there,* have a chance to strike again?

I lose everyone…I can't lose Noah, too.

CHAPTER NINE

"You're not supposed to sleep," Noah told Claire as he leveled a firm stare her way. "Not for a few more hours."

So the doctors had said. They'd agreed to release her, as long as Noah made sure that Claire wasn't alone.

He didn't plan to leave her side any time soon.

They were back in his suite. Claire was wearing a pair of yoga pants and a loose top. There was a small bandage on the side of her head. The doctors had stitched her up, but the wound was right on her hair-line, so no one would even be able to see it once she was healed.

Heal fast, baby.

"Since I don't feel sleepy, that shouldn't really be a problem," Claire murmured. She was gazing toward the large windows that looked out over the skyline.

Claire hadn't looked Noah in the eye, not since he'd left her hospital room in order to talk with Trace.

When he'd gone back, Claire had been too quiet. Withdrawn.

Afraid?

"You're safe," he said, and his fingers trailed over her arm.

Claire flinched. "It's not me that I'm worried about." Then her head turned and she finally stared into his eyes. "It's you."

He had to laugh. "I'm not afraid of this guy." If Claire only knew how many hell-holes he'd fought in during his military days...

But I don't want her knowing.

The laughter stilled as she gazed at him.

"Maybe you should be afraid." Claire's body shifted slightly against the couch. "If you nearly die, it's okay to fear some."

He hadn't been afraid, not since his parents had died. Even when he'd been battling the enemy — in ice, in sand, in the dankest forest he'd ever imagined — Noah hadn't been afraid.

But I was scared when she was so still on that sidewalk. Fear had come back then, and he wouldn't forget the feel of its icy claws raking into him.

"I don't want you to die for me," Claire said.

He leaned toward her. His finger slid down her arm. She didn't flinch at his touch that time. *So much better.* "I have no intention of dying for you."

He thought some of the tension left her shoulders. "Good."

But I would kill for you. I think that would be far more effective.

"The police are working," he murmured, "bringing in their bomb experts. I'm sure they'll compare this blast with the one that took out Ethan. Bombers often have a signature. It'll take some time, but the authorities will be able to determine if the attacker was the same."

"What if we don't have time?"

His fingers lightly caressed her. "We have all the time we need."

"Not if he's hunting."

He hated the fear in her eyes. "I'm good at hunting, too."

Her teeth pressed into her lower lip. "Your time…in the military."

"And after." He had his own demolitions expert coming in. Drake had stayed down in Alabama to learn more about the blast that killed Ethan, but he was already on his way up to New York.

"You killed, didn't you?"

He glanced away from her. "Men die in battle all the time."

"That's not what I asked."

"And you shouldn't ask questions that you don't truly want answered." He looked back at her. "You don't want to know, not really, do you?"

Her fingers curled around the pillow on the couch. "Why would you say that?"

"Because it's true. People like to see the surface, not the darkness underneath." Life was easier that way.

Claire shook her head. "I've seen your darkness all along."

Her words caught him by surprise.

"But you have to tell me your secrets," Claire said as her eyes gleamed. "You know every one of mine. No matter how painful, you know. Don't you think I deserve to hear yours, too?"

He rose from the couch. Paced away from her. "What if you don't like what you hear?"

I don't want to lose her.

He hadn't actually had anyone to lose, not since his parents. But Claire — she mattered to him.

"Have you liked what you've heard about me?" He heard the rustle of the couch cushions as Claire rose. "A woman who tried to kill herself when she was sixteen. I mean, hey, she's got to be some prize—"

"*Stop.*" He whirled back toward her. "You're a survivor. Everything I've learned about you has just strengthened that belief."

Her gaze searched his. "Most people pity me…or else they think I'm…pretending. That I'm a manipulator."

"I see you for what you are."

"Let me see you that way, too." She stepped toward him. Kept coming until her fingers lifted and pressed against his chest, right over his heart. "I'm going to ask you some questions now, and I want you to know that your answers won't ever leave this room."

Her touch singed him.

"Have you killed?"

"Yes."

"In battle?"

"During my tours, and then...after. Trace, Drake, and I set up a security team of our own."

She waited, watching him with a gaze that seemed to see straight into his soul. The way her gaze always did.

And he found himself saying more. "We focused on retrieving very high-end assets. Businessmen, dignitaries who'd been in the wrong place and been taken. Some of those guys were held for money, some held in hopes of a power swap."

Her head tilted as she studied him. "And your job was to get those people out?"

"Normal channels wouldn't work. Uncle Sam didn't want the wreckage coming back to his door...so our team worked those cases." His lips twisted. "That's how I got my start in the hotel business." Talk about a career change. "One of those guys thanked me with a hotel."

"Um, that's quite a thank you."

He inclined his head. It sure had been, but seeing as how he'd taken two bullets for the guy on that mission, Noah thought they'd come out of the deal square. "I had my own money, too, money left from my parents. I saved every dime while I was working with Trace and Drake, and then one day, I decided that I was done with that world."

The world of killing and death and blood.

"I got out. I started fresh." He looked down at her hand. It looked so delicate against him.

"You don't seem so bad to me," Claire told him.

Tell her. "I've killed with guns. With knives. I've attacked with my hands when they were the only weapons left to me. Killing is a talent I have, one that the government just honed even more for me."

"But that's not who you are now."

"That's who I will always be. When I see a threat, I want to eliminate it." He couldn't get more blunt than that. "And that's what I do."

Her lashes lowered. "Why don't women last more than a night with you?"

"What?"

"Drake said—"

Drake talked too much.

"He said that your lovers come and go. One time is it for you."

"I like sex." She'd asked for his secrets. He'd give her what he could. "I satisfy the need, then I move on."

"One time, then done?"

"I know that makes me sound like a bastard, but ties just screw with your head." He'd seen it happen. First with Drake—and the man had been to hell and back because of that painful mistake. Then the same weakness had twisted Trace.

Claire's hand pulled away from Noah, but she still stood close to him. "Why am I still here?"

Because I need you to be.

"Haven't you satisfied the-the 'need' yet?"

"No," he said, voice roughening, "I haven't. That's the problem with you and me."

Her tongue swiped over her lower lip.

Yeah, that's the problem.

"The need doesn't stop with you. The more I have you, the more it grows. The more I want." Until he felt like the need was consuming him. "And I don't want gentle and easy. I don't want rose petals sprinkled on the ground. I want you naked and moaning. I want you screaming and clawing my back. I want everything that I can get from you."

I want to own you.

And he was starting to think…

The way you already own me.

Claire stared up at him.

"Scared yet?" Noah had to push her.

Claire shook her head.

You should be, Claire. With every moment that passes, I get hooked on you even more. He'd seen Drake spiral, he'd seen Trace sink into near madness.

And now I'm on the brink.

The suite's phone rang. Its pealing cry seemed to echo around them. Noah didn't move.

She still doesn't know all that I've done. When she did, what would happen?

The phone rang again. Swearing, Noah headed toward it. "*What?*" Noah snapped.

"Sir, it's Janelle at the concierge desk." Her voice was soft as she said, "I know that you said no visitors were allowed up to your floor, but there's a very insistent gentleman here right now."

Noah glanced over his shoulder at Claire. "What's his name?"

"Austin Harrison."

Harrison? His hold tightened on the phone. He'd done his research. He knew Austin was the senator's other son. Three years older than Ethan, Austin had seemed to make keeping a low profile his priority. "You're shitting me."

"No, no, I'm not."

"Keep him right there. I'm on my way." He slammed down the phone and marched for the door.

Claire beat him to that door. She blocked his path with her body. "Who's here?"

"I'm heading downstairs for just a moment. I'll be right back and—"

"No. No way. The last time you tried to go off on your own, a building exploded." She crossed her arms over her chest and glared at him. "Who's here?"

"Austin Harrison."

Shock had her mouth dropping.

"And I'm going downstairs to talk with him while you, baby, are staying right up here."

"I'm coming—"

"Concussion, Claire." Gently, but firmly, he picked her up and carried her back to the couch. He put her down on the cushions. Pulled a blanket over her. Kissed her. "You stay here, and I'll go deal with the bastard at the door."

Her lips pressed into a determined line.

He wasn't going to argue with Claire. The last thing she needed right then was a confrontation. He headed for the door. Opened it —

Talk about a bastard at the door.

Drake had his hand raised to knock.

"No one is supposed to get up to this floor." Noah glared at the two guards near the elevator. Guards who'd been sent over from Weston Securities. Guards who were apparently damn inadequate.

"Trace told them I was clear." Drake smiled. "Come on, you know that you can trust me."

Yeah, he did. And that was why he yanked the guy in the suite. "Keep Claire company until I get back."

"Uh, wait, where are you —"

Noah shut the door behind him and stalked to the elevator.

Austin Harrison.

Well, he'd met the other two members of the family. Time to see if Austin was as much of a dick as they were.

***

The guy had just twisted her into knots and walked away. Claire shoved off her blanket and jumped to her feet. She was going after him and —

"I think the idea was for us both to stay put." Drake flashed her a broad smile. "So don't think you can just bat those big baby blues at me, and get out of here."

She glared at him.

His smile slowly faded. "You look like shit."

He was always such a charmer.

Drake's hand lifted toward her face.

Instantly, Claire stepped back.

"Easy," he murmured as he advanced. "I just want to see the damage."

She forced herself to stay still. "It's just a scratch."

"A scratch that's got you purple and black on your temple." His head cocked and his fingers feathered over her cheek. "And I'm guessing the bandage is covering some stitches?"

"A few."

He whistled. "Bet that made Noah go insane."

She pushed his hand away. "Nearly getting blown up made us both react that way."

His hand caught hers. "Explain it to me."

"What?"

"I've seen Noah touch you, and you act like a cat getting stroked."

She did *not*.

"But I come close, and you tense up like you're afraid I'll hit you." His voice and eyes had gone flat. "I don't know what Noah told you about my past, but I only did what I *had* to do. Killing my lover—hell, no, that wasn't my plan. She went rogue. Turned on us all—"

Wow. "He didn't tell me anything."

She knew Drake had killed in Chicago, but that had been a fight-or-die situation. As for his past... "Like you told me before, your past is your own."

"So you don't back away from me because you think I'm a monster beneath the skin?"

His words made her pause. Made her realize... "I back away because I think everyone has a monster inside."

Wasn't that what she'd learned from Ethan?

From herself?

***

Austin Harrison stood near the concierge desk in the lobby. Noah marched toward the guy, letting his gaze sweep over the last remaining Harrison.

The guy was tall, broad-shouldered. Dressed in a suit. Austin appeared tense, wary—good, because he should be.

His hair was a dark blond, and it currently looked as if the guy had spent hours shoving his hands through it.

"This way," Noah said, turning sharply to the right. He wasn't about to have a public fight with Harrison. No, it was far better to do that in private.

Where no one can see what I'll do.

Noah took the guy back to the hotel manager's office. The manager, Louis, had conveniently cleared out, per Noah's orders during a quick phone call mid-elevator ride.

Austin didn't speak until they were secured inside. As soon as the door shut, though, the guy said, "I'm not a threat to you. Or to Claire Kramer."

"I'm not so sure of that."

Austin swallowed. His Adam's apple bobbed. "Whatever you're doing...just...stop, okay? I'm not going to hurt her."

"What I'm doing?"

Austin's gaze jerked around the office. "My father. Ethan."

He thinks I killed them?

"I don't want to be next on Claire's revenge list."

"You think Claire has a list?" Had the guy not heard about the bombing? It had been all over the news. *How the hell would he have missed that?*

"If I were her, I would," Austin muttered as he yanked a hand through his hair. "I'd want revenge. Payback."

"You aren't Claire." *She doesn't think like that.*

Austin's hand fell to his side. His eyes met Noah's. "I know you're fucking her."

"Yes, I am." He wasn't about to deny something that gave him such satisfaction.

Austin exhaled on a rough sigh. "Are you killing for her, too?"

Everyone sure seemed to think so. "You should turn on the news. The radio. Read a paper."

Austin's eyebrows scrunched. "Wh-what?"

"But maybe you were flying up here, maybe you missed that huge story, so I'll just brief you." He rolled back his shoulders. "Someone tried to kill me *and* Claire with a bomb last night."

Austin backed up a step. He banged into the desk.

"Claire isn't the one who went after your bastard of a father or your sick freak of a brother. Someone else out there did that. Probably the same someone who tried to kill us."

"*Why?*"

"I think we have to ask the bastard killing that particular question." He studied the man before him. "You don't reek of booze like your father."

Austin flinched.

"Are you as insane as your brother?"

"I'm *nothing* like Ethan."

The two looked alike. The similarity was clear as day. "You're the older brother. So when you were growing up, did you know what Ethan was? Did you see it?"

Austin walked toward the window on the right. "I saw it. Ethan was always hurting those weaker than he was. I told my father that he needed help, but that wasn't the way my old man worked. Harrisons don't need help. We don't need anything." He looked back at Noah. "I came here because I don't want to die."

Noah crossed his arms over his chest. "And you thought you were next on Claire's list?"

"It's…because I didn't do anything. I didn't help her. I didn't stop him. Ethan talked about her. So much. About how he couldn't live without her. How he *wouldn't* live without her. How he'd do anything to prove his love to her."

Noah held his body perfectly still. "Did you know he was planning to kill her parents?"

Austin stared down at the floor. "No. Dear God…*no*. He was bad before Claire, he hurt some other girls, seemed to get off on the power rush, but with her, something broke in him." Then Austin squared his shoulders. His head lifted. His eyes met Noah's. "She's here, isn't she?"

Noah glanced around the room. "I just see you and me."

"In the hotel," Austin snapped. "If you're here, then she has to be close. Look, the PI called me and said —"

Noah jumped on that. "You mean Sloan Hall?"

"Yes, Hall. He said you and Claire were together. I'm not paying the guy anymore. That was my father's madness. Let Claire know that she's free, okay?"

"Sloan Hall is dead."

Austin's eyes widened.

"He was shot in the head."

A shudder slid over Austin's body.

"So I don't think you have to worry about paying him," Noah murmured. "I do think you may have to worry about watching your ass."

***

"Claire, I need a list of your enemies."

She'd put a bit more distance between herself and Drake.

"You moved around jobs quite a bit," Drake continued as he rubbed his chin. "So maybe you—"

"I didn't exactly have an option on the job front. Senator Harrison made sure my past had a way of being brought to the attention of my bosses. If they didn't fire me immediately, he just exerted a little more…pressure on them."

He seemed to absorb that. "Senator Harrison was your enemy."

Uh, yes. "Obviously."

"Who else?"

"Ethan was locked away." She shook her head. "As far as I know, there isn't anyone else." No one who hated her enough to kill.

He started to pace. He headed toward the door that led out onto the balcony. For a moment, he gazed at the city, then he tossed a hard glance back at her. "Come on, tell me the truth. You've got lovers that were burned. Maybe one of them is—"

"Noah."

He frowned at her.

"Noah is my lover. There hasn't been anyone else. Just Noah…and Ethan."

"I'm supposed to believe that? Come on, try again."

Claire heaved out a sigh. "It's the truth. Why would I take a lover when—"

"When you can't even usually stand to be touched." He leaned back against the balcony door. "So why does Noah get the free pass?"

"Excuse me?"

"What's so different about him? Because, sweetheart—"

She tensed at that endearment. Ethan had always called her that. She hated the word *sweetheart*.

"—if you want to talk about a man having a monster inside, Noah is your guy."

Now he was trying to scare her away from Noah? "I'm not afraid of him."

Silence. Good. Maybe it would last until Noah came—

"I am," Drake said.

Her gaze flew to his face. He looked completely serious.

"I know what it's like when a man gets too lost in a woman. When he loses his control."

Drake was confused. "Noah isn't…lost in me."

"Noah clings so tightly to his control for a reason. If he breaks, I don't want to see what happens."

***

"I'd like to apologize to Claire."

Noah didn't plan to let this guy anywhere near Claire. "I'll be sure and pass that along to her."

Austin's jaw hardened. "I'm not like them. I want to make this right."

"Then walk away from her and never look back."

Austin blew out a hard breath. Then he turned and stormed for the door. His hand curled around the knob. His shoulders stiffened. "I think it's my fault."

Noah slowly uncrossed his arms. "What's your fault?"

Austin spun back toward him. "Before he died, Ethan said…he told me that I was the one who saw her first. I'd forgotten about that. It was so long ago. Another life."

Noah advanced on him.

"I must've made some comment. Said I was going to ask her out. Ethan was always so competitive with me. I said I liked her, so *he* had to cut me out. *He went after her first.*" He gave a miserable shake of his head. "I brought Claire to his attention. He wanted to one up me, and he did it—"

"By taking the girl you wanted."

"Ethan hated me." His hands were shaking. "I realized just how much…at the end."

"The dead can't hate anymore. They can't do anything."

Austin nodded but his shoulders slumped. "I want to tell her myself. Just say how sorry I am."

"No."

"Look, I—"

"No one in the Harrison family ever needs to see Claire Kramer again. You say you're sorry? Then prove it. Stay the hell out of her life. Claire doesn't need you and she doesn't need your apologies."

Austin's lips pressed into a thin line.

Noah stood toe-to-toe with the man. "Claire isn't your concern anymore."

"How do you fit into this?" Austin's shoulders straightened. "You and Claire are lovers, okay, fine but—"

"Claire is mine." That was all that needed to be said. "Now, Harrison, seeing as how your business *isn't* in New York, I'd advise you to get out of my town."

Austin held his gaze.

Noah waited. This guy would be leaving town, one way of another.

Then Austin sighed. "Right. No business in New York, and no one left in Alabama. Maybe it's time for me to try something new."

"Maybe." Noah yanked open the door. "But stay away from Claire."

Austin stepped into the hallway. But he lingered. *Lingered.* "I guess I had this wrong."

He sure as fuck had.

"If…if someone is after you and Claire — you protect her, got it?"

A warning, from that jerk?

"I figure she's been through enough," Austin whispered, and then he finally walked away.

Noah stared after the guy. *Yes, she has.* It was time for Claire to know more than just blood and death.

***

Noah York would be a problem.

The man's guard was up. It wouldn't be so easy to lure him into another attack.

And Noah would have men watching Claire. Making sure she didn't slip away.

He thinks Claire is his.

Noah was dead wrong.

An attack would come again. He just had to be careful. Had to wait and plan. Had to draw out his enemy.

And I know just how to do it.

Noah had left loose ends in D.C. Those ends would come back…and bite the guy in the ass.

CHAPTER TEN

"We're going out tonight," Noah said as he strode into Claire's office.

Claire smoothed her hand over the faint ridge near her hair-line. The stitches had come out yesterday. The doctors had given her the all-clear.

It had been eight days since the bombing.

Eight days during which Noah had treated her as if she were going to shatter if he touched her too hard.

He made love to her each night. Slow, tender sex. His control was always in place. He made sure she came, and then, he found his pleasure.

He held her during the night.

And he had a giant wall between them during the day.

Something had changed. Something was *off* between them. His stare was too guarded when he looked at her. His voice was too careful.

His touch was too careful.

Is he already finished with me? And he just doesn't know how to tell me? Maybe her time with him was up.

"There's a big party tonight in the hotel's main ballroom—"

"I know," Claire told him, slightly annoyed. "I've been working on details for it most of the week." Only he hadn't exactly been around to see that. The guys from Weston Securities weren't camped out by Noah's suite any longer, but Claire still had a guard. Drake was the one who tailed her like a shadow during the day. While Noah—she wasn't sure where he went.

Or what he had been doing.

The party that night was to celebrate the one year anniversary of the opening of the New York branch of York Towers. It was supposed to be an epic event, with all the local power brokers in attendance. Claire had figured she'd be working behind the scenes, and she already had a to-do list that stretched a mile long for—

"You'll be my date," Noah said.

Her brows climbed. "Thanks for the invitation." Yes, her voice had bite. *Something is so wrong.* He was barely looking at her.

But at her snapped words, his gaze *did* shoot to her. "I'll have a dress sent up for you."

"You already did that, remember?" Claire pushed to her feet. "The first day. You bought me a whole wardrobe. I don't need anything else."

"You'll need this." He turned away. "Head upstairs. It will be there within the hour."

What? "Noah, stop."

Surprisingly, he did. Noah glanced back at her, and, of course, his gaze was guarded. No expression was on his face. She felt like screaming. Instead, Claire managed to semi-calmly ask, "What's happening?"

"We're getting ready for a party."

Her teeth snapped together. "You know what I mean. Things are different between us." Was it because she'd pushed him to reveal more of his past? Was he trying to shut her out now?

"Nothing has changed." He turned back for the door.

Liar, liar.

"Are we finished?" The question slipped from her. She'd more than passed his one night limit, so maybe it was time for her to go and he just didn't know how to tell her because of the train wreck that was her life. But there'd been no more attacks. No more—

"No, Claire," the words were growled and Noah didn't look back at her, "we're far from finished."

***

When Noah entered his suite, he found Drake lounging on the couch. Drake glanced over at him, brows raised. "Don't you look fancy?"

"Fuck off, Drake." He was already wearing his tux. He'd changed earlier, before Claire had made it up to the suite. He'd slipped in long enough to see the dress that he'd ordered for her. Then he'd headed back downstairs to make sure the staff was set on security guidelines for the night. When he'd left the suite, Drake hadn't been there.

"In the last thirty minutes, you're the second person to tell me that I should fuck off." Drake gestured toward the closed bedroom door. "Claire told me the same thing when I asked why she had tears in her eyes."

Noah's fingers tightened around the small, discrete box in his hands. "Claire was crying?"

"No." Drake rose, slowly unfurling from the couch. "Claire doesn't cry. She had tears in her eyes, but they never fell." He approached Noah and the guy's face held a hard flash of...anger? "But I think you probably know why they were there."

Are we finished? He'd hated that question. "Thanks for watching her this week. Trace went to D.C. to chase down some leads, and—"

"Why were you trying so hard to stay away from her?" Drake asked him.

He looked down at the box. "She was hurt."

"And you were busy hunting."

Noah's gaze rose once more.

Drake laughed softly. "That's it, right? When you ran off each day, you were looking for the jerk-off who set that bomb. And you wanted me here because you knew I'd take a bullet for your lady."

"I haven't found him." He was turning up jackshit everywhere he turned. "Sloan Hall's crime scene was swept clean. There wasn't anything there. And at the Claymire Hotel bomb scene —"

"Nothing was left but rubble," Drake finished.

Unfortunately. "This guy isn't just going to vanish. Another attack is coming, and I have to be ready."

The bedroom door opened.

"Are you ready for her?" Drake whispered as he backed away.

Noah's gaze locked on Claire. *So beautiful.*

Her dress was the same blue shade as her eyes. It hugged her breasts, revealing the sexy curves of her body so perfectly. There was a long slit in the dress, one that flashed her gorgeous legs as she walked.

She looked sophisticated. Sexy.

Mine.

She'd tied ribbon around her wrists again, and, as he stared at her, Claire tucked her hands behind her back. "The dress wasn't necessary," she said quietly. "I had plenty of things to wear —"

"It was necessary for me." Because tonight, he had plans. Big plans.

I'm not going to wait for an attack. I want the asshole to bring it on. Noah had never been the type to hide from a fight.

"I figure you got things now," Drake murmured as he gave Noah a little salute. "See you at the party." He made his way to the door.

When Drake was gone, Claire's gaze dropped to Noah's hands. "What's that?"

"A present." He had to clear his throat because the words came out too rough and hard. "For you."

Her lips quirked a little at that. "Well, I was hoping you hadn't bought jewelry for yourself." She walked toward him. The slit in her dress parted, his cock jerked, and he had to remember —

Control.

"Stop that." Claire's voice held a surge of heat that surprised him.

"Stop what?" Now he was confused. "Getting you presents? Most women don't usually complain about gifts."

Claire gave a hard, negative shake of her head. "Stop shutting yourself off from me. I could actually see you doing it just then." She didn't reach for the jewelry box. "And I'm not most woman."

He knew that fact too well.

He opened the jewelry box. Offered the diamond bracelets to her.

Claire's breath caught. "Those are beautiful."

The diamonds caught the light, shining even more. Very rare, the natural blue diamonds had cost him a fortune—and they were worth every penny that he'd spent.

They were the same shade of blue as her dress.

The same shade to match her eyes.

"I had the bracelets specially made for you. I'd hoped they would be here sooner." He put the jewelry box down on the table. Reached for her right hand. His fingers slid over her wrist as he pulled the ribbon away. "You won't need this anymore." He took out one of the bracelets. The diamonds were surrounded by gold, a tight band that would slide over her wrist and hold easily in place.

He slid the first bracelet around her wrist. It fit her perfectly.

Then he removed the second ribbon from her skin. He eased the other bracelet into position around her wrist.

The bracelets were savage in their beauty. The blue diamonds gleamed, and the gold cuff design of the bracelets gave the jewelry a harder, sensual edge.

"Noah…"

His head lifted. He stared into Claire's eyes. "I don't want you to ever feel self-conscious again. Those scars don't define you." *They just prove you're stronger than death.* He stepped back. "We need to hurry downstairs. I should—"

"Thank you."

I don't want your thanks. I just want you. He straightened his tux. "There will be a large number of photographers and reporters in the hotel tonight, so you need to prepare for their questions."

Her fingers slid over the bracelet on her left wrist. "Am I supposed to be your assistant tonight? Or your lover?"

The question caught him off-guard. "You're both. I thought I made that clear."

Her fingers kept stroking the bracelet.

I want to see her in those bracelets and nothing else.

By the end of the night, he would.

"You don't fuck your employees, remember?"

"You're more than an employee." Soon, everyone would know that.

He offered her his arm. "Time to go." There would be no going back after this.

She touched him lightly. Her body pressed against his. The woman smelled delicious.

Her fingers curled around his arm. "I don't know what you're planning, but I'm worried."

"You shouldn't be." He caught her hand. Lifted it to his lips. Pressed a kiss to her knuckles. "I want you to trust me."

"I do."

The instant words seemed to slam into him. Noah forced a smile. "Then you have nothing to fear."

***

The packed hotel ballroom had Claire's knees knocking together. Energy filled the air. Laughter and drinks were flowing freely.

And it sure seemed like reporters were *everywhere.*

Claire and Noah had barely gotten past the gleaming, marble steps in the ballroom when the first set of reporters closed in.

Sure, the men were in perfectly cut tuxes and the women wore glittering gowns, but Claire could see the avid gleam in their eyes and —

"Noah York…" A redhead murmured as her lips rose in a smile that never met her eyes.

"Jennifer." He inclined his head.

"Are the rumors true?" she asked. Then Jennifer directed her stare at Claire. "Are you the infamous Claire Kramer?"

"Jennifer Swan sort of…manages the main gossip pages in town," Noah said to Claire as his finger stroked down her arm. "And, baby, being called 'infamous' is a good thing."

Wait, had he just called Claire 'baby' in front of all those people?

"Then the stories about the two of you being an item are true?" Jennifer demanded as she inched closer. "Interesting. Claire, how do you feel about—"

"Claire's my fiancée," Noah said, and his voice seemed to carry all the way across the ballroom. "So, yes, Jennifer, we're an item." He gave the group of reporters a wide smile. "And feel free to print that in the papers."

Cameras flashed then.

"Smile, Claire," Noah whispered. His lips brushed over her ear. She felt the sensual lick of his tongue against her.

Claire smiled.

And, just like that, with his one, earth-shattering announcement, she and Noah were the center of attention in that ballroom. Everyone was looking at them.

Some people were smiling. Some were whispering.

Claire wanted to vanish.

The crowd closed in tighter.

Noah climbed up a few steps, pulling her back up with him. Then Janelle was there—and she had a microphone in her hand. She offered it to Noah.

Noah planned this.

Now Claire knew why he'd wanted her to wear the perfect dress. His fiancée had to be perfect.

"On the first anniversary of this hotel…" Noah sounded so smooth and polished as he addressed the crowd around them. "It only seems fitting that I get to share news that has made me the happiest man on earth."

Liar, liar. She hated it when Noah lied.

He lifted her hand into the air. The blue diamonds around her wrist caught the light and seemed to shine even brighter. "Claire Kramer has just consented to be my wife."

Applause shook the ballroom.

Noah laughed. "And I want you all to celebrate with us. Bring out the champagne!"

And, at his order, the champagne flowed. As if they'd been waiting for that cue — and Claire suspected they had — waiters bustled out with dozens and dozens of champagne flutes. The champagne was distributed quickly.

She even found a flute placed in her hand.

Dazed, Claire's gaze shot around the room. She saw Drake in the back, leaning against a broad, white column. Like pretty much everyone else, he had a champagne flute in his hand. He lifted it toward her.

Trace Weston stood beside him. Trace had his hand around Skye's shoulders. Skye stared back at Claire. Did the other woman looked worried?

Do I look terrified? Because Claire sure felt that way.

Everyone was lifting up their flutes as they toasted to her and Noah. Noah had freed her hand when he took his own flute of champagne.

He offered her a grin. "To my future wife," Noah said, the microphone catching every word he uttered. "Claire, I always want you to be mine."

Their glasses touched lightly, and she knew what he'd just done.

The reporters. The people. The public display.

The killer had gone quiet, and Noah thought to draw him out again with show.

"Always mine," Noah whispered and his lips took hers.

***

Claire was running, and she knew it. Noah was surrounded by a throng of well-wishers, and it had been hard, but Claire had managed to slip away from the crowd.

And she was now dashing for the exit as quickly as she could.

"You didn't tell me you were planning to marry Noah." Skye slipped into Claire's path. She was smiling, but her eyes flickered with concern. "Congratulations. I hope you'll be—"

Claire caught Skye's hands. She brought her in close, as if she were hugging the other woman. "I didn't know this was going to happen. He never asked me to marry him. This is all some plan of his."

A plan that was ripping her apart. Noah didn't know how long she'd actually dreamed of having a life, a husband who loved her.

He didn't know how hard it had been for her to stand there while he pretended they were the perfect couple.

She eased back from Skye, but made sure to keep that terrible, fake smile on her face. In case others were watching. And they were.

Skye's gaze searched hers. "What plan?" Skye whispered.

"He's putting us in the spotlight. I think he wants the killer to come at him again."

"So Noah can catch the guy." Skye was gorgeous in a black dress that fit her like a glove. "But he's pulled you into the cross-fire, too." Anger roughened her words.

"I was always in the fire." That danger was nothing new. She'd been hunted since she was sixteen, in one way or another.

She eased away from Skye. "I just…I need to be alone for a few minutes." Then she'd get her control back. She'd stop feeling as if she were about to break apart. But when Claire looked around the ballroom, she saw Trace striding toward them. And Noah had pulled free of his throng and he was closing in, too.

"Buy me just a few minutes," Claire said.

Skye nodded.

Claire rushed for the doors. A few more steps, and she'd head outside and be able to breathe for a bit. She'd suck in some air on the balcony, pretend that everything was fine, and she'd be okay.

But she didn't make it to the balcony. A man's hand snaked out and caught her arm, and Claire opened her mouth to scream.

"No need for that," Drake said as his hold tightened around her. "You know you're safe with me."

He pulled her behind one of the huge, towering columns that lined the outskirts of the ballroom. He caged her against that column, and he lifted her left hand. "There's no ring here."

"No."

"You didn't look like a blushing bride-to-be up there."

"That's because I didn't know I was going to be one."

He exhaled. "He should've told you."

Drake seemed to surround her fully then, and, hidden behind that heavy column, no prying eyes could see them. "Did he tell you? Did you know what Noah was planning?" It was *her* life. Noah should never have pulled a stunt like this without talking to her first.

"Hell, no. The guy's always twisting up the game."

There was no anonymity for her now. Her face would be everywhere. In the papers. On the news. Everyone would know who she was. Worse, they'd know who she'd been.

"I need to get out of here," Claire said, nearly desperate. "Those people—it's too much. I feel like they're vultures circling in for the kill."

"Because that's exactly what they are." He stepped back, surprising her. Then he took her hand in his.

Claire's breath eased out.

"Interesting," Drake murmured.

What?

"Come on. I'll get you some freedom." Then he was guiding her though the ballroom's back doors. In moments, they were sliding into the private elevator. "You know, you're leaving your fiancé in the middle of your own party."

A shiver had her tensing. "I'll go back. I just need a few moments."

His hand still held hers.

"You didn't tense on me," Drake said as the elevator doors closed.

She stared at their hands. No, when he'd taken her fingers in his, she hadn't tensed. Claire had actually felt relieved by his touch then.

"Not afraid of me anymore?" Drake queried softly. "Did you decide that I don't have a monster inside?"

She pulled away from him. "I know you do." But, no, she wasn't afraid of him.

Maybe she should be.

"You don't belong in Noah's world."

Those words had her blinking in surprise.

"When this is all over, you need to leave. Run as fast and as far as you can, but be warned, Noah will follow you."

"W-why are you telling me this?"

His smile was sad. "Because I like you, and I don't want to see you ripped apart by the vultures that always circle him."

The elevator doors opened. Claire hurried out—

And she slammed right into Austin Harrison.

***

"She wants some time alone," Skye said as she put her little ex-ballerina body right in front of Noah. Like she was going to slow him down. "Give her that time," Skye ordered. Her hands were on her hips and a glower was on her face.

Noah started to brush by her, but then Trace slid up behind his wife. Trace lifted a brow. "I'd suggest you listen to that advice. I saw Claire's expression a few minutes ago. That woman is running scared."

And that was why he needed to get to her. He hadn't told Claire his plans beforehand because he'd known that she'd balk. But if he introduced her as his fiancée in front of everyone...*I gambled that she'd stay quiet. That the shock would keep her at my side.*

It had. For a time. But when the shock faded, Claire had sure run fast.

"She can't keep running from me," he said. She needed to listen to him. He had a damn fine plan in place.

"She's not running from you. She just wants to be able to *breathe* without every reporter in the room watching her." Skye's smile was grim. "I know how that feels."

He sucked in a sharp breath. "You think I screwed up tonight, don't you?"

"Yes." Skye didn't pull her punches.

His gaze hit Trace's.

His friend nodded. Dammit. They *both* thought he'd screwed up?

"I am protecting her." He expected Trace to get that. "She can't just keep hiding out at the Towers, waiting for that asshole out there to make a move." *He* couldn't do that. He'd never been the type to wait for an attack to come. "In battle, you always take the offensive if you want to—"

"This isn't battle," Skye said softly. "This is her life."

Shit.

"And do you really think she liked that her first proposal was a fake one?" Skye's voice sharpened even more. "*No* woman likes that."

He schooled his expression. "Who says it was a fake proposal?"

Trace brushed a kiss over Skye's cheek. "I didn't see a ring on her finger, just plenty of flash around her wrists. Those bracelets...were they supposed to show everyone that she was chained to you?"

No, the bracelets had been designed to show Claire that she didn't have to constantly worry about her scars. He hadn't wanted her to worry about pulling down her sleeves to hide the scars or finding ribbons to bind her wrists. "You don't understand my relationship with Claire."

Trace shook his head. "I'm starting to think you don't, either."

Noah's gaze scanned the ballroom. "I need to find her." He should be talking to Claire, not Trace. He had to make sure she realized that nothing had changed between them. *I'm not using her.*

Trace motioned toward the exit. "Drake took her upstairs."

"Then, excuse me, but I have an elevator to catch." He hurried by Trace.

"And some groveling to do," he heard his friend mutter.

Noah's jaw locked as he entered the elevator. There would be no groveling. Claire would realize that an engagement was perfect for them. The attacker had targeted him once, so this would be like waving a red flag in front of the guy's face. He'd come after Noah again but this time—

I'll be ready for him.

***

Claire scrambled back even as Drake surged forward. Drake grabbed Austin and slammed the guy into the nearest wall. "What the hell are you doing here?" Drake demanded.

Austin jerked in his grip, but Drake wasn't letting the guy go. "I-I just needed to see Claire!"

Her heart was about to burst out of her chest. Her hands were shaking, her stomach churning, and Claire couldn't look away from Austin's eyes—*it's like I'm seeing Ethan again.*

Only Austin...he'd never been like Ethan. Austin had been the good brother. The one who graduated at the top of his class. The one who'd held the door open for her when she used to work at the diner. He'd been the one who—

Came to tell me how sorry he was. When she'd been in the hospital, recovering from the suicide attempt, he'd been there.

"How did you get past security?" Drake's hold on the guy tightened even more.

"I-I bribed a guy downstairs. I heard about the party tonight and knew this would be my best chance to get in." Austin's voice was tight. His gaze was on Claire—pleading? "I just need a few minutes, that's all."

"You're about to get an ass beating, *that's* all you're getting," Drake snarled right back. "Then the fool who let you up here is getting fired."

Austin's gaze narrowed on Drake's furious face. "I know you. You were at my father's funeral."

Drake just glared at him.

Austin's skin paled. "You were there…and my brother…his car exploded…*when you were there!*"

"Yeah, and stop looking at me like I did that shit. His death is one that can't be tied to me." Drake dropped his hold on the guy. "You're one dumb bastard to come up here and—"

Austin knocked him back and ran toward Claire. His hands grabbed her shoulders. "I just need a minute!" His hold wasn't painful. Just desperate. "I have to tell you—"

The elevator dinged behind them. Claire heard the doors open. Awareness shot down her spine. Even though she couldn't see the occupant in that elevator, she *knew* who was inside.

"You shouldn't have come here," Claire told Austin, and she whirled just in time to see Noah step out of the elevator.

His gaze went first to her. Then to Austin—and the guy had just made the mistake of curling his fingers around her shoulder again.

Rage flashed over Noah's face, and he attacked.

CHAPTER ELEVEN

"No!" Claire yelled. She grabbed Noah's arms and tried to push him back. It was like trying to move a brick wall. "Noah, I'm okay!" She cast a frantic glance toward Austin. Did the guy realize how close he was to danger?

"I'm not here to hurt her," Austin said, his voice breaking with what sounded like fear. "I told you...I just—"

Drake locked his hand around the back of the Austin's neck. "You just need to stay away from her. That's what you need to do."

Austin winced, and Claire knew Drake's grip had to be painful.

"I'm not like them," Austin bit out.

No, no, he never had been.

Noah was still straining beneath Claire's hold. If he'd wanted, though, he could have easily broken free. She knew that. He was staying still, for her.

She looked back at Noah, and, staring into his eyes, Claire said, "I want to talk with him."

Noah shook his head. "Bad idea, baby. Anything he has to say—it's just gonna hurt you. *I don't want you hurt.*"

He couldn't protect her from everything. "I want to talk with him," she said again as she eased way from Noah. Claire shook her head. "But not here, in the hallway." She inclined her head toward the suite. "Let's go inside, and, um, Drake, do me a favor? Stop choking him."

Drake eased his hold.

Silence fell over their little group, and Claire marched toward the suite's door. She was scared and this could be a huge mistake, but…

Austin tried to help me. When he'd gone to visit her in the hospital so long ago, he'd given her money. Told her to get out of town. To start fresh.

Noah didn't know what Austin had done. She was the only one how knew.

They filed into the suite. Noah stayed close to Claire, and Drake kept a careful watch on Austin.

"Five minutes." Noah's golden eyes blazed at Austin. "Then you're done. If I ever see you around again—"

"I knew Ethan had a problem, long before he met you." Austin was staring at Claire. "He hurt a few others girls. Roughed them up. One girl even wound up in the hospital with a broken jaw. She'd made the mistake of trying to break up with him."

"Sounds like the jerk didn't take rejection so well," Drake muttered, disgust obvious in his voice.

No, he hadn't.

"I asked my dad to get him help, but Harrisons…we don't need help." Austin swallowed. The click of his Adam's apple seemed loud in that tense moment of silence. "At least, that's the line my father always used. He'd tell us that no Harrison needed help, and then, when we did mess up, he'd beat the shit out of us."

Claire stepped back. Noah immediately wrapped his arm around her shoulder.

"No one knew about that, right? I mean, a senator, beating on his kids. And it's not like he did it that often." Austin's stare turned distant. "Only when we screwed up." His voice dropped. "I learned not to screw up. So I didn't…" He cleared his throat. "I thought things were better as we got older, but it turns out that things were just better for me. My father kept hurting Ethan, and Ethan—"

"Kept hurting anyone who got in his way," Noah said flatly.

His face miserable, Austin nodded.

"The fact that your father abused him doesn't forgive the fact that your brother *killed*," Noah shot back. "Plenty of other people have hell for an upbringing and—"

"And we don't hurt those who are weaker than us." Drake's face was tight. His words echoed with bitter fury.

We don't hurt those...

She looked at Drake with new eyes, but he wasn't staring at her. His attention was centered completely on Austin.

"I'm not saying this to try and-and excuse what he did. I just thought..." Austin's hands fisted. *"It's my fault!"*

She flinched.

"I didn't help my little brother. I didn't stop my father. I didn't—" Austin's glittering stare found Claire's. "I didn't stop Ethan from seeing you. Hell, I'm the reason he even asked you out. He was in competition with me. My father did that, put us against each other—made us enemies when we should have just been brothers." His breath expelled in a hard rush. "Ethan took you because he thought he was taking something from me." He stepped toward her. "I am so sorry, Claire. So sorry."

Claire stared at him, lost. The powerful Harrison clan was gone. Austin stood before her, and he was crumbling right before her eyes.

"You didn't do this to me," she whispered.

His gaze held hers.

"You didn't shoot my parents. You didn't," she had to take a steadying breath as the memories surged through her, "you didn't find me on that dock and put a gun to my head. None of that was you. It was Ethan. Despite whatever else happened, *he* was the one. He chose to do it all."

They all had the right to choose in this life.

Austin's eyes lowered. "I've been checking through my father's records. I know he caused you to lose your jobs. He had that detective, Sloan, following you, and when you came to New York, he even got the guy to trash your hotel room here."

"Why?" Noah demanded, and fury vibrated in that word.

Austin's shoulders rolled in a helpless shrug. "Even at the end, my father still wanted to find some evidence to prove that Claire manipulated my brother. He was in denial, and he wasn't going to let that go. Not ever." He shook his head. "I think he wanted Sloan to find some kind of proof that would show Claire was guilty. Maybe he thought there would be something he could use against her in that hotel room."

"There was nothing," Claire said simply. "Because I didn't do it."

Austin held her stare. "I know."

Noah stepped in front of her then. "Your five minutes are up." He grabbed Austin's arm. "Time to kick your ass out."

Austin didn't fight Noah's grip. "No more investigators, Claire!" He called out as both Noah and Drake shoved him toward the door. "No more lost jobs! No more trouble from my family ever again, I swear!"

She took a tentative step forward.

"I know you never wanted money from me," Austin said, and he was right at the door now. "You didn't take it before, but if you need it — if you need *anything* — I want to help. I want to make this right. I *have* to make it right!"

There were some things that couldn't be made right.

"I'll take him downstairs," Drake said as he once again curled his fingers over the back of Austin's neck. "And I'll make sure he doesn't get up here again."

Noah leaned in toward Austin. "This was it. You had your say. Now stay away, understand?"

Austin nodded.

Then he was gone. Drake hauled Austin away and Noah slammed the door behind them.

He didn't speak. Neither did Claire.

The sound of her breathing seemed overly loud in that room. Her whole body was tense, and she pretty much wanted to sink into a puddle on the floor and just tell the world to go away.

But there were about two hundred people waiting down in the ballroom. This was supposed to be an engagement party. If they vanished for the rest of the night, what would people say?

So she squared her shoulders. She lifted her chin. Adjusted her bracelets. And she walked toward the door.

Noah didn't move.

She slid around him. Reached for the doorknob.

In a flash, he was behind her. His body curved over hers and his fingers wrapped around her hand.

His touch seemed to electrify her. Claire closed her eyes. She couldn't handle the intensity between them, not at that moment. "We...we have to get back."

"Not yet." He turned her around. Kept his grip on her right hand. "I need to know that you're okay."

The laughter that escaped from her held a ragged edge. "Okay doesn't quite describe me right now." She was too raw for *okay*.

"I didn't want him near you."

She shook her head. "Austin has never hurt me."

His eyes flickered. "He said he tried to give you money."

"He came to see me when I was in the hospital after my—" *Say it.* "After my suicide attempt. He wanted to give me money to leave town." She could still see the stark expression on his face. He'd been so pale and shaken. "But taking money from his family, I-I couldn't do it. I didn't want anything from them."

I just wanted to get away.

"Don't see him again, Claire. Promise me."

"He's not a threat to me—"

He put his forehead against hers. "I don't trust him, and I want you to stay away from the guy. And when I find out who let him up here, that jerk is done."

Claire put her left hand on his chest. "I don't like games."

His head lifted. His gaze gleamed.

"You should've told me what you had planned. I nearly passed out when you announced to those people that we were getting married." She pushed against his chest. She needed some space between them. Talking was too hard when he was that close. Her body was hyper-aware of him. Too attuned.

Too weak where he was concerned.

"I was afraid you'd say no," Noah admitted, and his words had her stilling. "If you knew what I wanted to do…"

She knew exactly what he wanted to do now. "You think this killer is fixated on me, don't you?"

"Yes."

At least he wasn't trying to deceive her anymore.

"He's picking off the people who've hurt me." She'd pieced this together. "And he wanted to eliminate you—"

"Because I'm standing between him and you."

Her voice lowered as she said, "You just put a big target on yourself. Didn't I tell you…*I don't want you dying for me?*"

"I'm not, but I'm also not going to just wait for the bastard to strike again. I pushed him, so now he'll push back. I'll be ready."

She was afraid he wouldn't be. "We don't know anything about this guy."

"Not true. He's good with demolitions, he uses a silencer when he hunts—"

Her brows climbed.

"He has to use the silencer because no one reported hearing gunshots."

"You keep saying 'he'—"

"A man called me. A man is focused on you." His pupils seemed to swallow the gold of his eyes. "He wants you, and he thinks that he is going to take you from me."

"So you decided to publicly tell the world that I was yours." The anger and fear twisted inside of her. "*My* life, Noah. You shouldn't have pulled this stunt without telling me first."

"I'm trying to let you have a life!" Noah snarled back.

His anger had her tensing. Noah had never really been angry with her before.

But he sure seemed furious then.

"I don't want you always looking over your shoulder. I don't want you wondering who is watching you or what some sick freak might do next to you. I want you to be free." A muscle flexed in his jaw. "And no matter what I have to do, I will get you that freedom."

Then he caught her chin. He tipped her head back, and his mouth crashed down on hers.

***

Drake escorted Austin Harrison out the back of the Towers. He stopped under a streetlight and jerked the guy close as he warned, "Don't forget what Noah told you. Stay away from Claire."

Austin nodded. "I'm done," he muttered.

"You'd better be." Drake shoved him away.

Austin straightened his suit. Fumbled in his pockets. Hesitated.

Does he want an ass-kicking?

"Why were you at the funeral?" Austin asked him.

"Let's just say it was a pit-stop for me."

Austin stared down at the ground. "If he hadn't died, Ethan would just have come after her again."

Drake tensed.

"He would have kept coming. He had pictures of her that he kept in his cell. *He wouldn't have stopped*. Not until Claire was dead." He swiped his hand over his face. "I knew that, and this time, I had to stop him."

Was the guy making a confession?

"I should've done it sooner." Austin turned away. Began to walk into the darkness of the night. "But it's hard to send your own brother to hell."

***

He had his hands on her, but Noah couldn't shake the feeling that Claire was about to slip right out of his fingers. She was kissing him back, her mouth moving so perfectly beneath his, the taste of champagne on his tongue.

Don't leave me.

The kiss became harder, rougher. His hands curled around her hips, and he pulled her forward. His cock shoved against the front of his pants. Just one kiss from Claire, and he was hard and swollen. Aching. He remembered the feel of her silken mouth on his cock. The way she'd licked him. Sucked him.

His fingers slid down, and he found the slit in her dress. He put his hand on her thigh. No stockings for Claire. Just silken, golden skin. He parted that slit a little more and his hand rose. He touched the light scrap of lace that shielded her sex.

She was wet for him.

We touch, we kiss, and we ignite.

At least he wasn't the only one addicted. For them, it worked both ways.

His mouth pulled from hers. He stared into her eyes. "I want to fuck you."

"Th-they're waiting..."

"Let them wait." He jerked on the panties, hard, and they tore. He needed her. There. *Right there.*

No foreplay. No sensual build-up to release.

He had to take her.

He would. He freed his cock. The damn thing sprang forward, so eager for her that moisture already beaded the tip.

He lifted Claire up. She had on her heels. Those incredibly sexy heels. He held her easily.

And he drove into her as deeply as he could.

You're mine, Claire. I'm not letting you go.

She thought the engagement was fake.

He withdrew. Thrust deep.

She didn't realize...

I did it so you'd be tied to me.

The sound of her moans filled his ears. Her sex was a tight, hot paradise around his cock. Squeezing him. Driving him out of his mind.

He had her pinned to the door. He thrust into her. Again and again. And his fingers strummed over her clit. He knew Claire's body better than she did. He'd made a point to learn all of her weak spots. To learn how she liked to be touched. To learn just how to make Claire—

Her sex clamped around him. She choked out his name. *Explode.*

He drove into her even harder. The base of his spine tightened, and he came, climaxing inside of her on a long, powerful, mind-numbing release that left his legs feeling weak.

He didn't let her go. He couldn't, not yet. He waited until his breathing evened, then he kissed her again.

This time, the kiss was soft. Slow.

He started to get hard inside of her again.

With Claire, he was always ready to go again.

His head lifted. Red stained her cheeks. Her eyes shined, and her lips were swollen from his mouth.

"Everyone is going to know what we did," Claire said.

Good. He wanted them to know.

Claire's mine. I'm not letting her go.

Even if he had to kill in order to keep her with him.

***

Noah had fucked Claire. Drake could tell. Sure, their clothes were perfectly in place again, but there was a flush on Claire's skin. A sensual gleam in her eyes.

And there was the obvious stamp of satisfaction and possession on Noah's face when he looked at her.

Oh, yeah, Noah had staked his claim all right. It would be apparent to every male in the room.

"He's got it bad," Trace murmured as he slid up to the bar beside Drake.

The band was playing now. Some low, romantic tune that got on Drake's nerves. "Guess you'd know," Drake said, glancing over at him. "Since Skye's made you crazy for years."

Trace's gaze was actually on Skye as she talked with Claire. "She's worth every minute of insanity."

Bullshit. Drake had been burned — damn near lethally — by a woman before. He didn't plan on ever getting onto the insanity-boat again. As far as he was concerned, no woman was worth that nightmare. "I think your men need to focus more on Austin Harrison."

Trace's brows climbed. "The brother?"

"Yes, the brother." Drake was done with champagne. He drained the whiskey he'd just been given. He motioned to Noah, and his friend started crossing the room toward him.

A few seconds later, Noah leveled his gaze on Drake. "You took care of him?"

"Sure did." He saluted him with his empty whiskey glass. "And I'm guessing you recently fired an employee?"

Noah nodded. "Five minutes ago. And I've doubled the security at the hotel."

"Good idea," Trace told him as his fingers tapped against the bar. "Seeing as how you're working so hard to get a killer to come after you."

Drake put his glass back down. No one was close enough to overhear them, but he still dropped his voice as he said, "I think the brother did it. I think he set up the bomb to kill Ethan Harrison."

The faint lines near Noah's eyes deepened. "His own brother?"

"Austin knew Ethan would be at that funeral. He knew which car his brother would arrive and leave in." Austin had all but admitted his guilt outside of the Towers. "He said that Ethan would never stop going after Claire."

"He wouldn't have." Noah's face had hardened. "He was counting down the days until he we was free. He was as hung up on her as he always was." Noah glanced over his shoulder, obviously looking for Claire.

He's not the only one hung up on her.

But Drake was going to let his buddy dig his own grave on that one. His fingers curled around the empty whiskey glass. "Austin said he didn't stop him before, but I think he made sure he stopped Ethan this time."

Trace was already pulling out his phone. Drake heard the guy giving orders for a deeper investigation on Austin Harrison. "I want to know every move he's made for the last three months," Trace said into the phone.

When Trace gave an order, Drake knew his agents scrambled to obey.

"I don't like the way he is with Claire," Drake added.

Noah glanced back at him.

"He looks at her the same way you do." And that fact worried Drake. "It can't be good." Drake just didn't get it. Claire was a pretty woman, sure, definitely. Great eyes. Hot body. And she was smart—that was always sexy.

But…

Ethan Harrison had gone crazy for her.

Noah—hell, Drake didn't even know what Noah was doing.

"She has to be fucking phenomenal in bed," Drake muttered, and he realized his mistake two seconds too late.

Because in those two seconds, Noah drove his fist into Drake's jaw. Noah had always possessed a killer punch, and that hit sent Drake flying off the barstool. He slammed into the floor, and the barstool fell beside him.

Shocked gasps filled the air.

The band stopped playing.

Drake looked up and saw Noah coming in for another hit. He braced himself, but Trace pulled Noah back.

"Noah?"

And then Claire was there. She ran toward Noah and put her hand on his shoulder. "What are you doing?"

The reporters would be splashing this news all over the place. Especially the gossip reporter, Jennifer Swan. She lived for drama like this.

Noah glared at Drake. "I was just having a little talk with my *friend.*"

Drake smiled. "I fell. Must've had too much to drink." He stood up and rubbed his jaw.

Skye hurried over and straightened his suit. "Falling is easy when you get a punch to the face," she murmured, her voice only carrying to him.

Yes, it was.

Claire's gaze darted between Noah and Drake. "This isn't the place. Not for…whatever is happening between you two."

Noah shook free of Trace. "Of course." He motioned to the band. "Play something slow. I want to dance with my fiancée." He pulled Claire into his arms. Started to walk past Drake. Then Noah slowed. He leaned in close to Drake and rasped, "Fucking phenomenal. You'd better believe it."

Then he took Claire onto the dance floor.

Drake shook his head. No one woman — and no sex — was worth the kind of hell Noah was courting.

***

The ringing of a phone woke Claire that night. She blinked as her hand stretched out, seeking Noah in the darkness.

He wasn't there.

The phone — her phone — rang again, vibrating from its position on the nightstand.

Claire flipped on the light. It shined down on her phone — and on the framed photo of her family. She'd brought that photo into Noah's suite because she'd wanted to keep it close. She needed it close.

Claire picked up her phone. She didn't recognize the number, so she answered, hesitantly, "H-hello?"

"*Claire…*"

Goosebumps rose on her arms because that was a voice that Claire could never, *would never* forget.

"I've missed you, Claire."

Her gaze darted back to the photograph of her family. *Mom. Dad...*

She jumped from the bed. Where was Noah?

"It's been so long..."

It couldn't be his voice. "You're dead."

Laughter. Soft. Familiar. "Did you really think death would keep me from you?"

She yanked open the bedroom door. Rushed forward. Noah wasn't in the outer room.

"You're my one and only. Always." The voice — *his voice* — thickened. "And I'll be your one and only. No one else, not for either of us."

She wouldn't say his name. He was *dead*. "Leave me alone." Her body was shaking. She seemed to be splintering apart. *Dead. Dead. Dead. He's dead* —

"I'll see you soon, Claire."

The line went dead.

Claire didn't move. She could barely breathe as the suite seemed to whirl around her.

She didn't know how long she stood there, shaking, naked, but the suite door opened eventually. Noah stepped inside.

"Claire?" He hurried toward her.

She still had the phone clenched in her hand.

"Claire, what the hell is happening?"

She tried to talk, but her tongue felt too thick in her mouth.

He yanked the phone from her. His fingers flew across the screen as he checked her call log. "That's the same number that called me before the explosion at the Claymire Hotel. That's Sloan Hall's number."

Claire managed to shake her head. "I...know his voice." A woman didn't forget the voice of the man who'd wrecked her world.

"What? Claire, I couldn't understand you." His hand closed around her shoulder. "Dammit, baby, you feel ice cold."

She was. "He said…I was his 'one and only' — he always said that." At first, those words had made her feel special.

Then they'd made her terrified.

"Who was on the phone, baby? Who was on the phone?" She stared into his eyes. "Ethan."

Noah immediately tried to call the number back.

"I know it was him." She could hear his voice in her mind, looping endlessly. "He's not dead."

Noah had the phone to his ear.

"And he's going to come for me."

***

"Hey, Gwen, there's a package on your desk!"

Gwen waved at the cop who'd just passed her. "Thanks, John." She'd worked a double shift, and she was dead tired. She just wanted to get home and curl up with — and around — Lane.

She strode to her desk. Gwen frowned at the big brown envelope there. No return address. "Hey, John, when was this —"

John was gone. And, at close to 4 a.m., the bullpen was deserted. Sighing, she opened the package. She should probably wait but that damn curiosity of hers never let her hold back.

She slit open the side of the envelope. Photographs tumbled out.

Claire Kramer.

Gwen easily recognized the other woman, even though the photos were grainy and dark. She thumbed through the images. About eight pictures.

At Senator Harrison's hotel in D.C. Gwen's eyes narrowed.

Claire was standing right outside of the hotel. The pictures were even date and time stamped for her.

The times could be faked, of course, but…

What if the images were legit?

Then Gwen got to the last photograph. According to the time stamp on it, the image had been captured ten minutes after the last shot of Claire.

There was a man in this picture. A man rushing into the senator's hotel. The image only showed the side of the man's face, but she recognized him, too.

Noah York.

"I'll be damned," she whispered. She'd thought Claire had acted alone, but it looked like the lady had gotten some help from her lover. "And now I've got you," Gwen said. She reached for her phone. It was time for her to use some of her own power in this town. Favors were owed to her, and it was time they were called in.

CHAPTER TWELVE

"I'm not crazy," Claire said as she stalked toward Noah's desk around noon.

He glanced up at her. Damn, but she looked good in black. "I don't remember saying you were."

She was still wearing the bracelets he'd given her. As far as Noah knew, Claire hadn't taken those bracelets off. Now, as soon as he found the perfect ring to match her eyes, they'd be—

"You don't think Ethan Harrison called me last night."

He had to be very careful here. "A cemetery full of people saw him die."

"I don't care what they saw. I *heard* him." Her hands slapped down on his desk. "I need you to believe me. That whole engagement scene last night, it was designed to draw out the killer, right? Guess what? It worked even better than you'd hoped. Ethan is the killer. He's—"

"He can't be." Noah rose. Walked around the desk so that he could stand close to her. "He was in jail when his father was killed. Alibis don't get much better than that."

"Then maybe he hired someone to kill his father! I don't know how he did it." She gulped. "I just know he called me. He called using Sloan's phone, so maybe he killed Sloan, too. He killed Sloan and he set the bomb and—"

Noah caught her hands. "Breathe, baby."

She sucked in a shuddering breath. "I don't want to do this again."

She was breaking his heart. He pulled her closer. Put her right against that aching heart. "He's gone. Whoever called last night — hell, it's someone who was trying to mess with you." That someone would pay. "The guy who called you must've got some of Ethan Harrison's recordings. Ethan did a ton of interviews over the years. With a little splicing, it would be easy enough to run his words together and make it *seem* like he was calling you."

Her hands pushed against his shoulders as she looked up at him. "Why would someone do that?"

"To screw with your head."

She flinched.

"Think about the call. Did he respond to any questions that you asked him? Or was it just his voice? Rambling?" Because Noah had even used a tactic like this one before, on an enemy when he needed to get a guard to back away. A little voice manipulation, some splicing of a recording, and bam, he'd gotten exactly what he needed.

"I said he was dead." Claire's voice was leaden. "And he asked if I thought death could keep him from me."

Rage surged within Noah, but he held tight to his control.

Claire's long lashes swept down. "He said there wouldn't be anyone else, not for him and not for me."

"It *wasn't* him."

A knock sounded at his door. A visitor was the last thing he wanted. "Not now!"

But the door opened anyway. "Payback," Trace muttered as he came inside. "You did the same thing to me once."

Noah's eyes narrowed on him. "This isn't the time, Trace. I need to talk with Claire." He had to chase the fear from her eyes.

"I'm here about Claire." Trace's gaze slid to her. "My men tracked down Sloan Hall's phone."

Finally. Some damn progress.

"Did you find Ethan?" Claire asked, voice sharp.

Trace glanced at Noah.

Noah shook his head.

Trace cleared his throat. "We just found the phone. It had been left at the Hamlet Hotel."

Fuck. The phone had been left at the same hotel Claire had stayed in when she first came to New York? The caller was definitely enjoying his head games.

"I did some talking to the staff there," Trace continued with a slow nod. "Turned out they remembered seeing a man who fit Sloan's description, right around the time Claire checked in to the place."

"He trashed her room," Noah said. But that was exactly what Austin had told them.

"I think so." Trace rubbed the back of his neck. "There were no prints on the recovered phone. It had been wiped clean and dumped at the Hamlet's front desk." His lips twisted. "You know the security at that place is crap, so, of course, no one saw anyone actually leave the phone."

That would have been too much to ask for.

Claire stepped away from Noah. "Do you have agents down in Alabama?"

Trace nodded. "I sent them down after I heard about the explosion at the cemetery."

"Are they sure Ethan is dead?"

Noah rubbed his chest. The ache there just got worse.

"I mean, maybe he got out before the car exploded. Maybe he—"

"He was in the back of the cop car," Trace said softly, "so he wouldn't have been able to open those doors. He was trapped in there."

Her hands twisted together. "I know his voice. That wasn't a recording last night. It was *him*. He called me!"

Noah had to touch her again. He reached for Claire.

She flinched away.

That one move hurt. She hadn't pulled away from him, not since the beginning. "Claire?"

She whirled to stare into his eyes. "I need you to believe me. I've believed you, everything you said, right from the beginning." Tears glinted in her eyes. "He's alive, and he's going to come after me."

Then she started backing toward the door. "I need to get away. He knows that I'm at the Towers. I can't stay here."

She was trying to run again.

"Claire."

She stilled. He *hated* the fear in her eyes.

"You said you believed in me, right?" Noah asked her. Did she even realize how important those words were to him?

Her head moved in a faint nod.

Trace silently watched them.

"Then believe that I won't let anything happen to you. Whoever called you, I'm going to get him. I will stop him. You don't need to fear anything when I'm with you."

Her breath slowly eased out. Some of the wild panic seemed to fade from her eyes.

But then there was another knock at his door. Dammit. Why was everyone trying to rush inside his office?

Before he could call out, the door opened. Jonathan, one of his administrative assistants, rushed inside. "Sir, I'm so sorry. You said Mr. Weston was always clear and the others—"

Others?

A man and a woman came in behind Jonathan.

A tall, blond male. A petite and fierce woman—he would recognize her dark glare anywhere. "Detective Lazlo."

She smiled. It was a shark's smile.

Jonathan glanced around with wide eyes.

"That's all, Jonathan," Noah said because he didn't want the guy hearing what was to come.

Jonathan scurried away and shut the door behind him as quickly as possible.

Noah's glance slid over Gwen Lazlo. She had an envelope in her hand. *This isn't good.* He caught Claire's hand. Pulled her closer to him. Trace had taken up a position to Noah's right. "Detectives, what brings you both to New York, and so far away from your jurisdiction?"

Gwen's smile widened. "I hear congratulations are in order."

"You came this far to congratulate me? I'm touched."

Gwen's attention focused on Claire. "You don't exactly look like a thrilled bride-to-be, though. What's wrong? Did you discover some not so great news about the soon-to-be-hubby?"

"I-I don't know what you're talking about." Claire hadn't tried to slip away from Noah again. Good.

Noah looked up and found the blond's gaze locked on him. Lane Scott. He'd run a check on the guy. Both Lane and Gwen were supposed to be very good at their jobs. Honest cops who worked hard.

So why are they here?

Gwen lifted the envelope in her hand. "I got a package last night. Seems someone in D.C. managed to take a few photos during your last stay in *my* city."

He knew this wasn't going to be good.

Gwen crossed the room and spilled the contents of the envelope on his desk. "This is you, Claire. Right in front of the senator's hotel."

"I never went *inside* his hotel." Claire's voice was flat. "I didn't see him."

"No, I don't think you did." Gwen's fingers brushed through the photographs.

Noah caught sight of the next image. *Shit.*

Gwen's index finger tapped on the picture of Noah's face. "But York here, he went inside."

Because Noah was staring at Claire when the detective made her announcement, he saw the ripple of shock that went over Claire's face.

"I don't remember you mentioning to us that you'd been to see the senator right before he died," Lane murmured. "Want to tell us why you didn't mention that fact before?"

Not particularly, but it seemed like there wasn't a choice then. "I *didn't* see him before he died."

Claire was staring down at the picture. He wondered what she was thinking. *Keep believing in me, baby.*

Her eyes rose. Met his.

"I got to the hotel after he was dead. His door was open. I went inside, just a foot or two, and I saw him." He'd intended to warn the senator off. To tell the man to stay the hell away from Claire.

But his warning hadn't been necessary.

"We're supposed to buy that story?" Lane demanded. "I don't think so."

"Buy whatever you want." Noah kept his voice mild, and he managed to drag his gaze off Claire. "I didn't kill him."

Gwen was watching him with narrowed eyes. "You're used to getting exactly what you want, aren't you, York?"

"Most days," he allowed.

Trace had stepped closer to stare down at the photos.

"You walk in," Lane's voice had roughened. "You find a dead body, and you *don't* call the cops? Bullshit."

"I walked in," Noah said, "I found the dead body, and I got worried."

Claire jerked.

"Worried about Ms. Kramer?" Gwen scooped up the photos. "Because you thought *she'd* killed Harrison?"

He had to give them the truth here. "Yes."

Claire rocked back on her heels.

"I thought she'd killed him, and my first instinct was to get to her."

"Because…" Now Gwen's sharp-eyed stare raked him, then Claire. "Because Ms. Kramer has a history of instability, and you worried that the confrontation in the lobby had — what? Driven her over the edge?"

Claire's hands fisted at her sides.

"I just wanted to make sure she was safe," Noah said. Damn, this sucked. He wanted to grab Claire and pull her close. He wanted—

You're used to getting exactly what you want, aren't you? The detective's question had been spot-on.

Hell, yes, he was used to getting what he wanted. Noah shifted his body, and his hands curled around Claire's shoulders. "It wouldn't have mattered to me," he said as he stared into Claire's eyes. "I want you to know that."

"Uh, it wouldn't have mattered if she'd just killed a man?" Lane asked in disbelief.

Noah didn't take his gaze off Claire. "I needed to find you and see that you were safe." His breath heaved out. "You were, and I realized damn fast that you hadn't killed the senator." His eyes searched hers. For once, Claire seemed closed off from him. He couldn't tell what she was thinking or feeling and that drove him crazy. "My priority is protecting you, it has been from the beginning."

Not because of some debt he owed.

Because she was…Claire.

"Another little interesting coincidence we found," Gwen announced, drawing Noah's attention. "When I was down in Alabama, I met a man named Drake Archer."

Hell. Noah kept his hold on Claire as he waited for Gwen to drop another bombshell.

"It turned out the guy has a military record, one linked to you and…." She inclined her head toward a silent Trace. "You, too, Mr. Weston. You are Trace Weston, correct? Because you look just like the pictures I saw online."

"I'm Weston," Trace agreed. His expression could have been carved from stone.

Lane whistled. "Seems you three were quite the deadly team back in the day."

Back then, and now.

Suspicion shone in Gwen's eyes. "Archer had demolitions training. I'm thinking it would be pretty easy for him to rig a car to explode."

Yes, it would be. Noah let his brows climb. "So now you think I've got my friends killing, too?"

"I think you get what you want...just like I said before." She flashed another hard grin. "This time, though, I'm about to get what *I* want."

"Trace..." He growled his friend's name because he knew what was coming. "Stay with Claire."

"You're a person of interest in the murder of Senator Harrison." Gwen pulled a small, white envelope out of her jacket pocket. "And I have the authority to take you in for additional questioning."

"You're going to drag me back to D.C.?"

"No, I'll be dragging you down to the NYPD. We're cooperating with them, you see. Because we think the murders of a PI named Sloan Hall and Senator Harrison are connected. Same MO. And the ballistics match proved the killer used the same gun for both crimes."

Claire gave a frantic shake of her head. "You're wrong. Noah didn't kill Sloan. He was with me! He didn't—"

"Every minute? Was he really with you every, single minute?" Lane pressed, his doubt obvious. "Because I'm betting he could have slipped away, and I think you know that, too."

Claire swallowed. "Noah didn't do it."

"Then he can just explain to us who did kill the senator and Sloan Hall...he can explain all that down at the NYPD." Lane slapped his hand on Noah's shoulder. "Let's go, York."

"Call my lawyer," Noah said to Trace. Because he knew the cops were about to go after him with every bit of power they had.

Lane pushed him past Claire.

"Stay with Trace," he told her. "*Stay with him.*"

"Noah?" Worry darkened her eyes.

"I'll be back before you know it." But he would be damned if he'd leave her unprotected until he got this shit sorted out.

A few minutes later, Noah found himself being pushed into the back of Lane and Gwen's unmarked car. At least it wasn't a patrol car, but he knew word about this incident would spread through the city like wildfire. Engaged one night, arrested the next. A scandal like that would make headlines.

The cops climbed in the front of the vehicle. Before Lane could turn the key, Noah drawled, "Are you both really sure you want to go up against me?"

Gwen glanced back at him. "Am I supposed to be afraid of you?"

Yes.

"We do our jobs, and we don't care how much power you have."

Under other circumstances, Noah would like Gwen Lazlo. But since she was trying to toss his ass in jail... "Fair enough. But don't say I didn't warn you." Because they were about to find out just how much influence he had in the Big Apple.

***

For a moment, Claire stood frozen in Noah's office. No, that *hadn't* just happened. As the shock faded, she turned and rushed for the door.

"Wait." Trace grabbed her arm. "You don't want to go after them."

"They're *arresting* him. For murder!"

And he'd thought I killed Senator Harrison? Noah had thought she was a killer, and he'd still protected her.

Trace shook his head. "They're not arresting him. They're questioning Noah. The cops think they can push him into making some kind of mistake." He laughed. "They don't know Noah well."

He pulled out his phone. Called a lawyer. She tried to stop her knees from shaking. When he ended the call, Claire blurted, "They don't know Noah well, but you do." *I thought I did, too.*

Trace put the phone back into his pocket. "I've seen the man survive hours of torture, and he never broke."

"Wh-what?"

His eyes slid over her face. "But I guess Noah doesn't want you knowing about that time, does he? I never wanted it touching Skye, either."

Her head was about to explode. "When was Noah tortured?" The idea of him being hurt that way made her sick.

"In one way or another, I think the guy's been tortured most of his life."

"That's a really shitty answer," Claire snapped, fed up and pushed too far.

Trace blinked at her.

"*Who hurt Noah?*" Because she had the fierce desire to hurt them right back.

"One of our missions went to hell. Noah paid the price."

Her icy breath chilled her lungs.

"Noah has seen more death than most people can imagine, and because of that, the guy doesn't get real close to other people."

Neither did she, or at least she hadn't, until Noah. "And he holds tight to his control."

Trace nodded. "Noticed that, huh?"

It was hard not to notice it.

"Consider his control a good thing," Trace told her. "Because I've seen him lose it before, and when Noah breaks…" He gave a long sigh. "Men die."

She backed away from him. "That was war. That was—"

"Noah values his control more than he values anything else, because he knows how dangerous he is without it."

"*Why* are you telling me this?" Was he trying to scare her? Test her?

"Because I think you need to know exactly who you're dealing with." He crossed his arms over his chest. Noah had just been hauled away by cops. They should both be rushing out after him, but Trace was locking his steely gaze on her. "If you can't handle him, all of him, then you need to pull back."

She shook her head. Pulling back wasn't an option. Noah needed her then.

"I see what's happening between you. It may already be too late for him, and if you can't take him—all of him—then you'll wreck him."

"I-I'd never hurt Noah."

"Are you sure about that? Because I saw your face when you looked at that photo of him at the senator's hotel. For an instant, you were terrified." He took a step toward her. "You thought he might have killed, and terror consumed you. He thought that you might have done the same thing, and he protected you."

"Stop it! It's not the same—you don't understand!"

"I understand that Noah is my friend. And the biggest threat that the man has ever faced…she's standing right in front of me."

Claire straightened her spine. Focused on trying to calm her racing heart. "You don't know me. And you don't know how Noah is with me." She wouldn't let this man intimidate her. "And now you need to get out of my way because I'm not just going to stay in this place while he gets questioned. He was with me when Sloan was killed. *Every minute.*" Trace wisely backed away. She marched for the door. "And I'll make those cops believe me."

Trace called her name, but Claire didn't stop. She hurried through the hotel. Ran by the doormen. The street outside was so busy. Packed with cars. She raised her hand, ready to hail her own taxi, and her gaze flew around the area as—

Ethan Harrison.

He was standing across the street from the hotel. His hands were shoved into the pockets of the long, black coat that he wore. His eyes—his eyes were on her. He was watching her.

Then he smiled.

"Claire!" Trace yelled from behind her.

Ethan turned away.

Trace's hand closed over her shoulder. "Claire, come on, look, I'll get us down to the station—"

She yanked away from him and ran into the street. "*Ethan!*" Cars honked. Brakes squealed. Trace roared her name.

Ethan didn't slow.

She ran faster, and Claire could see him—

She was shoved through the air. Claire slammed onto the cement with an impact that rattled her bones.

Trace rolled her over, swearing. "Dammit, Claire, that car almost hit you!" His hands patted over her body. "Are you hurt? I didn't think I was going to get to you in time."

She shoved his hands off her, shoved *him* off her, and leapt to her feet. "Ethan!"

"Ethan?" Trace echoed.

Not bothering to respond, Claire ran down the sidewalk. There were so many people. So many—but where was Ethan? Where had he gone?

"He was here," Claire whispered. "He *is here*. I just have to find him." She whirled around. Looked to the left. The right. Bodies passed her in a blur as she kept searching for the man with the bright blond hair.

The man who should be dead.

***

Two New York detectives had joined the little party. One of the guys was named Sean Fuller, and the other guy, well, he hadn't volunteered his name.

"So…" Gwen pulled out the chair across from him. She was obviously the leader of the party. "Why don't we cut through the bull?"

He was seated at a wobbly little table in an interrogation room. They'd put a cup of coffee in front of him. The air blew overhead in a too-cold stream.

He smiled at her. "What do you want to know?"

His smile seemed to make her hesitate. She probably expected him to be nervous. Bring the tycoon downtown, throw him in interrogation, make him crack. Yes, he was sure that had been the general plan.

That plan was screwed.

"I want to know…would you kill for Claire Kramer?"

"Yes."

Gwen blinked.

"But *have* I killed for her?" He shrugged. "Not yet."

Gwen and Lane shared a long look. "So you're *planning* to kill?" Gwen asked carefully.

"I'm planning to keep Claire safe. Someone planted a bomb at one of my hotels recently. I'm sure you're aware of that." The news had been flashed in a constant stream on TV. "I won't just stand by while someone tries to hurt my fiancée."

Noah figured he had about ten more minutes before his lawyer burst in, so he'd keep playing this game a bit longer.

"Tell us about your visit to Senator Harrison's hotel room in D.C.," Gwen directed.

Sighing, Noah leaned forward. "The guy was being a total dick. Seemed to me like he was borderline insane. That insanity must run in the Harrison family."

Lane grunted.

The two New York detectives just frowned. *Ah, are you two holding back because you just want me to be pissed at your D.C. counterparts? Worried I'll come after you?* Because the New York cops did look nervous as they glanced his way. One of the guys had even started to sweat.

Noah stretched and took his time answering. "I wanted to deliver a personal message to Colby Harrison. The senator needed to realize that he wouldn't be able to threaten or harass Claire ever again."

Gwen's eyebrows arched. "And had he been harassing her?"

"Yes." He kept his hands flat on the table. "That's where Sloan Hall came in. The Harrisons hired him to keep watch on Claire. For years, they've been stalking her."

"Bet that pissed you off," Lane tossed out. "Knowing they were trying to hurt your lady."

Pissed didn't begin to cover the way he felt.

"So I guess it's no wonder you shot the senator and Sloan Hall," Lane continued as he rubbed his chin. "You wanted to make sure they didn't hurt her again."

Gwen's fingers tapped on the table. "I don't understand…"

Noah waited for her to continue.

"When did you meet Claire Kramer?"

"A few months ago, in Chicago."

"And what? It was love at first sight?" Her words mocked the idea. "I don't see that happening for a guy like you."

He smiled at her again. "Maybe I'm the romantic sort."

"I think you're the intense sort. You're also the *sort* who goes from woman to woman, night after night."

His reputation sure seemed to get around. Had the lady been talking to Drake? "Not anymore."

"Right…not anymore…not since Claire." She tilted her head to the right and a line appeared between her brows. "What is it about her? Why the change for Ms. Kramer?"

"Claire's a survivor. I admire that."

"Because you're a survivor, too?"

Ah, he should have seen that coming.

Gwen rifled through some files that waited on the table. "You survived your parents' death, didn't you? You were the only survivor when the boat sank."

"Yes."

"So you and Claire…it's like to like?"

"I don't know what you mean."

Gwen gave a little frustrated growl. "Survivor to survivor. You both lost the ones closest to you, and you had to keep going."

That door was going to open any second but he'd humor the lady a bit longer. "I'm with Claire because she's what I need." After so many years of going through the motions of life, she actually made him *feel* alive. She made him want to start thinking about a future.

"And are you what Claire needs? Someone who is willing to...kill for her?"

"Didn't she have that before?" Lane questioned, the words rapping out.

Noah's gaze cut to his. "You don't want to go there with me."

Now it was Lane's turn to smile. "Don't I? There were lots of stories circulating about Claire Kramer. Her parents were too strict, and they didn't want her seeing her lover, so she decided to just get rid of them. She slipped away, giving herself the perfect alibi, and she got her lover to come and —"

Noah started laughing. "There went your badge."

Lane's smile vanished.

"You should be careful what you say about Claire," Noah continued. His voice had dropped to a lethal softness. "I have a very long memory, and I don't forgive easily."

Lane's eyes turned to slits. "You threatening me?"

"I get that you want to ask your questions. Nailing me for these murders would probably make all your damn careers, but it's not going to happen." Noah rose. "And if you keep screwing with me, you will find yourself *without* any career."

The door opened. Only his lawyer didn't stand there. Claire did. Her eyes were big, haunted, and her face was far too pale. Trace was right beside her. The guy's lip was bleeding, and he had scratches on the side of his face. *What. The. Hell?*

"Noah didn't do it," Claire announced. "He didn't kill Sloan Hall." Her words tumbled together because she was speaking so quickly. "Ethan Harrison did."

CHAPTER THIRTEEN

"You think I'm crazy, don't you?" Claire asked as she turned to face Gwen Laszlo. The detective had taken Claire back to York Towers, and they were just entering the suite that Claire shared with Noah.

"I think you're under a lot of stress." Gwen pushed back her shoulders, and Claire saw the gun holster on the detective's side. "I was there when the patrol car exploded. You can trust me on this. Ethan Harrison is in hell right now."

The cops had sent a team to search the streets near York Towers. They'd searched for several hours. Turned up nothing. Claire had been the only one to see Ethan. Even Trace hadn't noticed the guy.

Noah was downstairs in the lobby. The cops had finally let him go, and Claire needed him to hurry up there so they could talk. *He'll believe me this time.*

"You came up here because you wanted to question me," Claire said wearily as she shoved back her hair. "We both know that's your plan."

Gwen searched her eyes. "I'm worried about you."

"Because I'm seeing dead men?"

"Because you have a very dangerous taste in men."

Claire flinched. "No, I don't." She turned and started pacing toward the window. She eased out of her coat, tossed it onto the couch. She started to remove her gloves. "I don't have…"

Claire's words trailed away. Her picture was on the floor. The picture of Claire, Sara, and her parents — the only thing that had been salvaged from her time at the Hamlet Hotel. The frame was gone, and the photo...there were large X's on all the faces. An X on Sara's face. An X on Claire's mother. An X on her father.

An X on me.

"Claire?" Gwen continued. "I'm worried because you could be in trouble, and you don't even realize — "

She grabbed the photo from the floor. "He was here." She whirled toward Gwen. "He was *here* — "

Claire saw the gun. The one aimed right at the back of Gwen's head. Gwen was looking at Claire. The detective didn't see the threat behind her.

Claire screamed and lunged forward. Her body collided with Gwen's and they slammed into the floor. There was no explosion of sound, no blast as the gun fired but...

"Gwen?" Claire whispered. She'd tried to move so fast. Her trembling hand touched Gwen's head, and she felt the sticky wetness of blood.

There was no blast because a silencer was on the gun.

"You weren't fast enough, Claire." The dark, rumbling voice mocked her.

She looked up and saw that, this time, the gun was pointed straight at her.

***

Noah paused in front of the elevator. "You coming up, detective?"

Lane gave him a grim smile. "I think I'll wait down here. There are a few of your staff members that I wanted to chat with."

The guy was so obvious. "I know you came to grill them, just like I know your partner is up there questioning Claire right now." The cop was probably trying to make Claire feel more comfortable by questioning her in a place that would put Claire at ease.

No interrogation room for her, huh? Trying a different approach?

Lane seemed to brace his body as he studied Noah. "Your lawyer got you out of there, but that doesn't mean you're free."

"You need to get your ass back on a plane to D.C.," Noah told him bluntly. He stepped onto the elevator. "I think you've worn out your welcome in New York."

The doors began to close.

Lane's hand flew out and stopped that closure as he curled his fingers around the door on the left. "Do you think Claire saw Ethan Harrison today?"

Noah stared back at him.

"I mean, if my lover told me that the man who tried to kill her, the man who murdered her parents…if she told me that asshole had been in town, standing less than thirty feet from her, I'd freak the hell out," Lane said.

"Move your hand." *Or I'll move it for you.*

"But your buddy Weston didn't see the guy, did he? Just Claire, and I don't exactly see you freaking the hell out."

"Because I'm not the type to do that." *I need to get upstairs to Claire.*

"Or else you don't believe her. Do you think she's having another breakdown? Is all the stress too much for her?"

"Claire isn't going to break." Anger hummed in his words.

"She did before. And they barely got her to the hospital in time."

"Move. Your. Hand."

Lane shook his head. "You didn't answer me."

The sonofabitch was pushing too far—

"Mr. York!" Janelle's frantic voice caught Noah's attention. He looked over Lane's shoulder and saw Janelle, running toward him. All of the color was gone from her face.

Noah shoved Lane out of his way. "What's happening?"

"G-Greg…one of our bellmen…I just found him…" Janelle's fingers were shaking as she pointed toward the staff door on the far right. "Someone shot him. In the head. H-he's dead."

Lane immediately lunged toward the staff door.

But Noah spun around and leapt back into the elevator. He only had one thought.

Claire.

***

The light glinted off the gunman's blond hair. His green eyes gleamed at her. "You're on your knees again, Claire, and there's a gun pointed at your head. Brings back memories, doesn't it?"

Her left hand was still pressed to Gwen's head, but her right was beside the cop's body. Just inches from Gwen's holster. "Why are you doing this?" Claire whispered as she looked up at the killer—

Not Ethan Harrison.

Austin. *Austin Harrison.*

The *good* brother smiled down at her. "You ruined my life, Claire."

She shook her head.

Rage flashed across his face. *"Yes!* You did! You destroyed everything."

"I-I never wanted Ethan to—"

"Say his name again, and I'll put a bullet in your brain."

She stared at the gun. A long silencer covered the tip of the weapon. "Aren't you planning to do that, anyway?"

"Actually…no." He motioned with the weapon. "Get up. I'm not my brother. I don't need you to beg me."

She rose. Claire kept her right hand behind the leg of her pants.

"You just killed a cop." He shook his head. "You should never have gotten out of that mental health facility all those years ago. You just aren't well."

"I-I didn't kill anyone."

"You fucking killed me!" His rage exploded again. "You ruined my life! My family lost everything because of you!"

"I lost my family," Claire said, keeping her voice low. He didn't realize that Gwen was still alive. Claire did. The blood matted Gwen's hair, but the wound wasn't deep. Claire had knocked the cop aside in time. The bullet had grazed over her, but it hadn't driven into Gwen's skull. She just needed to keep Austin from realizing that Gwen was still alive. Because if he discovered the truth, Claire knew he'd shoot the cop again in an instant.

"Your family was trash. They didn't matter."

Her eyes narrowed. *Don't talk about my family that way.* "They weren't murderers so I'd say they mattered a whole hell of a lot more than the Harrison clan."

"You should have just let him screw you! Until he was done!" Spittle flew from Austin's mouth. "Then he would've walked away. Ethan liked to be the one to leave. It gave him—"

"Power," Claire finished.

Because power was so important to the Harrisons.

"You broke him. And when Ethan fell, he took my father down with him." His smile flashed again, chilling her. "Of course, the old man always was a twisted bastard. Didn't realize quite how much, not until Ethan told me…"

The gun was inches from her chest.

"Walk toward the balcony." He jerked the weapon toward the balcony door. "It's a phenomenal view out there. A real helpful bellman let me see it earlier. I flashed some cash and got a free pass up here." He licked his lips. "Did I mention that folks here are bribed too easily? No matter. I made sure to tie up those loose ends this time."

Claire walked, backward, toward the balcony. Her hands were still down.

"I was supposed to be president." A muscle flexed along his jaw. "I was groomed for that position. I spent so many years being *perfect* for that."

She didn't speak.

"Then the dream was gone. Scandal was all my family knew. Scandal because of *you*."

"I thought—I thought you wanted to help me. In the hospital…"

"I wanted you to vanish. I figured that if you disappeared, there would still be some hope for me."

Claire opened the door and slipped out onto the balcony. It was cold out there, and the wind sent her hair whipping around her face.

"It's a killer view, isn't it?" Austin asked as he followed her out.

Claire glanced over and saw the lights of the city below. *Killer.*

"My father drained our fortune tracking you. Trying to free Ethan. He used all of his money, and even though I was working my ass off, he took mine, too, and I had *nothing*."

"Austin, you—you don't need to—"

"I know exactly what I need to do. I need to get rid of the problems in my life. I need to be free. It's time for my new start." His shoulders straightened. His hold on the gun was rock-steady. "That's what I've been doing, you see. Cleaning house. My father was a dead weight, so I had to get rid of him."

Her breath choked out.

"He never would've stopped. He would have bled me bone dry as he tried to free Ethan, but that just couldn't happen. If Ethan ever got out, hell, he'd go after you again, and the scandal would be even worse."

"You're here with a gun. You just shot a cop." *He's crazy.* "You think the scandal isn't going to be bad from this? You need to think again."

He laughed. "Ah, Claire, I didn't shoot a cop. You did." He lifted the gun, and she saw that he wore black gloves. "No fingerprints from me, and you…you're wearing gloves right now because it was cold outside and you didn't get the chance to take them off when you came back to the suite."

He was right.

"You shot the cop because she realized you had killed Senator Harrison and his PI, Sloan. And after you shot her, you panicked. You knew there was no escape, so you did the only thing you could do...you then took your own life."

A dull ringing filled Claire's ears. "No."

"You tried suicide before. You just didn't try hard enough." He nodded toward her. "Don't worry. You'll do better this time. A jump from this height will make sure you end up in the morgue."

"Y-you said you had help in the hotel." *A bellman.* "The cops will find him. The cops will get him to talk and—"

"The dead don't talk."

His words had her heartbeat stuttering.

"And, by the way," he added darkly, "you killed the bellman, too. Even used this same gun for the crime."

Claire wouldn't look over the edge of the balcony again. "*Why* would I have killed him? I don't—"

"You're crazy, Claire. You've been seeing my dead brother this week. Getting phone calls from him." He laughed. "Talk about perfect timing! When I heard that shit, I couldn't believe how wonderfully things were falling into place."

Her heartbeat shook her chest. "Don't do this. Please."

"I'm not doing it. You are. You killed all those folks. And now, you're going to jump over the edge of that balcony, and you're going to kill yourself."

"I-I won't do it."

"You've hurt enough people." He advanced toward her with slow, gliding steps. "It's time for the nightmare to be over. You caused all of this—"

"No!"

"Now you'll be the one to end it."

She braced herself. Where was Noah? He'd been downstairs, talking with Lane. Noah should be coming up to the suite at any moment.

Would Austin shoot Noah, too?

Claire couldn't let that happen. "I'm not going to jump."

"Yes, you will." His grin flashed. "Because if you don't, I'll go downstairs. I'll find your lover. And I'll put a bullet in his brain."

A tear slipped down Claire's cheek. "You were the one who planted the bomb at his other hotel."

"What?" His brows rose. "Damn, maybe you are crazy."

No, he was. "You've been planning to kill Noah all along."

"*You destroyed everything, Claire! I had a great future. I could've had —*"

Claire lifted the gun that she'd taken from Gwen's holster. She'd hidden that gun so carefully.

Not anymore.

Austin's mouth hung open as he stared at the weapon.

"I'm not going over that balcony," Claire told him. The weapon was shaking in her grip. "And you're not going to hurt Noah."

His gaze dipped to the weapon, then back to her face. He laughed at her. "You don't have what it takes to pull that trigger."

"I do." Actually, it was taking all of her strength *not* to pull it right then. "I've lost everyone close to me. My parents. My sister. I won't lose Noah. I'd do anything to protect him." Claire pulled in a deep breath. "So drop your weapon, or I will shoot you."

He took another step toward her. "You *bitch!* You don't get to tell me what—"

"*Claire!*" Noah's roar reached them, spilling through the open balcony door.

Claire didn't take her eyes off Austin. "You're going to be arrested," Claire told him. "Gwen's not dead. She'll recover. She'll tell everyone it wasn't me who shot her. She'll—"

"I'm not going to jail!"

"Yes, you are. You're going to jail just like Ethan did. Your whole family—you're the crazy ones!"

Then Noah was there. He ran onto the balcony. "Claire!"

Austin whirled toward Noah. He brought his gun up, aiming right at Noah.

"No!" Claire screamed.

Austin's hand jerked.

Claire fired her weapon even as Austin shot at Noah. Her bullet hit Austin in the shoulder, and he stumbled, falling forward.

Claire raced past him, hurrying toward Noah. He'd fallen too. *Please, God, not Noah, not Noah.*

Noah's head lifted. "Fucking asshole!" And he tried to charge at Austin.

Claire threw her arms around Noah. He was alive. He was safe. They were *both* alive. "I love you." The words burst from her.

Noah stiffened. His arms tightened around her then, squeezing her so much that he stole her breath.

"No!" Austin's snarling voice. "You don't escape, Claire! Not this time!"

She tried to look back, but Noah grabbed Claire and shoved her behind him.

"Neither of you escape," Austin shouted.

Noah had put his body in front of Claire. He'd yanked the gun from her hand.

Gunshots filled the night.

But...

Austin's gun had been equipped with a silencer. She shouldn't have been able to hear so many shots. Claire craned her neck to see around Noah.

"No one shoots my partner."

She looked to the left. Lane was there, standing on the balcony, his weapon still drawn. Pointed at Austin.

Her gaze flew back to Austin. He was on his feet, but staggering. Under the lights of the balcony, she could see the dark balloon of blood on his chest. From several wounds.

Noah had a gun aimed at Austin, too. Noah and Lane had both shot the guy. That was why she'd heard the sound of so many gunshots.

Austin sank to his knees. "Claire…"

"Go to hell," she whispered back to him.

And, he did. Austin tumbled back, and the blood pooled beneath him.

***

"You're going to be okay."

Claire's head turned at the husky words. Gwen had just been loaded onto a stretcher, and Lane was right beside her, holding tightly to her hand.

"It's barely a scratch, love," Lane told her. "Just another kick-ass battle wound for you to show off to the guys back in D.C."

Claire stepped toward them. Gwen's eyes were open. She whispered something to Lane—

"I love you, too," he told her as he bent to kiss her hand.

Then the EMTs wheeled Gwen out of the suite. Claire watched her go, frozen, heart-sick. Gwen had been hurt because of her. A hotel bellman had been found with a gunshot wound to the head. When Austin had said that he had tied up loose ends, the sonofabitch had meant it.

His body was still out on the balcony. Cops and crime scene techs swarmed around him.

"Are you okay?" At the gruff question, Claire looked up and found Drake standing near the doorway.

She nodded.

"Claire…" He sighed her name. "Stop trying to bullshit me." Then she found herself being yanked into his arms. "You look like you're about to shatter."

She felt that way. "I-I thought Austin wasn't like them." Maybe that was what hurt the most.

"Noah wants you out of here." Easing back, Drake stared down at her. "He has to talk with the cops, but he wanted me to take you downstairs so you'd be safe."

And all she wanted was…Noah.

She'd told him that she loved him. She hadn't meant for those words to spill out. In that one instant, she'd just been so afraid and her guard had lowered.

"The cops will want to talk with me, too." Her gaze darted back to the balcony. Noah was out there with the cops.

"Come with me, Claire. You don't need to—hell, you don't need to watch them bring out the body."

No, she didn't want to watch that. "Noah killed him." Her voice was just for his ears. "Didn't he?"

"He told me they didn't know yet if Lane's bullet or his ended the bastard. Either way, I figure it's good riddance." He turned, and with a steady hold on her, Drake led her to the door.

She didn't look back when they slipped out of that suite. The EMTs and Gwen were already gone. Claire glanced down and realized she still had blood on her hands.

A few moments later, the elevator dinged. She and Drake slipped inside when the doors parted. Then, as soon as they were alone and on their way down, Claire confessed, "I didn't want him to do it."

Drake lifted a brow.

"I never wanted Noah to kill for me."

"I know."

She sucked in a gulp of air. "Why did it have to happen like this?"

With his eyes on her, Drake shook his head. "You're not responsible, got it? Austin Harrison is to blame. The man was twisted, and he needed to be put down."

"It's not that simple."

"To me, it is. And for Noah, the choice was kill or be killed. He did just what he'd been trained to do."

I love you.

She stared at her blood-stained hands. "What's going to happen now?"

"I'd say that's up to you and Noah."

Noah hadn't said much. That was the problem. After Austin had fallen, Noah had pushed her inside the suite as fast as he could. His hands had roamed over her, checking for injuries, and when he'd been satisfied that she was unharmed, he'd let her go.

I love you. "I think I made a mistake." She straightened her shoulders.

The elevator stopped. The doors opened, and she hurried to exit. But Drake caught her shoulder. "What mistake?"

Swallowing, Claire looked over at him. "I fell for Noah." He'd gotten right past her guard. "Austin wanted to hurt him. I couldn't let that happen. I-I was the one to fire the first shot."

"Because you were saving Noah."

She had saved him, barely. Austin's bullet hadn't hit Noah. She licked her lips. "I shot first because I love Noah."

And everyone I love gets hurt.

***

"Austin Harrison." Lane shook his head as he watched the body get bagged and tagged. "Never seen crazy run in a family as much as it did in that one."

A thick knot of tension curled at the top of Noah's spine. "He was going to kill Claire." Every time he thought of just how close he'd come to losing her...*I'll have nightmares forever about that moment.*

His hands fisted.

When he'd rushed into the suite, he'd found Gwen on the floor. There'd been so much blood around her, but her eyes had been opening. She'd been whispering for Claire.

Noah had been shouting for her.

He'd burst onto that balcony. Seen Austin with his gun—

Then Claire fired. Her bullet had found its mark, and Austin's shot had gone wild.

She'd fired and then run right into Noah's arms.

"I think Claire is finally going to be free," Lane said, his eyes still on the black body bag. "There aren't any Harrisons left to try and wreck her life anymore."

So it would seem.

"The New York detectives are going to be taking over." Lane finally pulled his gaze off the body bag and inclined his head toward the two suits in the corner. "The press will go wild, but I figure a guy like you is used to handling the press."

"I am, but Claire isn't." His eyes locked on the New York detectives. "After we answer their questions, I'm going to take Claire away from the city. I don't want her steps dogged by every reporter within a fifty mile radius."

"I'd do the same damn thing in your position." Lane offered his hand. "I know we didn't exactly get off on the right foot, York."

"You mean because you thought I was a killer?" Noah took his hand. Shook it once.

"Hell, I *know* you're a killer. I've got friends at the Pentagon, so I got my hands on your military records." Lane gave him a hard grin. "I mean because I thought you were a pompous rich jerk who was playing games in my city."

Noah smiled. "I like you, Detective."

"No, but you respect me, and that's just as good." Lane hesitated. "I really hope my bullet was the one that ended that bastard's life." His jaw hardened. "*No one hurts my Gwen.*"

And no one hurts Claire.

Noah realized that he and the detective had quite a few things in common.

When the detective walked away, Noah glanced around the suite. He'd seen Drake leading Claire away minutes before, and he was glad that she had escaped from the death that clung to that place. Claire had seen enough death.

It was time for her to live.

I love you.

Those words had been so soft that Noah hadn't been sure he'd heard them, not at first. Then he'd looked into Claire's eyes and *seen* her love.

"Mr. York?"

He glanced to the right. One of the New York detectives was coming toward him. More questions. He and Claire would both have their turn being grilled. But as soon as they got the all-clear…

I'll get you out of here, Claire. They'd go back to the Hamptons. They'd walk on the beach. Fuck on the balcony.

Live.

And there wouldn't be any more fear for Claire. Because Noah wasn't going to let her out of his sight anytime soon.

Seeing her on that balcony had scared a good fifteen — *twenty?* — years of his life away. In that one instant, when Austin had swung with his gun up, Noah had realized one very, very important fact.

I can't live without Claire.

Love or obsession? Claire had asked the question once. She'd wondered if there was a difference between the two things.

For a while now, Noah had thought that he would kill for her.

Yet in that one, desperate moment, he'd been ready to die for her.

Love, Claire. It's love, not just obsession.

CHAPTER FOURTEEN

The last twenty-four hours had been hell. Claire climbed the steps to Noah's beach house, feeling exhaustion pressing over every inch of her body.

There had been questions. Then more questions. Detectives who grilled her. Detectives who seemed to comfort her.

There had been reporters. Dozens of them. Camped out around the hotel. Waiting outside of the police station.

They'd shouted at her. Snapped images.

She'd already seen a few newspaper headlines. *Another Harrison Driven to Kill?*

She hadn't driven Austin to do anything.

But the press loved a story about sex and murder. Claire knew she'd be in the headlines for a long time to come.

"Claire?" Noah's fingers brushed over her arm. She realized that she'd just stopped in front of the door. "Baby, what is it?" He turned her in his arms so that she stared up at him.

Night had fallen again, but the house was lit. Gleaming from within. Noah had called his caretaker earlier and told him to prepare the house.

She knew he'd wanted her to have a place to hide. *Escape.* "I'm sorry that my nightmare spilled over onto you. Sometimes, I know you have to wish that I'd never walked into your hotel."

He shook his head. "I never wish that. The day you walked into my hotel was one of the best days of my life."

What?

His head lowered toward her, and Noah's lips took hers. The kiss was long, slow, and so thorough. So...Noah.

When he ended the kiss, he stared down at her with eyes that seemed to blaze with emotion. The problem was that Claire couldn't read that emotion. Need? Lust? Or something more?

She wanted it be to something more so badly.

"Let's go inside, or I'll take you right here."

Her own eyes widened at that, and Claire hurried to get inside the beach house. Noah locked the door behind her, and she stopped by the couch, wondering—

"You scared me."

He'd said the words like an accusation. Claire turned and blinked at him. "I, um, didn't mean to." She'd been trying to save him.

"You shot Austin. A damn ballsy move, but then you ran toward me." His eyes glinted. "The guy still had his weapon. I could see him trying to get it up and aimed, and you were between him and me. *He could've shot you.*"

"That wasn't his plan." Noah hadn't been there when the cops questioned her so he didn't realize... "He wanted me to jump from the balcony. A bullet to my head wouldn't have worked with the suicide story he was trying to create."

"Suicide?"

"I broke once, so he thought everyone would easily buy the story that I broke again."

Only about five feet separated her and Noah. He started walking toward her, *stalking* forward, and he eliminated that space quickly. His fingers closed around her shoulders. "I never would've bought that story."

Still trying to understand the emotion in his eyes, Claire searched his gaze.

"I haven't been afraid for a long time. Not in the military. Not during my...extra stints with Trace and Drake. Hell, not since that boat sank and my world changed. I was afraid then. Fucking terrified, and there was nothing I could do to save the people I loved most."

Her heart ached for him.

"I'd planned to kill the man who was after you." He said this bluntly, easily, as if death didn't matter to him. "It was an easy choice. Someone was hurting you. I had to stop him. So I used the engagement, thinking that it would draw him out."

"It did."

"*It drew him to come after you, not me.*" His hold on her tightened. "That was never what I intended. I never wanted you to be hurt or to be afraid or—"

"I know," she said, cutting through his words. And she did.

But Noah shook his head. "I've screwed up a lot with you. Made mistakes. Blundered my way around, and that's not my way. I can usually charm women, but when I'm with you, I feel like I can barely speak sometimes."

That didn't sound like Noah. "You seem so confident to me."

"It's a lie. Most days with you, I'm just trying to figure out what I can do to keep you close." He exhaled slowly. "After we met in Chicago, I...wanted to see you again. But you vanished after Sara's funeral. You just disappeared. I figured that was a sign you weren't interested in me, and that I should just forget about you." He paused. "But you're not easy to forget."

"Neither are you." She'd tried to forget him after Chicago, but he'd started to slip into her dreams. He'd made her feel, made her fantasize, and that had terrified her. So she'd run. Tried to start a new life—*only that hadn't worked.*

"When you walked into my hotel in New York, I knew the instant I saw you that I wasn't going to be able to let you go. I was going to do anything necessary in order to get you to stay in my bed and in my life."

Claire lifted her hand. Pressed it to his chest. She was still wearing the bracelets he'd given her, and the diamonds gleamed. "You're talking about sex."

"With you, I'm talking about forever."

Now it was hard for her to breathe. "You…you heard me when I said that I loved you." That was why he was doing this. He felt like he'd put her in danger with the engagement, and he was trying to make up

"Hell, yes, I heard you. Those were the most important words of my life. Do you really think I *wouldn't* hear them?" Then he dropped before her, sliding down on one knee.

It wasn't hard to breathe. It was *impossible.* Claire had just stopped breathing entirely.

"I want to marry you, Claire Kramer. This isn't some bullshit fake engagement. It's real. It's forever."

"Noah…" Claire felt her heart thundering in her chest. "The Press. You know what they'll say about me—"

"Screw them. I don't give a damn about them or what they have to say." His fingers slid over the bracelet on her left wrist. "I care about you. I *love* you. Enough to kill for you. Enough to die for you. And, baby, enough to live for you, too. That's what I want to do. I want us to live together and make love and be happy for the next fifty years."

It sounded so good. So perfect. "Everyone I love…they all die."

"Not me, Claire. I'm not going anywhere. I'll be right by your side, from here on out."

Her eyes burned, and Claire had to blink away tears. "I don't want to lose you." Her fear. Her weakness—*him.* She loved him so much. And it was love, not obsession. Loving him…she wanted to put him first. Wanted him to be happy. Safe.

Loving him gave her hope. Without Noah, Claire didn't know what would happen to her.

"Say you'll marry me." Then he reached into the pocket of his coat. Pulled out a small, black box. When he opened that box, Claire saw a huge, blue diamond ring nestled inside. A ring to match her bracelets. To match… "Just like your eyes," Noah told her.

He was on his knees. Offering her everything that she had ever wanted.

And fear was there. Surrounding Claire. Choking her.

I lose everyone.

She stared into his eyes, and in that moment, Claire was finally able to read the emotion there. It was the emotion that had always been in his gaze, but she'd been too scared to see it for what it was.

Love.

Noah loved her.

And she loved him. "Yes," Claire whispered, and she threw herself against him. Noah fell back. They both hit the floor, but Claire didn't care. Her mouth was on his, and Claire was kissing Noah with all of the love and passion that she had.

This was her chance. Their chance. They could be happy. They could have everything that they wanted.

Noah was laughing and kissing her, too. They stripped in a tangle of limbs. He put the ring on her finger. Sealed it with a kiss. Then he was thrusting into her. Claiming her with a fast and hot lust that stilled the laughter.

The sex was intense. Hard. Consuming. Their fingers linked. Their eyes held.

There was no fear. It was gone.

There was only pleasure. Love.

It wasn't about control or power.

Just pleasure.

Claire called his name when she came.

And when he came, Noah kissed her. There was lust in that kiss. Raw need.

So much love.

She wrapped her arms around him. Held him as tightly as she could.

This was an ending she'd never seen coming. Wrapped in a lover's arms. Dreaming of a future.

Life.

Hope.

***

Claire slipped from Noah's bed. He felt the mattress shift as she rose, and Noah opened his eyes. He enjoyed the view of her back and her perfect heart-shaped ass before Claire slipped on her clothes.

Frowning, he sat up. He didn't care that he was stark naked. He'd rather hoped Claire would join him for an early morning round of mind-blowing sex.

He'd never get enough of her.

"Where are you going?"

Claire tensed and glanced back at him. Then the tension drained away, and she smiled. "Just for a walk. The sun's coming up, and I thought that I'd watch it. Seems like a good way to start a new life."

He rose from the bed and pulled on a pair of jeans and snagged a sweatshirt. "I'll come with you." Because it did seem like a damn good way to start their life together.

And I want to be with you, Claire.

Their fingers twined together as they headed out of the house. They walked down the steps. Their toes sank into the sand. Claire laughed a little then, and she flashed him the smile that had first stolen his heart.

The smile that started with the little curve of her bottom lip. The smile that made her dimples wink. The smile that ended when it reached her eyes and made them shine.

He pulled her close. The wind was chilly against them, and he wanted to warm her. Noah sank his hands into the thickness of her hair and kissed her. Noah took his time with that kiss, savoring Claire. She'd always be the sweetest thing that he'd ever tasted.

When he pulled away, Noah knew there was one more thing he needed to share with his Claire. She'd proven just how much she loved him.

It was Noah's turn to prove his love to her.

"I want to take you out today," he told her as he kept her close. "On the boat."

Claire searched his eyes. "Are you sure?"

"It's time to put the past to rest. For both of us." And he wanted to show Claire that he'd share all of his life with her. The good and the bad.

They walked toward the boat. It gleamed, already set in the water. The day was clear and bright. The waves were easy. It was the perfect weather for a trip out.

"We don't have to do this," Claire said, stopping him on the dock. "You don't have to—"

"You'll be the first woman I've taken out with me, and you'll be the woman who stands by my side for the rest of my life." This mattered to him. *She* mattered.

Claire smiled again. Damn but he loved her smile.

They climbed on board. Noah untied the vessel. He started the engine. The boat roared to life, and soon, they were pulling away from the dock and heading out toward that rising sun.

Claire slipped below the deck. Noah's hands tightened on the wheel as the salty scent of the water filled his nose. He'd expected to feel the pain from his past as soon as he got on the water. He usually did. But he didn't feel those old ghosts this time. Because she was with him? "Claire?" Noah called.

She didn't answer.

The boat was forty feet long, so Claire could still be exploring below deck. He waited a few more moments.

But Claire didn't come back up.

A tendril of unease snaked through Noah. He killed the engine. Left the boat drifting a bit. "Claire, is everything okay?"

Then he saw the top of her blonde head as she climbed back up. Her face became visible, and his heart stopped when he saw the fear heavy in her expression.

Not just fear—*terror.*

Then Noah saw the gun barrel pressed under Claire's chin. She kept rising, climbing up from below deck, and soon the man who held her was visible, too.

Blond hair. Green eyes. A smile that was smug and evil.

"I told you she was my one and only," Ethan Harrison said. "You should've believed me."

Every muscle in Noah's body locked down. "I thought you were still in the city."

"Wh-what?" Claire gasped. The gun barrel shoved harder against her skin.

Noah glanced at her face. The desperation in her eyes undid him. "You said that you saw him," Noah said simply. "I believed you."

"Th-that's why you wanted me out of New York so badly?"

Noah nodded. Yes. It hadn't been about the reporters. The escape to the Hamptons had been about protecting Claire. Trace and his men were tearing apart the city. Noah had thought Claire would be safe at his beach house.

He'd been wrong. Noah focused on Ethan once more. The man's gaze was wild, too bright with intensity, and his fingers trembled around the weapon. "You need to move that gun. I know you don't want to hurt Claire."

"No." Ethan lifted the weapon, just an inch. "I love Claire, and she loves me." He kept a tight grip on her. "But Claire has to be punished. She let you touch her. I saw…"

Claire shook her head. "Ethan, *no*."

"I'm going to kill him," Ethan told her. He pressed a kiss to Claire's temple. "Then we'll be together. We'll sail away, and no one will ever bother us again."

That wouldn't happen. Noah would not let that bastard take Claire. "Sloan Hall. You found out about this place through him, didn't you, Harrison?"

Ethan smiled. "You know my brother killed him? Right before I could." He laughed. "And Austin always pretended to be so perfect!"

"How'd you get away?" Claire whispered. She pressed back against Ethan, and the man's gaze jumped to her.

"I had to get away. I had to come for you." The gun pushed back against her skin once more. "York visited me in that damn prison. Talked as if you were his. I knew I had to find a way to you then…"

Fuck. *He'd* caused Ethan to escape?

"You faked that car bomb." Claire's voice was so calm it surprised Noah. Her eyes were lit with terror, but her voice was flat.

"I didn't fake it. It was a very, very real bomb. Just ask those dumb cops who were there…oh, wait, nothing's left of them now." He laughed again.

The boat kept drifting in the water.

"I called in my favors," Ethan said, his lips curving. "Warden Quill still owed my family, so he set things up for me."

The warden?

"Quill made sure the back doors of that patrol car were…a little broken. I could get out, easy. And I did. Right before the dumb prick turned the key in the ignition, I jumped out and slipped into the woods."

Noah realized that Ethan was damn proud of himself. The guy was talking and talking…and not even realizing that Noah was reaching for the knife he kept stashed near the wheel. The knife had been used the few times he'd fished, and he always kept it close at hand when he was on deck.

It was the only weapon he had available, but Noah was good with a knife. Very, very good.

"I slipped through the woods." Ethan just sounded boastful now. "You remember those woods, don't you, Claire? They led to the little bayou. We made love there. Our first time." He inhaled deeply, as if drinking in her scent. "I missed you so much." He pulled her even closer, but kept the gun against her. "Did you miss me?"

Claire was staring right at Noah as she said, "Yes."

Noah tensed.

"I missed you so much," Claire repeated to Ethan, her voice wooden. Then she lowered her lashes. Cleared her throat, and said again, "*I missed you.*" But emotion was in those words, shaking them.

Satisfaction flashed across Ethan's face. "I told you. Claire's mine. She'll always be mine." Then he lifted the gun and pointed it at Noah. "And you're dead—"

"No!" Ethan's grip on her had loosened and Claire whirled in his arms. She put her hands on Ethan's chest. "He doesn't matter. You and I...we matter."

Noah took a slow, gliding step forward.

Ethan had lowered the gun to Claire's side.

"Let's just leave him," Claire said, her words flying out quickly. "Make him jump off the boat. You and I—we can keep going on this ride, and no one will stop us. No one will ever find us."

Ethan's blond eyebrows lowered. "But I want to kill him. He *touched* you. He thought he'd take you from me."

Noah took another step forward. Claire stood between him and his target.

"No one will do that," Claire said. Her hands were curving around Ethan's shoulders. "You're my-my one and only. We'll be together always." She glanced back over her shoulder. Her gaze held Noah's for just a moment. "He doesn't matter." Then she looked back at Ethan. "*Please*, just let him go."

Ethan smiled at her. Noah caught the flash of his grin. "I love it when you beg me." Then he kissed her.

Noah leapt forward.

A gunshot blasted.

Noah's entire world stopped then.

Claire staggered back from Ethan.

"But you're begging for *him*," Ethan shouted at her. "For *his* life, and you know what that tells me?" He lifted his gun, preparing to shoot it again. *Preparing to shoot Claire again.*

Claire's blood was dripping onto the boat.

A roaring filled Noah's ears. He didn't even realize that he was the one making that sound.

"It tells me that you love him!" Ethan fired again.

Noah shoved Claire to the side. The bullet drove into Noah's shoulder, but he didn't even feel the impact. He was too busy holding Claire.

There was blood on her shirt. The bastard had *shot* her, at point blank range. The bullet had sank into Claire's stomach, and she stared up at Noah as tears poured down her face. "L-love...s-sorry..."

"No, Claire, you're okay," he told her, frantic. *"You're okay!"*

"No, she's not," Ethan snapped. "You're both dead. And you're in just the position I like. On your knees." His laughter grated in Noah's ears. *"Look up at me, asshole.* The last thing I want Claire to see is you dying."

Carefully, oh, so carefully, Noah eased Claire down on the deck. "I love you," he whispered. Did she realize just how much? That she was his whole world?

That world was bleeding out in front of him.

He looked up. "I told you what would happen if you ever came near Claire again."

Ethan advanced on him. His fingers gripped the gun tightly. "I'm the one with the power here. Claire should've been true to me! You ruined everything! Now you are going to die!"

Noah shook his head. "I told you to forget Claire. And I told you that if you didn't..." Noah lunged up. With his left hand, he grabbed Ethan's hand-the hand that held gun—and he broke the man's wrist. "I said you'd be a dead man." Noah's right hand drove his knife into Ethan's chest. Right into the bastard's heart.

Ethan's breath choked out. He stared at Noah with wide, stunned eyes. "Pl-please..."

Noah twisted that knife. "You'll never hurt her again." He yanked the knife back.

Blood poured from Ethan's wound. The man fell back. And, furious, snarling, Noah, plunged the knife into Ethan's throat.

Go join your bastard father and brother in hell.

Then Noah spun around. He fell to his knees beside Claire. "Baby, baby, *look at me.*"

Her eyes had closed. When he touched her, Claire's skin was so cold.

"Don't do this, Claire. Please, please don't leave me." He was begging her, and he didn't care. Noah would have done anything for Claire right then.

Her lashes lifted. Her eyes — the blue seemed so dim — met his. "Love...y-you..."

He pushed down on her stomach, trying to apply pressure to her wound. "Fight for me. You love me, so that means you have to fight." He kissed her, desperate, breaking. "Fight to stay with me. Because I don't want to be without you, Claire. I don't think I can be. Please, baby, *hold on.*"

He lifted his head. Her lips started to curl. The smile that began with her bottom lip.

"Changed...me..." she whispered.

The smile wasn't flashing her dimples. It wasn't reaching her eyes. It had to reach her eyes.

"I was...yours..."

"You still are." He grabbed for the boat's radio. Called for help even as he kept applying pressure to her wound. "And I'm yours. Yours — always. Do you hear me, Claire? Always. This isn't the end for us. We've just started. We're getting married. I'm going to buy you so many blue diamonds that you get sick of them, and I'm going to make you scream over and over again when you and I are in bed and I make — "

Her eyes had closed once more.

"Claire?" No, no. "Get me help!" he yelled into the radio. "She needs a helicopter! I need a life flight for her. Dammit, I'm out on the water and I need — "

Claire.

His hand was on her wound. She was terrifyingly still on that deck. The water was all around him, blue for miles. No help in sight.

If they stayed there and waited for help to come, Claire would be dead.

"Live for me," he begged her. "Please, God, Claire, *live for me.*"

He lifted her up, holding her as best he could even while he kept trying to put pressure on that wound. His left arm wrapped around her, and she hung limply against him.

His mother had been limp like that. So long ago. He'd thought that she'd just passed out. But…

Still holding her, Noah sent the boat racing forward. It bounced against the waves at first, then cut through the water.

He kept holding Claire.

He'd always hold her.

Because she was the only thing that mattered to him.

"Please hold on, Claire," he said, and he knew he was begging her. "Just…hold on. *Don't leave me.*"

CHAPTER FIFTEEN

When the helicopter landed at the hospital, Drake tensed. He was inside the hospital, watching from his position in the waiting area. He saw the figures jump from the chopper, and, a few moments later, the medical attendants ran forward, pushing the small figure on the gurney toward the hospital's emergency room entrance.

Noah was right beside that gurney.

The emergency room doors flew open. Drake had only a flash of Claire. The doctors were working on her. Yelling. Saying that she'd lost too much blood.

Fuck, not her.

Claire vanished as the operating room doors swung closed. Drake glanced over his shoulder. Now Noah stood just inside the emergency room waiting area. His shirt was covered with blood. So were his hands.

Cautiously, Drake approached his friend. He could see that Noah was on the edge. The very dangerous edge that he'd always sensed with Noah.

"He was on the boat," Noah said, and his voice stopped Drake. That low, deadly whisper—Noah normally only used it in battle. "I wanted to take Claire out and show her that she could know all of me...*but he was on my boat. Ethan Harrison was on my fucking boat.*"

Trace had called Drake to let him know about the deadly situation. Trace had told him to haul ass to the hospital, and Drake knew that Trace would be arriving there any minute, too.

"She was trying to protect me." Noah's eyes were haunted. "She told him to let me go. That she'd stay with him." His hands had fisted. "She would've done it, too. I saw it in her eyes. If he'd let me go, she would have gone away with that bastard and let him hurt her. Let him kill her. *For me.*"

"Noah…" He put his hand on Noah's shoulder.

Noah shoved him back. "*I didn't move fast enough.*"

Drake swallowed. "I don't…I don't know what you mean."

"He knew she loved me. Ethan knew. I was going to attack him, but I didn't move fast enough." Grief ravaged his face. "He shot her in front of me. We were out on that water, and I couldn't help her. There was too much blood. I kept telling her to hold on. To hold on…"

The ER doors burst open again. Trace stood there, breath heaving, as his gaze flew around the waiting area. He saw Noah and Drake, and he rushed toward them.

"But she didn't open her eyes again," Noah whispered. His head sagged forward. "I need her to open her eyes. *I. Need. Her.*"

Drake couldn't even lie to his friend and tell him that Claire would be all right. She'd been so pale — ghost white — on that gurney. And he hadn't even been able to see her breathing. Drake cleared his throat. "She's a fighter."

"I told her to fight for me. I begged her." Noah swiped a hand over his cheek. When his hand fell again, Drake saw a line of blood on his face. Claire's blood. "But I don't even know if she could hear me."

When Trace came up to the men, his gaze went straight to Noah. "Tell me what I can do."

Noah's attention was on the shut operating room doors. "I used to envy you, Trace. You always loved Skye. She loved you. You seemed to have it all."

Trace's face reflected his worry.

"I didn't know it would…hurt so much." Noah rubbed his chest. "It feels like someone is clawing my heart out right now."

"Because you love her," Trace said.

Noah's head sagged forward. "I'd kill for her. I'd die for her." His shoulders rolled back and his face slowly lifted. "But how can I live *without* her?"

"You won't have to," Trace told him, voice fierce. "You got her to the hospital. This isn't like the time with your parents. The doctors are in there, and they'll get her sewn up. She's going to make it." Maybe Trace's words were a lie, but Drake was glad Trace had said them. Drake didn't like the haunted, desperate look in Noah's eyes.

Noah's gaze flickered to Drake. "She loves me."

"Yes, I figured that one out pretty fast."

"I love her."

"That one was obvious, too," Drake muttered. "When you stopped the revolving bedroom door routine you enjoyed so much."

Trace exhaled on a long, rough sigh. "I don't know how Ethan Harrison managed to get all the way up to New York. He must've had help and-"

"The warden helped him." Noah's voice was flat. "So we need to destroy him."

Trace nodded. "Consider it done." He backed away.

Drake knew Trace had found his way to "help" Noah. Within the hour, Drake figured that the warden would be in either police custody or in the custody of Trace's agents. The man wouldn't get away.

Noah started to pace then, walking back and forth on the tiled floor of the waiting room. His gaze darted back to the operating room doors every few moments.

There was so much blood on the guy. Drake had to ask, "Noah, are you all right? Do I need to get a doctor for you?" The last thing he wanted was for Noah to keel over. The guy could be so focused on Claire that he was ignoring his own injuries.

Noah stopped pacing. "I think I got shot. Maybe my shoulder? It doesn't matter."

Uh, yes, it did. Drake motioned to a nurse.

Noah looked down at his clothes. "Most of the blood is Claire's...and Ethan Harrison's."

"He's dead." Drake had gotten that bit of information from Trace on his way over and —

"I stabbed him in the heart and drove my knife into the bastard's throat." Noah started pacing once more. The nurse nervously hovered nearby. "He'll never hurt Claire again."

Drake whistled soundlessly. No, Ethan would never hurt Claire again. And if Claire didn't survive the surgery...he knew that Noah York would never be the same again, either.

He's lost control. He's gone over the edge.

Claire would be the only one who could bring him back.

***

She looked so pale against the white covers.

Noah pulled his chair closer to Claire's bed. She was connected to about five different beeping machines, and an IV fed into her left arm.

Her eyes were closed. Her wound stitched up.

The anesthesia was still in her system, but the doctors had assured him that Claire *would* be waking up soon. The surgery had been a full success.

She was going to make it.

He could actually breathe again.

Noah reached for Claire's hand. His fingers threaded through hers. He just needed to hold her. To feel her, warm and alive, against him.

"That was too close," he rasped to her. "Please, baby, don't ever do that to me again." Because for a while there, his whole world had gone dark.

He bowed his head, and he kept holding her.

***

When Claire opened her eyes, the first thing she saw
was...Noah. He was in the chair right next to her bed. And
his gaze was on her.

She tried to smile at him.

He immediately leaned forward. "Baby?" His hand was
holding hers. So warm and strong.

But that was Noah. Her strong, sexy Noah.

"I...it's over..." Her throat was desert dry, so she
swallowed and finished, "isn't it?"

His fingers tightened around hers. "Ethan's dead."

She didn't remember him dying. She remembered a
gunshot. Remembered falling. Remembered Noah begging
her to hold on.

She'd tried so hard to hold on to him. "Didn't...want you
hurt..." The machines beeped around her.

"You were going to trade your life for mine." He shook
his head. The faint lines around his eyes and mouth were
deeper, and Noah looked more grim than she'd ever seen him
before. "That shit just wasn't working. *No one* takes you from
me. You're mine, Claire and—"

"You're mine," she whispered back.

She could see her ring gleaming on her finger. The
bracelets were gone, but the ring was still there. Noah had
asked her to spend her life with him.

And, even though Ethan had tried to take that life
away...*I'm still here.* "I wasn't...leaving you."

He pressed a tender kiss to her lips. "Good. Because I was
ready to fight death to get you back." His jaw clenched. "I
love you, Claire Kramer, more than I ever thought it was
possible to love anyone or anything."

That was how she felt about him. No, Claire hadn't
thought that she *could* love. Then Noah had walked into her
life. He'd changed everything for her.

"We're not having a long engagement," his voice warmed
as he stared into her eyes. His hand still held hers. "I...can't
wait. I need you too much."

And she needed him.

"As soon as you're out of this hospital, we're heading to Vegas. Or, hell, we'll go any place you want. I just want you with me." He kissed her again. "Always, Claire. Always."

There was no other place she wanted to be. "Always, Noah," she swore, and the love she felt for him filled her. "Forever."

***

The chapel was covered in roses. Noah knew they were Claire's favorite, so he'd made sure the florist he used in Vegas brought in as many roses as possible.

He suspected that every rose in Vegas was in that little chapel.

The Justice of the Peace smiled as Claire walked down the aisle.

She wore a simple white dress. Her bracelets gleamed around her wrists, but the blue reminding him so much of her eyes.

Her eyes had gotten to him from the very first moment. If the eyes were the windows to the soul, then Claire's soul was perfect. Beautiful.

Drake walked Claire down the aisle. The guy was grinning as he put Claire's hand into Noah's.

And when he touched her, some of the tension Noah felt eased away. Trace stood behind Noah. The guy was his best man. Skye was Claire's matron of honor, and she wore a grin nearly as big as Drake's.

The Justice of the Peace started speaking. Noah didn't look away from Claire. He'd never thought he'd be getting married. Never thought this was the life he'd have.

But without her, I don't have a life.

"Noah?" Claire whispered as alarm flickered in her gaze.

He tensed and leaned toward her. Then Noah became aware of the silence. All around them.

"You're supposed to repeat after him," Claire said, nibbling her lower lip. "I...is everything okay? You haven't...haven't changed your mind?"

"Hell, no, I haven't." He'd just gotten lost in her eyes, and he hadn't heard a word the Justice of the Peace said. He curled his fingers under her chin and kissed her. A deep, long kiss, as he savored the sweetness that was his Claire.

The Justice of the Peace cleared his throat. "That comes later."

No, it came any damn time Noah wanted.

After a moment, after he'd enjoyed her, Noah lifted his head. The uncertainty was gone from Claire's gaze.

"Ah...repeat after me," the Justice mumbled. "I, Noah Robert York, take Claire Cassandra Kramer to be my lawfully wedded wife, to have and to hold—"

"To hold forever," Noah promised her, cutting through the other man's words. "I'll love you forever, Claire."

She smiled at him. Her lower lip curled. The dimples winked. Her eyes glinted.

And he knew that he'd spend the rest of his life loving this woman.

Claire was his, and that was only fitting because the woman truly owned him, body and soul.

###

AUTHOR'S NOTE

Thank you so much for taking the time to read MINE TO HOLD. I hope you enjoyed the story. If you would like to learn about my upcoming releases, you can subscribe to my newsletter (http://www.cynthiaeden.com/newsletter/). You can also visit my website (www.cynthiaeden.com) for information about my books.

EXCERPT

Want to try one of Cynthia Eden's sexy paranormal tales? A VAMPIRE'S CHRISTMAS CAROL will be available on 11/11/13...but you can read this excerpt now:

Unedited Excerpt from A VAMPIRE'S CHRISTMAS CAROL by Cynthia Eden

Lust clawed through him. The need, the red-hot desire, seemed to burn Ben from the inside. He grabbed Addison and yanked her against him. His mouth locked on hers. He'd always tried to be so careful with her in the past. He'd played the gentleman because she *mattered*.

He wasn't a gentleman any longer. Ben wasn't even sure what he was. He just knew he needed Addison naked, and he had to be *in* her.

He carried her back to his bedroom. He ignored the glittering New York skyline. She was the only thing he could see. Desire pounded through him. His cock was so swollen that he hurt and—

His teeth were extending. Stretching in his mouth.

Ben dropped Addison on the bed and stepped back, horrified.

What is happening to me?

"Ben?" Addison sat up on the bed and pushed back her blond hair. "What's wrong?"

She was so beautiful staring up at him. Looking at him with those wide, dark eyes.

I'm going to hurt her. He grabbed tight for the control that he'd held so easily in the past. Only that control was broken. Shattered. "You need to leave."

Addison sucked in a sharp breath. Pain flashed over her face. "I thought...you said you loved me."

He did love her, and that was why she needed to get the fuck away from him. "Something is different." He turned away from her so that she wouldn't see the fangs that were now fully extended.

Fangs. When did I get fangs?

***

A VAMPIRE'S CHRISTMAS CAROL
Available on 11/11/13

This holiday season has bite...

HER WORKS

E-book only titles by Cynthia Eden
- BOUND IN DEATH
- BLEED FOR ME
- FOREVER BOUND (A Vampire & Werewolf Romance Anthology that includes the following titles: BOUND BY BLOOD, BOUND IN DARKESSS, BOUND IN SIN and BOUND BY THE NIGHT)

Please note: All of the BOUND stories are also available separately:
- BOUND BY BLOOD
- BOUND IN DARKNESS
- BOUND IN SIN
- BOUND BY THE NIGHT

List of Cynthia Eden's romantic suspense titles:
- MINE TO TAKE (Mine, Book 1)
- MINE TO KEEP (Mine, Book 2)
- FIRST TASTE OF DARKNESS
- DIE FOR ME
- DEADLY FEAR (Deadly, Book 1)
- DEADLY HEAT (Deadly, Book 2)
- DEADLY LIES (Deadly, Book 3)
- ALPHA ONE (Shadow Agents, Book 1)
- GUARDIAN RANGER (Shadow Agents, Book 2)
- SHARPSHOOTER (Shadow Agents, Book 3)
- GLITTER AND GUNFIRE (Shadow Agents, Book 4)

List of Cynthia Eden's paranormal romance titles:

- THE WOLF WITHIN
- HOWL FOR IT
- ANGEL OF DARKNESS (Fallen, Book 1)
- ANGEL BETRAYED (Fallen, Book 2)
- ANGEL IN CHAINS (Fallen, Book 3)
- AVENGING ANGEL (Fallen, Book 4)
- NEVER CRY WOLF
- ETERNAL HUNTER (Night Watch, Book 1)
- I'LL BE SLAYING YOU (Night Watch, Book 2)
- ETERNAL FLAME (Night Watch, Book 3)
- HOTTER AFTER MIDNIGHT (Midnight, Book 1)
- MIDNIGHT SINS (Midnight, Book 2)
- MIDNIGHT'S MASTER (Midnight, Book 3)
- IMMORTAL DANGER
- WHEN HE WAS BAD (anthology)
- EVERLASTING BAD BOYS (anthology)
- BELONG TO THE NIGHT (anthology)

ABOUT THE AUTHOR

Award-winning author Cynthia Eden writes dark tales of paranormal romance and romantic suspense. She is a *New York Times, USA Today, Digital Book World,* and *IndieReader* best-seller. Cynthia is also a two-time finalist for the RITA® award (she was a finalist both in the romantic suspense category and in the paranormal romance category). Since she began writing full-time in 2005, Cynthia has written over thirty novels and novellas.

Cynthia is a southern girl who loves horror movies, chocolate, and happy endings. More information about Cynthia and her books may be found at: http://www.cynthiaeden.com or on her Facebook page at: http://www.facebook.com/cynthiaedenfanpage. Cynthia is also on Twitter at http://www.twitter.com/cynthiaeden.

CPSIA information can be obtained at www.ICGtesting.com
Printed in the USA
LVOW05s1554300914

406573LV00017B/1073/P